P9-DVO-472

PRAISE FOR ANDY JONES

'Frank, funny and bittersweet . . . this is a book with its heart firmly in the right place.'

—*Louise Candlish*

'Touching, funny and real, Andy Jones . . . had me laughing one minute and crying the next. I loved it.'

—*Jane Costello*

'At my age I am still amazed when a writer with the gift of the written word can make me care about a character so much that I can be reduced to tears one minute and laughing the next – but [with *The Two of Us*] this author manages to do just that.'

—*The Sun*

'Honest, heartfelt and real, Jones has poured heart and soul into his words . . . the emotions are constant . . . be it laughter or hurt, you will experience it all as you journey through the pages.'

—*The Love of a Good Book*

'If you want a book which takes you on an emotional rollercoaster of such incredible highs and lows, this is no doubt the book for you.'

—*Compelling Reads*

'Like *One Day* and *Me Before You*, *The Two of Us* almost reads like a screenplay for a hit film and I would not be surprised if we see this on the big screen in a year or two. Like all good romcoms it is heartwarming, poignant, frustrating and its ending feels like a big, warm hug.'

—*Hollikins, Goodreads*

CALGARY PUBLIC LIBRARY

AUG -- 2017

'Beautifully written and wonderfully engaging.'

—*Daily Mail*

'[*The Trouble with Henry and Zoe* is] one of the few novels that deserves to be mentioned in the same breath as *One Day.* Everything you could want from a romcom and then some.'

—*The Sun*

ALSO BY ANDY JONES

The Two of Us
The Trouble with Henry and Zoe
Untogether Lives

GIRL

ANDY JONES

LAKE UNION
PUBLISHING

This is a work of fiction. Names, characters, organizations, places, events, and incidents are either products of the author's imagination or are used fictitiously.

Text copyright © 2017 Andy Jones
All rights reserved.

No part of this book may be reproduced, or stored in a retrieval system, or transmitted in any form or by any means, electronic, mechanical, photocopying, recording, or otherwise, without express written permission of the publisher.

Published by Lake Union Publishing, Seattle

www.apub.com

Amazon, the Amazon logo, and Lake Union Publishing are trademarks of Amazon.com, Inc., or its affiliates.

ISBN-13: 9781503942295
ISBN-10: 1503942295

Cover design by Emma Rogers

Printed in the United States of America

Revised edition of *Girl 99*, first published in Great Britain in 2012 by Andy Jones.

To my brother, Martin

PROLOGUE

Reasons why I shouldn't have slept with the girl who's singing in my shower:

1. We have slept together before.
2. Several times.
3. To the extent where she now has a favourite mug in my kitchen.
4. And a favourite side of my bed.
5. We work together.
6. She likes me.
7. I like her.
8. But not in the same way that she likes me.
9. She's a lovely girl.
10. But a terrible singer.

This list is not exhaustive, but it serves its purpose. You get my point.

The first time I slept with Holly was fine. We were single, consenting, slightly drunk, rather horny adults. Why not? No harm done. The second time, less so. You've upped the ante; it's not so easy to dismiss as 'just one of those things'. Because it wasn't 'just one', was it? It was just two. And so on, exponentially, with each subsequent 'thing'. Last night was thing number five, and now she's singing 'Lovely Day' in my shower. *Add that to the list.*

In terms of direct impact on my life, however, sleeping with Holly still doesn't top the act of kissing her in the first place, in the back of a taxi after the office Christmas party. That and thinking it might be a good idea to admit this indiscretion to my girlfriend Sadie. Now my ex-girlfriend Sadie.

DECEMBER

A LITTLE OVER FOUR MONTHS EARLIER

Chapter One

Traditionally, I'm a big fan of Christmas – I love turkey, stuffing and bread sauce; I like presents; I'm rather partial to sleeping off a bottle of wine in front of a James Bond movie. According to the listings, this afternoon's Double-O is *Thunderball* – the one where Sean Connery massages the villain's mistress with a mink glove he had presumably packed along with all his other spy gadgets. Well, I won't be needing one of those today, that's for sure. Sadie was due to come back with me this year, our first Christmas together, but I've well and truly stuffed that, to coin a festive phrase.

Even if she were here, there's no way Dad would sanction us sleeping in the same room. 'My house, Thomas; my rules.' But if Sadie were at least in the house, sleeping in my old single bed while I took the sofa, at least then I could have snuck up here for a Christmas quickie while Dad's at Mass. *Jesus.* Very nearly thirty-one years old and reduced to sneaking into my girlfriend's – if I had one, which I don't, not anymore – bedroom. *Happy sodding Christmas, Thomas.*

I haven't slept on a decent mattress for three weeks (since suffering some sort of brain spasm and confessing to Sadie about kissing Holly) and my spine aches like it's been concertinaed inside a small wooden box. Which, in a way, it has. I'm six foot three and a half, and this bed is about three and a half inches shorter than that. This bed where I had my first sexual experience. I was alone then, too.

Pornographic magazines would briefly enter circulation at school, and while I had glimpsed the contents, I'd never managed to take ownership, however temporarily, of this rare and tantalising material. My friend Keith, however, lived in a house full of books. The stairs and hallway were lined with shelves bent under the weight of accumulated lit. Creased spines in washed-out colours, bearing the names of a thousand authors. Some – Dickens, Stoker – were familiar, the majority not. Henry Miller, for example, author of *Plexus*, *Nexus*, and the more obviously titled *Sexus*. No pictures, but enough dirty words and startling acts to stimulate a barely teenage boy. Probably I would have worn the pages translucent if Dad hadn't somehow found the dog-eared novel hidden beneath the underlay, beneath the carpet, beneath my bed.

To call Dad a religious zealot would be unfair. I went to a Catholic school and in my experience he was no more dogmatic, fearful or close-minded than many of my friends' parents. And certainly less fervent than the majority of my teachers. He was moderately relaxed about church attendance and only minimally irritated by casual blasphemy. Even so, the discovery of my 'pornographic' literature was met with the full weight of the established Roman tradition.

We burned *Sexus* together – my father holding up occasional pages in the coal tongs and asking, sincerely, 'Do you enjoy reading this filth, Thomas?' 'Aren't you embarrassed, son?'

Yes, and of fucking course yes, I screamed inside my skull, while I shook my head and watched another page go up in smoke and cinders.

But that wasn't the worst thing. No, the real toe-curler was being taken to Father McKinley for a 'talk'. This was the highest sanction, more terrible than any grounding, arse-smacking or pocket-money freeze. It was a long, humiliating session. Veiny-faced, hairy-nosed Father Mac was keenly interested in what happened between the pages of this 'dorty book', and what, exactly, I had been doing while reading it. And even though this wasn't an official confession in the sacramental sense, he gave me a forty-rosary penance and a piece of advice I'll never forget. Next time I was troubled by 'wrong notions and belligerent loins', I was to bite the thumb of my ('you're right-handed, aren't you, boy?') right hand, and bite it hard, until the temptation passed.

No biting, however, is required this morning. And it's not simply my miniature bed that's responsible for my diminished libido – the entire room is wrong. The walls are black now – dotted here and there with glow-in-the-dark stars – and where there were once posters of Madonna and Kylie, there is now a six-packed actor wearing a towel, and a come-hither rapper beginning the process of unbuttoning his jeans. A small bookcase is heaving with A. A. Milne, Enid Blyton, Jacqueline Wilson, Jane Austen and Stephanie Meyer; last night I read *Love Lessons* – it's not bad, but it's not really my thing.

I was thirteen when my parents sat me down and told me I should start getting used to the idea that I was no longer an only child. Who was most surprised is a three-way split, but the news was as exciting as it was unexpected. For the next six months I fluctuated between wishing for a brother and wishing for a sister, but when six pounds and five ounces of Bianca arrived the following spring, it was impossible to imagine any alternative. I took to the role of very big brother with gusto, and over the next three and a half years, I fed Bea her bottle, sang nursery rhymes, coloured in, read bedtime stories and watched even more cartoons than usual.

Baby Bea started nursery school the same month I left for university, and I don't mind telling you it was a tearful goodbye for all involved. Over the years that followed, Bianca slowly appropriated my bedroom, using it as a playroom, den, study and, I have no doubt, somewhere to snog boys and hang out of the window smoking cigarettes. Her own bedroom is across the hallway, the walls painted a soothing shade of pale grey and hung with tasteful prints of famous paintings. Whereas the walls of my room have been through more shades of pink than Brighton beach on the first day of summer, and most of the rainbow besides. Girls progress through the spectrum in their own sequence and at their own pace, but they all begin with pink and end in black. Bianca made the transition faster than most, I think, reaching for the dark emulsion shortly after her eighth birthday and our mother's death from breast cancer. Almost nine years ago now.

Maybe that's why the room feels so small – all the layers of paint. It's like sleeping inside some kind of macabre doll's house.

So even if Sadie was here in my old bedroom, and even if I did sneak upstairs and climb in beside her, even then I doubt I could raise the necessary enthusiasm to commit any kind of sin. It feels wrong just thinking about it.

So now you know all about my bedroom. That's good.

Dad won't be back from Mass for an hour or more, so I decide to wake myself up with a gentle jog. Before I leave, I knock on Bea's bedroom door and wish her a happy Christmas. When she doesn't answer, I knock again and tell her I think Santa's been.

Whatever she shouts is muffled beneath several layers of bedding, and it sounds far from festive.

Where I run takes me through a small wood and onto a country road bordered by a muddy quilt of farmers' fields. After thirty-odd minutes that feel like twice as long, I arrive at the playing fields of St Francis of Assisi Roman Catholic School, a little over four miles from Dad's house. Normally I'd just be warming up, but my pulse is high and it feels as if long-dormant pockets of my lungs are being peeled apart with every breath.

I must have run this route hundreds of times as a schoolboy and it should be no surprise that this is where my feet take me when my brain stays out of the way. Known to the students as Sweet F. A. High, this is the school where Mum used to teach English to predominantly – me included – uninterested children.

You might think having a parent who teaches in your school would act as a deterrent to bullies. But, in my experience, it only acts as an incentive: 'Read us a story, bookworm', 'Kiss this, Romeo', 'Eat this, Oliver', and et cetera, most of it initiated by thug-cum-comedian Declan 'Deck' Chambers. It would be an exaggeration, I think, to say that I ran to avoid sharing a bus journey with Deck Chambers. I ran because I was good at it and I enjoyed it. I represented the school and then the county at the 10,000 metres, and there are a few ribbons and trophies in a box somewhere in Dad's attic. Nevertheless, on the days when I ran, it certainly was a bonus to get whacked around the back of the head with a book. In a way, I resent myself for taking it as much as I despise Declan Chambers for dishing it out. And not smacking the bastard square in the mouth with a spiked track shoe is something I will always deeply regret.

I stretch my calves against the goalposts, drop to the mud and grind out thirty press-ups. I was born lanky, Mum used to say, and by the time I was thirteen I was the tallest kid in my year and relatively useful as a goalkeeper. Not that I gave much of a shit about football, but the kudos of playing for the first team offset a small amount of the stigma that goes with being an English teacher's son. Hanging from the crossbar now, the metal is wet and cold and I slip off twice during the course of nine chin-ups. Names I don't know are etched into the paintwork, some in love hearts, others associated with boasts or insults, a few simply announcing the author's existence.

Mum started to show at the beginning of my third year. 'Life begins at forty,' she joked on her birthday that October, and I remember catching Dad – almost a decade older than his wife – blowing air from the corner of his mouth, a gesture that spoke more of anxiety than amusement.

At school, my persecutors had a new angle. Instead of my mother's profession, they shifted focus to her condition and inferred proclivities. Asking had I heard my parents screwing three months ago, did they do it often, was Mum a screamer? Deck Chambers would re-enact the conception, humping thin air, slapping a pair of invisible buttocks and grunting, 'How's that Missus Ferguson?' 'Keep your voice down, darling, we mustn't wake little Tommy.'

But as vile and humiliating as this was, I found the baby noises harder to bear. Maybe because they were aimed at my mother instead of me. We'd be in her class when someone – almost invariably Declan Chambers – would make a mewling noise from the back of the class. Then someone else joined in, then another and another. Maybe a dozen kids all bawling and squawking and shouting *goo-goo ga-ga*. Mum would try to ignore it, but it was as obvious as her red face that the taunts were hitting their mark. Sometimes I'd join in.

With the exception of a few superficial amendments – satellite dish, prefab outbuildings, new goalposts – the school hasn't changed much in the thirteen years since I left. But who am I to pass judgement? I dig a sharp stone out of the mud, scratch my name onto one of the goalposts and set off running towards another Ferguson family Christmas.

᚜᚛

I'm on my second sherry and peeling my four-hundredth vegetable when Bianca shuffles into the kitchen, still wearing her pyjamas, one cheek pink and pillow-creased, her hair high and wild as an owl's nest.

'Happy Christmas, Goat Boy,' she says, kissing my cheek and stealing a carrot from the chopping board.

The nickname was coined by my mother in reference to my star sign, a strategy that only really pays off for Leos and Sagittarians.

'Hey, Daffy.'

Bianca punches me on the shoulder, and the older she gets the harder she hits. Still, it's nothing less than I deserve. I was twenty-eight when I gave my then thirteen-year-old sister the nickname Daffy, derived from our shared assumption that Bianca had been an unplanned addition to the family. The Mistake, The Gaff, Gaffy, Daffy. Silly, for sure, but it helped pull Bea out of a gloomy patch and the nickname (a secret one, between the two of us) stuck.

'Time is it?'

'Well, you've missed half of Christmas already. Time was, you'd be up at five – "Has he been yet? Has he, has he, has he?"'

'Count yourself lucky, then.'

Bea fetches a sherry glass and pours herself a measure, watching me out of the corner of her eye, defying me to comment.

'Are you hungry?' I ask her.

Bea shakes her head, clinks her glass against mine. 'Where's Dad?'

I drop two rounds of bread into the toaster, nevertheless. 'Snoozing in front of the TV. You're as bad as each other.'

'So, what have you done with Sadie?'

I shrug noncommittally. 'I haven't done anything, we're just . . . it's complicated.'

'Bollocks,' says my baby sister. 'She dumped you, didn't she? Why? What did you do?'

'Nothing. I . . . she didn't dump me, it was just, we both just—'

'Blah, blah, bullshit.' Bianca snatches a mushroom and wrinkles her nose in disapproval. 'You know,' she says, 'I was never convinced.'

'Convinced about what?'

'Sadie. Come on, Goat Boy, keep up.'

'I thought we'd dropped that. And anyway, you said she was lovely.'

Bianca shrugs. 'She's your girlfriend – *was* – what else am I going to say?'

'Well, now's your chance,' I tell her. 'What, in your opinion, *was* wrong with her?'

'It's not so much that there was anything *wrong*, I suppose. I just didn't really reckon she was "The One", you know.'

'Oh, you didn't?'

'Feminine intuition, innit.'

11

'Well, it looks like you were right, doesn't it? Bravo.'

Bianca cocks her head immodestly and sips her sherry.

'Anyway,' she says, 'you're too pretty for her.'

'Sod off.'

'Well, you are. I'd kill for those eyelashes.'

The toast pops, and I spread one piece with peanut butter and one with jam before sandwiching them together. Bea washes her face in the sink and dries it on the front of her pyjama top. I cut the toast into four triangles, like I have done since she was a toddler.

'Here.'

Bea tuts, but she takes the toast. Mum's wedding ring hangs on a chain around her neck, and as Bea eats and stares out of the window, she worries the gold band. Mum got the diagnosis when Bianca was five and I was in my second year at university. A tumour in her right breast, and she fought the cancer for three years before it finally beat her in the summer just a few months before her forty-ninth birthday. To some extent, a gradual decline prepares you for death – you begin the process of grieving early, easing into your bereavement and moving towards acceptance. For Bianca, though, the three years in which Mum lost her hair, during which her skin sagged and darkened, those years simply gave her the time to learn and understand what death is and what it means. It was harder for Bea, and I think it still is. I had Mum for my entire childhood, but Bea had her for only eight short years – and at only sixteen now, a difficult and confusing time as she transitions into womanhood, I imagine she feels Mum's absence keenly.

Tears move slowly down my sister's cheeks; they hang and drop from either side of her jaw.

'You okay?'

'Silly,' she says. 'You'd think I'd be over it by now.'

'Christmas,' I say. 'I miss her, too.'

Bianca nods, wipes her eyes on her sleeve. 'Well, I don't know about you, Goat Boy, but I am going to get shedded.'

'Now?'

Bianca pulls a face designed to reflect the depths of my stupidity. 'Later. There's a thing at the Tivoli.'

'Thing?'

'Band. DJ.'

'On Christmas sodding Day?'

Bea rolls her eyes. 'Night actually. You sound like Dad.'

'And he's okay with this?'

In a single lazy blink, Bea slips from derision to solicitation. 'Actually, I was wondering if you might have a word.'

'Bea, don't put me in the middle.'

She shrugs. 'You kind of already are. Right then, Goat Boy, get the spuds on while I take a shower.'

Bea clumps upstairs, leaving me to clean up the kitchen and figure out how I'm going to mediate a resolution between my hormonal sister and fretful father. The problem is, I can see both of their positions – her need for independence and his compulsion to protect – and whether I like it or not, Bea's right, I am stuck slap bang in the middle.

❦

Mum invented 'play for your presents' at around the time she started wearing a headscarf. At a time when her children were more amenable to that kind of nonsense.

'The minister's cat is delightful,' says Dad.

'Diabolical,' I say.

'Diarrhetic,' says Bea, rounding off the 'D's.

We would play Charades, Twenty Questions, Elephant's Foot Umbrella Stand and – the English teacher's favourite – The Minister's Cat. Dad keeps the tradition alive, and the romantic in me hopes generations of Fergusons will do the same. If nothing else, we'll acquire a formidable arsenal of adjectives.

'The minister's cat is energetic.'

'Euphoric.'

'Eviscerated.'

Presents are awarded arbitrarily throughout play, not so much as a reward, more as a means of pacing out what would have been a paper-tearing frenzy when Bea was six and halfway through her Cadbury's selection pack.

'Good one,' says Dad. 'Shall we?'

We each take a wrapped parcel from our own pile. Dad unwraps a jumper from Bianca, Bianca opens perfume from me, I open snowboard goggles from Bianca. Everyone seems genuinely pleased; we hug, kiss, clink our glasses.

'The minister's cat is . . . flatulent,' says Dad, and we all smile ruefully at this old favourite of Mum's.

'Frisky,' I say.

'Fidgety,' says Bianca, giving me a sideways glance.

'The minister's cat is—'

'Going out?' interrupts Bianca.

Dad looks at Bea, looks at me. I shrug.

'Bianca,' he says, 'we've had this. You're sixteen.'

'Nearly seventeen.'

'Well, *nearly* isn't actually, is it?'

Bea juts her chin at me, demanding my input.

'I . . . I went when I was . . . sixteen?'

'Not with my permission,' says Dad.

'I came back, though.'

Dad inhales deeply, holds the breath for a count before releasing it. It's hard to decipher the gesture, but I sense he is beginning to yield. Some people harden with age, but Dad has gone the other way. He's softened a lot since his book-burning days, maybe due to age and perspective, maybe in response to my mother's passing, probably in part due to both. And the truth is, in most matters (excluding those concerning erotic lit), he has always been reasonably permissive. Even so, protocol demands he doesn't make it too easy.

'Sharon's going,' says Bea. 'And Kelly.'

'Well, if they were going to jump—'

'Do not,' says Bea, 'do the cliff thing. Or the hand-in-the-fire thing. It's so predictable.'

Dad looks at me to confirm this, and I nod, mime putting my hand in a fire and flinching, in the hopes it will lighten the mood.

'It's a club, Dad, not a . . .' Bea throws her hands in the air, '. . . a war zone. 's not even a good club.'

'Then why d'you want to go?'

'Because' – as if explaining to a person with severely limited comprehension – 'everyone else is.'

'Perx, I suppose.'

'What's Perx?' I ask.

'My boyfriend, if you must know.'

'I thought he was called David.'

'It's short for percussion,' says Bianca, again with the defiance. 'He's a drummer.'

'He's a plonker,' Dad mutters under his breath.

Bianca grabs two fistfuls of her hair. 'God! It's so unf—'

'Fine,' says Dad.

'*What?*' Me and Bianca in unison.

'Thomas will pick you up at midnight.'

'But—' Again from both brother and sister.

'Well, someone has to collect her,' Dad says, choosing to answer me first.

Bianca widens her eyes at me: *Pleeeaaase.*

So much for the nice bottle of red that's breathing in the kitchen. 'Fine. Of course.'

'Midnight,' reiterates Dad. 'And if you get legless, you get grounded.'

Bea pretends to sulk about this but she can't maintain the act. 'The minister's cat is gratified.'

Under the pretence of making myself a drink, I sneak up to my black bedroom and check my phone for messages.

There are none.

How I feel about that – disappointed or relieved – I honestly don't know. And I don't know if it's possible to experience both at the same time but, if it is, then that would explain the knot in my stomach. After several seconds weighing the pros and cons, I call Sadie but her phone goes straight to voicemail. I get stage fright, hang up and text instead: Happy Xmas Xx. And I regret the second 'x' the minute I hit the send button. Three kisses would be overdoing it, obviously; three is a romantic volley and our days of romantic volleys are, if not behind us, then definitely on hold. One kiss, on the other hand, would be only slightly more personal than a full stop – you see it sitting there at the end of the sentence but it doesn't register on the emotional scale. No kisses would appear plain sulky. Which is why I opted for *one and a half* kisses – 'Xx', one upper- and one lower-case kiss. But what I ended up with, of course, was two kisses. *Kiss kiss*. Which is a tad too cute for our current situation. Particularly when you consider the pivotal role kissing played in our break-up. Why didn't I go the whole hog roast and text Happy kissmas, with a smiley face and giant kiss made up of two-dozen smaller kisses? At least that might have been perceived as ironic.

And does it really matter one way or the other?

Bianca said Sadie wasn't 'The One' for me. But should this come as any kind of surprise?

Of the seven billion – *7,000,000,000!* – humans out there, how likely is it that your One works in your office, drinks in your local, goes to your school, turns up at your Halloween party? You've got more chance of winning the lottery with a found ticket. Of course Sadie wasn't The One. A better question would be: *is* there a One?

I sincerely hope not. I mean, what kind of cruel trick would that be? How could you ever rest, ever be happy, knowing that somewhere – in some house, high-rise, hovel, hut, shack, castle, tower, palace or frigging igloo – your One, your only, is patiently waiting for you to arrive and sweep her clean off her snowshoes. And it's not that I'm some hopeless unromantic. Love, monogamy, happily ever after – I believe in all of those things, *want* all of those things, really I do. But I don't believe they're going to arrive on the end of a lightning bolt. I don't believe that capital 'O' comes fully formed. Rather, there are various, potential, lowercase 'ones' – the few, the several, the many – but not 'The One'. And with patience, perseverance and an open mind, maybe, if you're lucky, one of those ones will turn into a . . . fuck, what do I know?

My mobile chirrups the arrival of a new text message and I wince reflexively.

Sadie: Ho Ho Ho.

No kisses.

And if it's funny or not, I really can't tell.

⁕

The predictable news is that teenage girls will be teenage girls. Whether or not my little sister qualifies as legless would depend on the extent of your literalism. While Bea has retained possession of her lower limbs, neither of them is of any use beyond filling out a pair of tight jeans. Right now they are folded beneath her as she slumps in front of the upstairs toilet. The good news is – and the irony has not escaped me – Dad is passed out drunk in his armchair, so Bea can retch, puke and cry with impunity.

'Your sick is blue,' I tell her.

'Wicked.'

'It's nothing to be proud of, Bea.'

'The drink,' she says, around a mouthful of spittle. 'Blue Wicked.'

'The minister's cat was being droll.'

'Yeah? Well the minister's cat can fu— *fuuurgghhh*.' Retch, spit, *pfft, pfft, pfft*.

'Did you have fun?'

Bea shakes her head. I'd hold her hair, but it's full of hairspray and is the only part of my sister still capable of self-support.

'Perx trouble?'

'Don't gloat.'

'I'm not, sis. You can talk to me, you know? About anything.'

Bea makes a noise that could be gratitude, cynicism or the beginnings of another gastric upheaval. 'Are you going to tell Dad?'

'Not this time,' I tell her.

'Fucking men.'

And that's Christmas.

Chapter Two

The drive back to London takes all of Queen's *Greatest Hits* and *The Beatles 1962–1966*, plus most of *The Essential Johnny Cash* – all Sadie's. I'm mumbling along to 'A Boy Named Sue' when it occurs to me that Sadie's CD collection consists entirely of compilations. Spread out on the passenger seat are the Carpenters' *Gold*, *L'indispensable Elvis*, *Motown Chartbusters Volume 6*, etc. And isn't it all a little contrived? A touch rose-tinted? Where are the not-so-great hits – the 'Ob-La-Di, Ob-La-Da's, the 'Radio Ga Ga's, the lows that define the highs and make for an honest account of an artist's output? If I were to compile the highlights from mine and Sadie's relationship, you'd see the holidays, posh restaurants, presents, parties, sex, cosying up on the sofa . . . and you'd think: *Great relationship*. But you'd be missing the arguments and insecurities, the nights apart, the weekends lost to work, the bored Sunday afternoons, the faked headaches, failed orgasms and infidelities. That said, we were only together thirteen months, which is a little premature for *Tom and Sadie Gold*.

But I'm not listening to Sadie's eclectic collection out of any kind of sentimentality; it's just that my own CDs are in the flat in London. Forty-eight hours ago, I couldn't get out of London fast enough. It didn't enter my mind to bring music; it's a miracle I packed two pairs of underpants. Sadie leaves her stuff wherever she drops it: knickers in the bathroom, banana skins on the coffee table, CDs in the Mini. And while I feel justified moaning about the milk turning sour on the countertop, it is handy having a supply of music in the glovebox. Besides, the car is half Sadie's. A couple of months after she moved into my flat, we spent a weekend in Devon for a wedding. And at some point during the delayed and diverted, eight-hour taxi, train, coach and tube journey back to London, we decided it might be handy to own a car. Sadie decided it should be a brand-new Mini Cooper.

It's tempting to say it seemed like a good idea at the time, but I'm not sure that it did. It certainly doesn't now.

I liked Sadie the first time I met her.

We were at a Halloween party. Sadie was dressed as Uncle Fester. I was meant to be Frankenstein's monster, but when I was introduced to Sadie I reinvented myself as Lurch from *The Addams Family*. We talked easily, agreeing for the most part but comfortable in our discrepancies too. An instant item, we posed for photographs, got drunk, went to Sadie's place, had sex, removed our make-up and had sex again. We arranged to meet at a Bonfire Night party the following weekend. Sadie arrived late and tear-streaked and informed me she'd just dumped her boyfriend. A boyfriend I hadn't – up until that exact moment – known existed.

Sadie is very close to being beautiful – and some people would tell you she's all the way there. Tall and slim, pouty lips, intelligent eyes, moulded cheekbones; tick, tick, tick. Instant attraction for sure, but my heart did not go *boom*. For no reason I could put my finger on, I had reservations, but they were small nebulous doubtlings, easily attributed to new-girlfriend nerves. Also, this smart, sexy woman had just unhitched from her boyfriend, apparently on account of me, and I felt obliged to at least complete the basic inventory of new-couple dates: restaurant, cinema, National Gallery and so on.

December arrived, and while the doubts hadn't entirely dispersed, it was now Christmas party season and we had plenty of distractions and festive fun to buoy us along. In January we went skiing. For Valentine's Day we went to Paris. In March, work took Sadie to Zurich for ten days and me to Slovenia for eight. Sadie's dad was ill in April. It was her birthday in May. By June we'd been dating for seven months and we did what all couples do in summer: we went on holiday to Palma. And one night, drunk on wine and the sunset and the next best thing to love, I asked Sadie to move in. I remember waking up the next morning and thinking even then that I'd acted in haste. And now I know that I did. It's easier, I think, to know when something's wrong that when it's right, but it's knowledge we resist – because the alternative is an awful lot of lonely nights and microwave spaghetti Bolognese for one.

But I ignored the doubts that never really went away. Sadie moved in and for a while it was new and exciting. We bought a car, we went for drives, we slipped into complacency and then the Christmas party happened.

The company I produce commercials for is called Blank Slate, and this year's Blank Slate Christmas party coincided with the conclusion of my last shoot of the year. Meaning, after three thirteen-hour days of marshalling crew, nursing egos and making sure everyone had the right kind of milk in their lattes, I was hoarse, thirsty and exhausted. I needed a relaxing drink, but this wasn't that kind of party. This was an unabashed schmoozefest swarming with drunk clients we had either worked with in the past or hoped to work with in the future. Free beer for them, hard work for me. And in addition to the clients, there were the directors. We have nine on our roster, most of them talented, affable and amenable. But whether they're young, old, award-winning or jobbing, they all need reassuring that, *yes, you are a unique and special snowflake and the next big script that comes in . . . you, buddy, are top of the list.* I'm the youngest producer in the company, but far from the least experienced. I started straight out of college, I work hard and I like my job. The young pups see me as an ally. The old hacks view me as a soft touch. Net result: by the end of the night I probably had more saliva in my ear than beer down my throat. Several of the gang were talking about hitting a club, but I'd had all the saliva I could handle, so I ordered a cab and did a round of goodbyes and happy Christmases.

When I got to Holly the only thing holding her head up was the straw in her vodka tonic. This had been her first shoot as a runner, and after three days of fetching tea, fetching biscuits, fetching bacon sandwiches, fetching sushi, fetching cigarettes and magazines and skinny triple-shot Starbucks, she was falling asleep on her feet. We both live south of the river, so I offered her a lift. And she accepted. It was as simple and innocent as that. The idea of snogging her in the back seat hadn't even entered my head. Not at that stage.

We stared out of the windows in silence, watching the landmarks and London lights roll past. Holly yawned and slumped against me. My arm was squashed uncomfortably against the side of my body, so I slipped it around Holly's shoulders. Besides, it was cold. We crossed the river and Holly leaned across me, better to see the lights of Albert Bridge reflected in the Thames. Her hair was in my face, so I brushed it away from my cheek. And that's when it happened. She kissed me. I kissed her. We kissed. In that order. I told Holly that it was probably a bad idea. 'Yes, probably,' she said. Then she snogged me again, and I snogged her back, and we snogged all the way through Battersea and Clapham Common and Clapham South until the cab pulled up outside Holly's flat and she invited me inside. And despite the fact that Sadie was in Stockholm on business, and despite my straining erection, I declined politely. And that's all it was: a bit of harmless drunken snogging, and maybe a little groping. The cab driver grinned at me in the rear-view mirror. 'I'd've been up there like a rat up a drainpipe, pal.' I smiled nonchalantly and watched Holly go into her flat, feeling pretty pleased with myself for showing such restraint and character in the face of temptation.

Which is not how I felt when I woke the following morning. What had felt, eight hours previously, like nothing more than a harmless, festive faux pas, now lurked like a threatening silhouette in a dark corner of my mind. Say Holly developed a crush, pursued me, phoned drunk at midnight, sent texts, posted an indiscreet Christmas card . . . how then to explain it all away as a trivial indiscretion? No, the truth would set me free. Sadie would appreciate my honesty; if anything, it would reassure her of my fidelity. I mean, I turned down no-strings Christmas sex, for God's sake. If you can't trust a guy like that, then who can you trust?

Sadie returned from Stockholm on the Sunday. I kissed her like she'd been gone a year not a week, carried her bags up from the taxi, opened a bottle of wine. And the opportunity to offhandedly mention my amusing but harmless Holly encounter didn't present itself. Sadie gave me a hideous woolly jumper as an ironic early Christmas present. I cooked, and we opened a second bottle and caught up on what we'd each been doing for the past six days. Most of it, anyway, because this too seemed a less than ideal time to drop 'funny thing happened at the Christmas party' into the conversation. We finished our wine in front of the TV and, well, you know how people hate it when you talk over a good movie. We brushed our teeth, went to bed, had sex, and at no point during the proceedings did the perfect moment present itself for me to inform Sadie that I'd kissed the company receptionist on her first shoot as a runner. I was still half asleep when Sadie left for the office early on Monday morning.

So I emailed my confession just before lunchtime.

I clicked send, shuffled through to the kitchen, and had barely filled the kettle before Sadie called. And whether or not she appreciated my honesty didn't come up. She was more concerned about the fact that I couldn't be trusted to keep my hands to myself for one week while my live-in girlfriend was working sixteen-hour days in Stockholm: 'And you tell me this by email!' and 'Were you thinking of her when you screwed me last night?'

With regards to this last point, I decided, further candour was an inadvisable strategy. I explained that it was 'just a kiss', but this cut me little slack. My protestation that 'it wasn't as if I shagged her' did nothing to dampen Sadie's anger. I tried explaining the Jekyll and Hulk theorem I'd been working on over the weekend.

In a nutshell: The 'potion' or 'gamma rays' represent your lager or tequila or your large glass of Chardonnay. Now, in some individuals the potion releases pre-existing, but hitherto repressed, malevolent tendencies. In others, the gamma rays create an out-of-control creature that is completely incongruous with the hero's true and trustworthy persona. I, of course, fell into the latter camp. Sadie pointed out they were the same thing, and I magnanimously admitted that I hadn't thoroughly worked out all the finer philosophical details. Undeterred, I went on to assert that the main point still stood – neither Doctor Henry Jekyll nor Doctor Bruce Banner could be held entirely responsible for their temporary lapses. It was the potion, the gamma rays, the large goddamned glass of Chardonnay.

Also, Sadie contended, they're fictional fucking stories, this is the real fucking world, and a monster's still a fucking monster.

And, in a nutshell, I slept in the spare fucking room.

The mattress isn't as comfy in the spare room, and in the last six months I'd become used to the presence of another body beside me. I found it difficult to sleep, which gave me plenty of time to think. The major conclusion I kept coming back to was that it's surprisingly bloody hard to unpick what you want from what you don't want and what you think you should want.

On the Saturday we went for a meal to talk things through.

We both admitted our relationship had become somewhat rote, but I denied this was the impetus behind the kiss. 'So what exactly was the *impetus*?' 'Maybe it was the drink?' 'So that's an excuse?' 'No, just a reason.' 'Not a very good one.' Et cetera. No, I didn't regret asking Sadie to move in; yes, I still found her attractive; absolutely I still loved her.

The meal was (predictably) a tearful affair, during which (inevitably) my various shortcomings were aired rather more loudly than I thought absolutely necessary. But we seemed to be making progress and I was looking forward to, if not energetic dirty-talking sex, then at least a kiss and a cuddle in a bed with a soft mattress.

Sadie allowed me to hold her hand as we walked home; she didn't protest when I stroked the back of her hand with my thumb. My attempt at a kiss went less well. Sadie stepped away from me, wiped the back of her hand across her mouth, ran crying to the bedroom and slammed the door. I slunk off to the spare room and the lumpy mattress.

Fast-forward to the following Thursday and Sadie's office Christmas party.

Where she gave one her colleagues a hand job.

She tells me this at two-something a.m. after clattering through the front door and lurching into the spare room, where I'm trying to improvise a weapon out of a shoe because I think there's a home invasion in progress. Sadie plonks herself on the edge of the bed and asks am I awake. And although I'm not entirely lucid, I smile welcomingly and throw back a corner of duvet. 'Awake enough,' I tell her.

And Sadie smiles, savours the moment, then hits me with it. Not literally. She didn't give a colleague a hand job and then use the same warm palm to smack me across the face – although the effect could have been only slightly more shocking than this bald blurting out of the horrible facts.

'I've just given a colleague a hand job,' she says, as if this were akin to giving him a novelty mug in her capacity as his secret Santa.

I try to say something but it's as if the part of my brain where I store my vocabulary has been burgled, so I sit with my mouth hanging open and try not to visualise anything. Sadie's hair is a mess and her eyes are unfocused and her lipstick is smudged.

'Do you want to kiss me now?' Sadie asks matter-of-factly, and leans towards me.

I brace my hands against her shoulders, angling my face away from hers. 'Don't be—'

'Don't be what?' she says, slapping my hands aside and moving in again. 'What, Tom? What shouldn't I be?'

'Sadie,' I say, holding her off with one hand and trying to pull on my boxer shorts with the other. 'Listen, it's late, you're drunk—'

'Yeah, I'm pissed off my fucking face. It's my Doctor Hyde alter-id that did it. Don't blame me, blame the gamma rays.'

'I understand,' I say, getting up and backing out of the room. 'Can we just . . . Let me get you some water.'

Sadie follows me through the living room and into the kitchen. 'Why would I want water? Where's the fun in boring water?'

I fill a pint glass, nevertheless, and hand it to Sadie. Which, with hindsight, and now soaking wet in my boxer shorts at two-God-knows-what in the morning in the middle of December with no heating on, clearly wasn't too clever.

'Jesus, Sadie, will you just go to bed and pass out, please.'

'What? Wassamatter? Did I upset you? Have I let you down?'

I am teeth-chatteringly cold now, and my immediate priority is to do something about it before I die, but Sadie blocks the door as I attempt to walk past her. And when I try to manhandle her out of the way, she shouts, 'Don't you touch me! Don't you put your fucking hands on me.' And now the neighbours think I'm a wife beater.

I back away, raise one hand in a gesture of appeasement and attempt to dry myself with an already damp tea towel.

'Well,' Sadie says, 'I suppose that makes us even, doesn't it?'

I should be glad that Sadie appears to be calming down, and I really should keep my mouth shut. But 'even'?

'*Even!* How is a hand job the same as a kiss? On what planet does you wa— does what you did make us even, Sadie?'

'What you did was worse,' she says, and all the fight has drained out of her. 'You started it.'

'And you've finished it, hey?'

Sadie puts her fingers to her eyes and drags the tears across her cheeks in twin streaks of mascara. She shrugs. 'It's not as if I shagged him.'

I nod with a mixture of acknowledgement and resignation. There doesn't seem to be anything more to say, and I just want to go to bed.

Sadie bats her eyelids. 'Can I have another pint of water, please?' she says in a little-girl voice.

Despite myself, I laugh. Sadie laughs too; she laughs so much that snot bubbles out of her nose, which makes her laugh even harder and she collapses onto a chair, clutching her stomach. And then she bursts into tears.

I take advantage of the diversion to find a dry towel and throw on a jumper and a pair of jogging bottoms. Three minutes later, I find Sadie passed out on the sofa in the living room; she's tall but thin, and carrying her through to the bedroom requires no major heroics. Removing Sadie's shoes and jewellery feels acceptable, but I leave her clothes. I kiss her (on the forehead) and slink back to the spare room.

We had it all planned. Christmas with my family, Boxing Day with hers, then New Year's Eve up a mountain. Probably the most expensive time of year for a ski trip, but it fitted around work and the idea of champagne in the snow was too romantic to resist.

So much for romantic. With us unable even to sleep in the same bed, the idea of a week together in a cold cabin seemed more like an ordeal than an escape, but the chalet was booked and, Sadie insisted, at least one of us ought to go. I didn't know anyone who could join me at such short notice, but Sadie had a sister who needed a holiday. Not the holiday we had planned, but it would give us both some 'space to think'.

After all, Christmas Eve is a lousy time to admit you're breaking up.

We said our goodbyes on Christmas Eve morning, me carrying presents down to the Mini, Sadie packing her salopettes into her suitcase. A hug, a kiss on the cheek, Happy Christmas, Happy New Year.

Back at my flat on Boxing Day afternoon, the non-drop Norwegian spruce has shed most of its needles onto the floorboards, but I turn on the fairy lights, nevertheless. Well, it's Christmas, innit? The main bedroom looks like it's been burgled – the wardrobe doors hang agape and all of Sadie's shoes and bags and suits and coats and dresses are gone. The chest of drawers I bought for Sadie six months ago, they loll open and empty, her various items of underwear disappeared out of our communality. Sheets, pillows and duvet are piled high and scattered wide. The white oak trunk that moved in with Sadie has vanished, leaving a square of clean in the dust at the foot of the bed. She hasn't even left a card.

My first thought is *Good for her*, and to my surprise I find myself smiling. It's not that I'm happy; I'm quite the opposite in fact. I really did like Sadie, and I'm sad that things have ended the way they have – we'd have made good friends. But the reality is, we weren't destined to be together forever. Probably not even for thirteen months, and while her leaving isn't a cause for celebration, it was right and inevitable and now it's done.

From beneath the bed I retrieve a shoebox, in which I store a collection of photos, letters and cards. I archive this year's Christmas cards from Dad and Bianca and go to replace the box. The lid, though, now sits an annoying two millimetres too high for the box to slide beneath the bed, and it looks like I'm at that stage in my life where I need to start a second shoebox. Fleetingly, I consider tipping the whole lot into the wastebasket, but you can bet your inheritance someone will die within five minutes of the bin men driving off. And isn't that the real reason we hoard this semi-sentimental junk – out of guilt and fear and superstition?

And so, instead of emptying the whole shoebox into a bin bag, I root through the concert and theatre stubs and foreign maps and currency and postcards and football medals to see if there are any items I can safely dispose of. At the bottom of the box is a red leatherette diary with the year's date embossed across the top in gold. My parents' idea of an exciting Christmas present for a teenage boy. It makes me smile nevertheless – a mixture of affection, embarrassment and nostalgia. The December 25th entry details my haul for that year: *New Liverpool kit, Umbro goalie gloves. Batman and Robin DVD (shit film but Uma is smoking hot). Oasis, Radiohead, Björk (definitely would) CDs. Catcher in the Rye (whatever). Lynx Africa body wash and D.O.*

Boxing Day's entry informs me that the Bond movie was *Goldfinger* and that Dad let me drink two cans of Foster's lager. There is no entry for December 27th. In fact, there is only one more entry and I know exactly when it is. Friday, July 19th.

Lost my V!!! No. 1, Trudi R. Everything × 2. 8/10.

Not the most ingenious code, admittedly. If Mum or Dad had ever discovered my diary (hidden in the attic under a roll of fibreglass loft insulation) they would hardly have needed an Enigma machine to ascertain that I'd had sex with Trudi Roberts, twice, and that I'd given her a higher mark than my mother ever did for her English homework.

The party was at Georgina Hollingsworth's parents' house, the fifth form started in a month, and I suppose we all felt pretty grown up. In less than a year we could legally buy cigarettes, have sex, sign on. In two years we could drive; in three, drink. We could hardly wait. And, like most fifteen-year-olds, we had no intention of doing so. Drinking no-frills vodka neat from the bottle and sharing a step on the hallway stairs, Trudi and I were discussing our plans for life after GCSEs. I was going to stay on for A levels, and Trudi had secured a hairdressing apprenticeship at her auntie's salon in Chester. She said I had nice hair (which made a pleasant change from 'Coppertop'), we discussed a few styling possibilities, and before you could say 'flat-top' our mouths were full of each other's tongues. From the stairs we adjourned to a bedroom and started getting adventurous on top of a mountain of coats. Before we were able to venture too far, Trudi succumbed to altitude sickness and vomited, very coolly, into a bedside drawer. I escorted her outside for fresh air and, arms tight around each other's waists, we strolled around the block waiting for Trudi's nausea to subside. My inexperience and associated awkwardness seemed to swell outside the confining walls of Georgina's house and, not knowing how to proceed but suspecting that marvellous things might occur if I did, I steered myself and Trudi towards the nearby playing fields where teenage couples grew in pairs.

After I've weeded out a selection of ticket stubs and decades-old Christmas cards, I replace my diary in the shoebox and the shoebox beneath my bed. I tidy the bedroom, change the sheets, wash the dishes, vacuum the pine needles, shower, make coffee, take down the decorations and throw out the Christmas tree.

I've just disposed of the Norwegian spruce when Douglas, my seventy-one-year-old downstairs neighbour, comes to his door and invites me in for a cup of tea. An Ulster Scot with a dry sense of humour and a rare vernacular, Douglas is a good man to live above. Before working as a gas engineer, he spent eight years in the army, so I'm well covered in the event of domestic emergencies involving plumbing or intruders. Plus he's fastidious about making tea and only buys biscuits that are coated in chocolate. As we're sipping our lapsang souchong, the old traitor casually informs me that he helped Sadie load her things into a black cab approximately fifteen minutes after I left on Christmas Eve. Suggesting she didn't need that much space in which to think, after all. Douglas gives me a card and hot-water bottle for Christmas. 'Well, I thought you might need it now as you're on yer ain.' And if it's a joke, he tells it with a very straight face. After we finish our tea, Doug opens the Laphroaig I gave him two days ago, and we drink a toast to good health and old friends.

Back in my own flat, warmed now by the peaty whisky, I've still got over an hour before I'm due to meet El.

With nothing better to do, I slide out the shoebox from its hiding place.

Lost my V!!! No. 1, Trudi R. Everything × 2. 8/10.

I find a biro and beneath 'Trudi R.' write: *No. 2, Lisa McSomething.* I feel a little guilty and ever so slightly roguish that I can't remember the full name of only my second sexual conquest. Although I have less trouble recalling the name of Number 3, Samantha Fawcett.

And this is how I while away the remainder of Boxing Day afternoon. There are memories fond, fearful and vague. Several times I lose the thread, but certain landmarks guide me back on track. I know, for example, that my second year at university was one of my most prolific, and that during those three terms I slept with eleven women. This isn't an achievement for which I was awarded a certificate, nor did I record the statistic in any diary. I simply know the number. I also know that I slept with fifteen women during thirteen months travelling Asia and the Antipodes, and that I scored my half-century in the room that came with the bar manager's job at the Old Oak in Islington. And so on. And while I knew roughly how many women I'd slept with, I didn't know exactly. Until now. Now I have a diary full of names, numbers and question marks – the sexual history of Thomas William Ferguson, aged thirty years eleven months and one week old.

What would you think if I told you I was a virgin? Unusual for a man of my age, no? You'd probably want to know why. Was something wrong? Broken? Was I religious, or a member of some other weird cult?

What if I said I'd had only a single sexual encounter? Say we were in the pub and the subject came up. *How many people have you slept with?* We go around the table: *Five, fifteen, seven, twelve, twenty-seven.* You get to me and I say, 'One.'

'One!' You all shout in unison.

The first guy says, 'I thought five was low! What have you been doing?'

Mr Fifteen pulls a face: 'Were you in prison?'

'Or a coma?' says Mr Twenty-Seven.

Everybody laughs.

So we've established that none is weird, and one is laughable. Two might elicit a patronising coo. Three would be better, five better still. What about a thousand? You'd fall off your barstool, appalled. Somewhere along the way, more went from being better to worse. So where exactly did this shift occur? At what point does 'one' more become 'one too many'? Thirty? Forty? Fifty? Okay, let's say fifty. Why is fifty worse than forty-nine? What's so bad about fifty? Or fifty-one, or fifty-two?

What's so bad about eighty-five?

Chapter Three

'Eighty-five!' says El. 'You filthy fucking slag.'

Jiang, the waiter, smiles awkwardly.

My best friend is impulsive, irritable, excitable, aggressive, blunt, inappropriate, clumsy and prone to depression. Though not all the time, and not necessarily all at once. Also, it is unlikely that he will reach his fortieth birthday. Sufferers of Huntington's disease survive, on average, between ten and twenty years after the onset of symptoms. El was diagnosed seven years ago, at the age of twenty-five. He can expect to die from heart failure, choking, pneumonia or a fall. Suicide is also a popular choice. It's a rare condition, and El developed it unusually young. And while all of the above are well-documented side effects of Huntington's, it would be rash to dismiss El's damning assessment of my character as merely symptomatic of his disease. He's always been a wanker.

We met at Bristol University. I rowed for my first two years, until a shoulder impingement and an indiscretion with the stroke's girlfriend made it all too uncomfortable. For a while, El joined the team as a wannabe cox but, despite his small stature, he wasn't cut out for the job. He steered a true line and called a regular rhythm, but it's hard to row when you're laughing – and El made us laugh every time out. With jargon including *strokes*, *oars*, *hold it up*, and a *cox box* at his disposal, El could fit more double entendres into two thousand metres than Benny

Hill managed to stuff into forty-five minutes. Add to that a camped-up commentary of the various rowers' pecs, delts and 'glistening biceps', and we had no choice but to throw him permanently overboard.

Nevertheless, El remained a regular at races and in the club-house, and we've been friends ever since. After graduating, he moved to Glasgow to study for a PhD. It would have been easy for us to drift apart, but we visited often and spent large chunks of our holidays together. After gaining a few more letters after his name, El moved to London and found digs a twenty-minute tube ride from the place I was renting. It was like old times again, and it makes me smile at how lucky I am to still have him. Even if he is a wanker.

Jiang manages to find room on our already overloaded table for a side of mushroom fried rice, a plate of crispy seaweed and two bottles of Tsingtao. There's enough food for four here, of which El will eat less than a quarter. Every time, I tell him: *This is too much, we'll never get through it*; and every time, he laughs and orders one more dish. Five foot six with a hat and boots on, honest smile, mischievous eyes, El looks like the cute one from just about any boy band. The sort of guy mothers love, because he's just so downright adorable.

'Eighty-fucking-five,' he says through a mouthful of beef in oyster sauce.

I almost ask El why he doesn't just shout it to the whole restaurant, but odds are he'd do exactly that, so I keep my mouth shut and fill his glass for him.

'So Sadie,' says El, 'is actually eighty-five. Sadie-five.'

'Very good.'

'Yes, I thought so. So what's going on? Is it . . . ?' El draws his fork across his throat in a gesture meant, I assume, to communicate the death of my relationship with Sadie.

'Looks like it. Came back from Dad's and all her stuff's gone.'

El winces. 'And this is all because of that . . . whatsaname, the one from your office?'

'Holly.'

'That's the one. Seems a bit harsh.'

I haven't told El (I haven't told anybody) about the whole Sadie-giving-a-co-worker-a-hand-job thing. The excitement might finish the bugger off.

'And you just snogged her?' El says.

I nod.

'Well, that'll learn you. If you're going to cheat, cheat properly.'

I raise my beer. 'Words to live by.'

El reaches for his drink, but his arm spasms, knocking the glass to the floor where it smashes. 'FUCK! Fucking bastard.'

'It's all right,' I say, rising from my chair.

Before I can get to my feet, Jiang arrives on the scene with a dustpan and a wet rag. As if he was waiting in the wings for just such a disaster.

'Don't worry,' says Jiang. 'It's only glass.'

'Full of fucking beer,' El says, and laughs.

Jiang smiles. 'I'll get a mop.'

'And another Tsingtao,' says El. 'I might even drink some of it.'

Despite the facade, I know how much these ticks and twitches upset El. They are the only visible sign of his degeneration, and they're getting worse. Up until two years ago El worked in a research lab at UCL, adding unpronounceable chemicals to test tubes full of mutated bacteria. However, as the Huntington's advanced, El's declining mental faculties left him unable to cope with, or care about, the job. Plus, and to quote the man himself, a lab full of glass and poison is no place for a guy with a twitch. These days El stays at home, reads when he has the energy and watches movies when he doesn't. Fortunately, his long-term partner, Phil, is solvent enough that money is one thing El doesn't have to worry about.

Jiang pours El's beer and places the glass towards the centre of the table. I mouth a silent *thank you*, and he smiles graciously.

A few years into his diagnosis, with an unknown span of time slowly unspooling behind him, El pledged to see a small group of his best friends on as regular a basis as possible. To this end, he embarked upon El's Dead Good World Tour ('*Dead* good, geddit?'). Each of these friends has been assigned a particular restaurant, and they meet there between once and a few times a month. A guy from El's old lab takes him to an Italian, a former boyfriend treats him to Thai, and some friend called Fisher does Indian. I get China. We meet in the Lucky Dragon around once a fortnight and have been doing so for around eighteen months, so Jiang has pretty much got the hang of us. He knows about El's illness, and we come early in the evening when the restaurant is relatively quiet.

Carefully, El takes a sip of his beer. 'So,' he says, wiping his lips, 'what are you going to do about it?'

'About Sadie?'

'Fuck Sadie. Sadie's history.'

'Harsh.'

'But fair,' says El.

'So what are you talking about? What am I going to do about what?'

'Eighty-five,' El says, using his fork to trace the digits into his oyster sauce. 'That's almost a hundred.'

'Did Phil cook Christmas dinner?' I ask, sensing where this is going and not liking the look of the neighbourhood.

El shrugs, points his fork at me. 'You should go for your century.'

'Turkey and all the trimmings?'

'Say you're playing snooker or cricket,' El continues. 'And you rack up eighty-five points, runs, whatever. You don't quit. You get your head down and get on with it.'

'Fine,' I say. 'I'll do it. I'll put an ad in the paper.'

'Don't be facetious; I'm only trying to help.'

I take a long sip of my Tsingtao.

'Do you know how many people I've slept with?' El asks.

I sip more beer and shrug.

'Guess.'

'I don't know. Ten? Twenty?'

'Guess again.'

'A hundred,' I say.

'Do I look like a slag?'

I give El the finger.

He holds up four in return. 'Three men and' – he shudders – 'one woman.'

'I think that's sweet,' I say.

'It's pathetic. So, if not for yourself, do it for me. Think of it as having my share.'

'Christ, El, you're like a . . . like a dog with a hard-on.'

'Very apt.'

And this is how it goes for the next thirty-several minutes. I try, numerous times, to change topic, but El's train of thought is locomotive and will not be derailed. While I eat, he bombards me with rhetoric, both rational and ridiculous, and while El seems to have forgotten we're in a restaurant, I've eaten so much I'm sweating MSG. The sight of the remaining food is making me uncomfortable so I beckon Jiang over and he sets about clearing the dishes.

Balancing a kilo of uneaten food, Jiang asks with a straight face if we would like dessert. We order two coffees.

'What have you got to lose?' El continues. 'You might even meet someone nice.'

'Done that, didn't like it.'

'Think about all the nuns, priests and ugly people that don't sleep with anyone at all.'

'And your point is?'

'The point is,' says El, 'we need your hundred to maintain the global average.'

'What about porn stars and rock stars?'

'Exactly,' says El. 'Gene Simmons – from Kiss – he reckons he's shagged four *thousand* women.'

'Bullshit.'

'Read it in a magazine,' says El. 'Lemmy, the bloke with the warts from Motörhead, said he'd done over a thousand. Even Paul Daniels bonked seven hundred and something.'

'The magician?'

'Yep.'

'Utter bollocks.'

El shrugs.

'And how does all this fit your theory of me bringing up the global average?' I ask.

'Forget the global average.'

'Gladly.'

'But if Paul Daniels could convince seven hundred women to play with his magic wand, the very absolute least you can do is do a hundred. Otherwise it's just embarrassing.'

And El does have a point, albeit a blunt one distorted beneath the relentless mallet of his wonky sensibilities. The idea of being single again, and all the fun stuff that encapsulates, is not entirely unappealing. Not in the mathematical sense that El is advocating, just in the sense of having a good time and rebuilding my ego. Plus, and shame on me if it's wrong, I do like having sex with pretty ladies.

The waiter arrives with our coffees and bill, and I fish my credit card from my wallet.

'Jiang,' says El, 'how many people have you shagged?'

Jiang looks for a hole in the ground to reverse into, doesn't find one and looks to me appealingly.

'Sorry, Jiang, he's being a . . . he's just . . .' I hand him my credit card. 'Will you put it on this, please?'

'Was that inappropriate?' says El, after Jiang has retreated with my plastic.

'He'll get over it. You can leave the tip.'

El leans across the table and whispers, 'A hundred quid.'

'It's a little steep, mate.'

'For you. I'll bet you a hundred quid you can't do it.'

I pull a face designed to project utter exasperation and total refusal.

'Is that a yes?' says El.

'No, it's a no, you muppet.'

'I'll give you a year.'

'I don't want a year. And I don't want your hundred quid; you already owe me a meal.'

El blows a loud raspberry. 'When did you lose your virginity?' he asks.

'Difference does that make?'

'Conversation, innit? When'd you' – El slides his finger into the corner of his mouth and snaps it out with a loud pop – 'your cherry?'

'I was fifteen.'

'Dirty bugger. When, though? Date, and don't pretend you don't know.'

'July.'

'The . . .'

'Nineteenth.'

'Nice time of year for cherries,' says El, and I can't help but laugh. 'C-day,' he says, encouraged by my reaction. 'C for cock, C for cu—'

'Yes,' I say. 'I get it.'

'Well, you do seem to. Okay then – C-day plus one *thousand* pounds.'

This time I go for unadulterated incredulity.

'Good bet, yes?' says El.

'No. It's not. It's an absolutely awful bet.'

'That gives you . . .' El counts on his fingers. 'Four, five, six . . . almost seven months. What's that in weeks?'

'Twenty-eight . . . ish.'

'Okay. Twenty-eight-ish weeks to score fifteen runs. That's what . . . about one every two weeks-ish?'

El delights in mischief, it's one of the reasons I love him. But this bet, the almost autistic belligerence, it's not El. It's the insidious disease that's taking him over. And it's tiring.

'Fancy a pint on the way home?' I say.

'Does George Michael shit in the woods?'

'Well, if you shut up, I'll buy you one.'

El zips his mouth, locks it, throws away the key.

Then he says, 'You could start with that whatsaname, Holly.'

Eighty-five.

It sounds big all in one lump, but this is the product of almost sixteen years' work:

One plus two plus two plus five plus eleven plus nine plus fifteen plus seven plus eleven plus three plus two plus six plus four plus four plus three plus none equals eighty-five.

I've been consistent. I've been in the right place at the right time – eighty-five times, in fact. University, for example, is a place kids go to get drunk and have sex. You won't find it in any prospectus, but neither do you need a degree in social anthropology to appreciate the truth of the situation. I toured Asia. I worked in and lived above a bar. If you can't get laid in those situations, either you're not trying or you're absent a working set of genitalia. And I tried. I got myself out there, kept in shape, moisturised. Being tall helps, too. I'm easy to find in a dark, crowded bar for one thing. And it's not '*short*, dark and handsome', is it? That said, I'm hardly dark. In fact, if you asked one hundred people to name their least favourite hair colour, about ninety of them would pick mine. But at least it's not that boiled carrot colour; it's the copper variety or, as we like to call it, 'auburn'. And some people like it, thank you very much. Which – as we seem to be doing the 'big three' – brings us to handsome. Whether I am, I don't honestly know, but I'm not *not*; there's nothing obviously off. I have pale blue eyes, straight teeth, my ears lie flat to the sides of my head. And, if Bianca is to be believed, I have good eyelashes. I'd give myself six out of ten, maybe seven on a good day at the right angle in favourable light . . . Call it six and a half. I can live with that.

With one eye on the TV and the other on my list of conquests – as if I'm sneaking up on them – I'm able to overwrite several question marks with names and, in some cases, marks out of ten. At the bottom of the list, without making a higher-brain decision to do so, I write the words *Sadie-Five* – and I go over the capital 'S', turning it into an 8: *8adie-Five.* And I add a score: *7/10.*

Then, purely for fun, I write the numbers *86, 87, 88* and so on, all the way to *100*, which I decorate with stars and flags and fireworks.

Chapter Four

Sadie used to say, *Would you love me if I was fat?*

How fat? I'd ask.

An extra stone.

Of course.

Two stone?

More of you to love. And me – what if lost my hair?

Wouldn't bother me.

Lost a leg?

You'd never run away.

We'll grow fat together. Bald together. Old and toothless and grey together.

Romantic lies.

About four months after moving in, she pinched me on the love handle while she kissed me on the cheek, saying nothing but making her point nevertheless. I checked in the bathroom mirror, and no doubt about it, my waist was beginning to thicken – not much and not that you'd notice under clothes, but I've seen my father with his shirt off and the warning signs were there. A few weeks later, Sadie joined a gym and told me – more than once – that they did a discount membership for couples. I bought a rowing machine. But the sound of the fan used to annoy Sadie if she was anywhere in the flat. On the other hand, I only ever got the urge to use it when Sadie was home. Which, with the benefit of hindsight, was a warning sign of another kind.

This morning it takes eighteen minutes and forty-three seconds to row four thousand metres, which is a couple of minutes more and few thousand metres less than is ideal. My shoulder seems to be holding up, but my heart feels like it's trying to hammer its way out of my chest. Maybe it's all the Chinese food I've been eating, or maybe it's simply time I got myself back in shape.

I'm a single man, after all.

Following a long shower and a breakfast of coffee and thin air, my heart rate has finally dropped to somewhere in the double digits. It's New Year's Day in less than a week, so I resolve to get fit and get rid of these nascent love handles before they become the real thing. And, as any idiot knows, the first step in an effective fitness programme is to buy a fridge full of healthy food and a new pair of expensive trainers.

I'm gently buoyed by good intentions as I pull on my coat and head outside. I'm a long way from whistling a jaunty tune, but I do toss my car keys in the air as I step into the crisp December sunshine.

And then I drop them.

Some bastard has stolen my car.

That's the first thought that enters my head as I stare stupidly at the place where I'm pretty certain I parked it yesterday afternoon. People don't move other people's cars to the opposite side of the road or to nearby streets, but I zig-zag-zig up and down Poets' Corner, checking Spenser, Byron and Tennyson Roads just in case. If the Mini had a name, I'd probably call it out as if summoning a lost dog.

When I get back to the flat I'm hot and hoarse and sweaty so, before I call the police, I stop in the kitchen for a glass of water. Where, despite matters more pressing, I'm surprised to see that I've left the milk out – that's Sadie's trick, not mine. I am also reasonably confident that I didn't use the pink mug with a cat printed on it. And that if I had, I would have put it in the dishwasher afterwards. Not left it on the countertop next to . . .

Fuck.

. . . my little red diary.

Which I'm pretty certain I left in the living room.

Maybe, I tell myself, I inadvertently left the diary here last night. The way you might, when tired and distracted, put a knife in the fork drawer, milk in the bathroom cabinet, the remote in the fridge. There's a chance, I reason, that Sadie . . .

What the hell was she doing letting herself into the flat, anyway?!

. . . while drinking coffee in plain sight of an open diary in her ex-boyfriend's kitchen, wasn't in the slightest bit tempted to take a peek.

I approach the counter and pick up the diary as if it might be booby-trapped.

When there is no explosion, I open my eyes. When I see Sadie's red-inked handwriting, I nearly drop the book and run. Gouged into the paper, beneath *8adie-Five, 7/10,* are these words:

Eighty-six, fuck your sad self. PTO.

I turn the page: *The car's at the airport.*

Next page: *Borrowed your snowboard.*

Followed by: *Your boots were too small. Connor's an 11. Happy New Year, Sadie-Five X*

There are no more entries.

I guess Sadie decided not to take her sister skiing after all, opting instead for *Connor*, whoever the hell he is, although I can make a pretty good guess. Connor on my holiday, that I paid for, with my *ex*-girlfriend. Connor drinking my champagne in my snow. Connor with his big bastarding feet all over *my* snowboard.

Now I see what I have so far somehow missed.

Perhaps I should be thankful that Sadie thought to place my snowboard boots in the sink before filling each with a bottle of expensive Shiraz Cabernet. But I'm not.

Turning my back on the mess, I walk through to the living room, find my phone and send a text to El:

You're on.

MAY

A LITTLE MORE THAN FOUR MONTHS LATER

Chapter Five

Holly is still singing but she's relocated from the shower to the kitchen and segued from 'Lovely Day' to 'Do That to Me One More Time'. Talk about a theme tune. True to El's prediction, Holly was the eighty-sixth name on my list. She has also made guest appearances in between 88 and 89; 89 and 90; 91 and 92; and, after last night's antics, between 94 and whoever comes next.

Hanging on the wall in front of the rowing machine is a motivational poster of the sort normally found in gyms or advertising agency corridors. The framed print features a wide-angled shot of a single-man skull ploughing a furrow across an airbrushed lake. It's early and the shadows are long. Printed in italicised script across the dawn sky are the words: *Obstacles are what we see when we take our eyes off the goal.*

Naff, to be sure, but it's a nice picture and – annoying really – the thought does spur me on during the last five hundred metres of a 10k pull. It was a birthday present from Douglas, and I imagine he was pretty pleased with himself when he found it. Sadie would have hated it, and every time there was a knock at the door I'd have had to retrieve the picture from under the bed and hang it just in case the person at the door was Douglas asking could he use the rower for twenty minutes. He never has, but it's not beyond the bounds of possibility.

Holly – wet-haired, towel knotted around her cleavage – pads into the room, carrying two mugs of coffee in one hand and a plate of toast in the other.

'Milk no sugar, two slices, one jam one peanut butter.'

'Oh, right, thanks,' I say, not wanting to seem ungracious but at the same time not wanting to appear too comfortable with Holly knowing how I like my coffee or where I keep the peanut butter.

Holly has stayed here often enough now that she has a favourite mug – printed on the side is an image of the Loch Ness monster rearing up from the water. The words *One Day We'll Find It* are printed in curving script above a bright rainbow. Sadie picked it out as a souvenir from one of the many gift shops in the area. I chose a pen with an image of woman inside the top half of the barrel – when tipped a certain way, her kilt slips down to her knees. Printed on the bottom half of the barrel is the line *I saw it at Loch Ness!* The mug is one of the last remaining relics of Sadie's occupancy. In the four months since she left, I have gradually cleared away old papers, odd socks and dropped hair slides. But not the mug. I like the mug, the souvenir reminding me of more than a body of water in the Scottish Highlands. Sadie and I may not have been a match made in heaven, but we had more than a few good times, and this mug makes me remember them fondly.

The Mini, however, is a different matter. We are still joint owners of the car, and its presence – or absence, on the occasions when Sadie takes it – serve as a two-ton reminder of everything that went wrong. Around two weeks after Sadie emptied two bottles of wine into my ski boots, she came to take the car for a weekend, filling its boot with a few items she had left behind. She still has my snowboard, of course, but I'm too embarrassed to mention it, given the circumstances surrounding her taking it. We drank a cup of coffee at the kitchen table, making official what we already knew. Voices were raised, but only so far; there were tears, but only a couple of slow rollers; nothing was thrown, no one was slapped. We hugged on the doorstep, a kiss on the cheek as articulate as anything we'd said in anger or apology around the table.

After Sadie left I washed up the mugs, hers with a green monster grinning on the side. Whether she left it deliberately or not I don't know, and it makes me slightly uneasy watching Holly slowly appropriate my ex-girlfriend's mug. As if she is taking her place, which she isn't and which she won't.

I like Holly. There is nothing to dislike about her. Except, perhaps, for her indefatigable vigour, which isn't in itself a flaw but is nevertheless exhausting and occasionally irritating. Like a fairground – fun for a few hours while tipsy, but you can do without it first thing in the morning with a hangover.

Holly sits on the bed and the towel slips from her boobs. 'Oopsy.'

'Blimey,' I say, nodding at the bedside clock, 'is that really the time?'

'Not trying to get rid of me, are you?' says Holly in a tone of voice that suggests she doesn't for one second believe this to be the case.

'Don't be daft. Just don't want to make you late.'

Holly kisses my cheek. 'Sweet. Are you going in?'

'Yeah. Later. Just got to' – I hold an invisible phone to my ear – 'make a few calls. I'll be in before lunchtime.'

And not be seen walking in with the secretary-slash-runner who happens to be wearing the same T-shirt she was wearing last night.

Holly takes off the towel, envelops her head in its folds and dries her hair with unnerving vigour. Her breasts jounce and bounce like a pair of sugar-rushed babies.

This is the thing with Holly. She has an easy, guileless sexuality. And it's . . . well, *sexy*. The morning after the night before, I come across all modest and hide behind a towel, dressing gown, pair of undies – all three. Holly, on the other hand, it's not so much that she's comfortable with her nakedness, but that she's entirely oblivious to it. I can imagine her leaving the house for work and forgetting her clothes the way you might forget a watch or a woolly hat – an optional but non-essential accessory – and only realising she's naked when she goes to put her hand in her pocket for her bus pass. And she is as uninhibited in bed (or the kitchen or the hallway stairs or an empty tube carriage or on the rowing machine) as she is singing along to the office radio. She's twenty-three, healthy, maybe ten maybe twenty pounds overweight, but they're well-proportioned, springy, twenty-three-year-old, puppy-fattish pounds. She has a little tummy and more than a little bum, but she wears it well and probably would if there were another ten pounds on top. Riding cowgirl with reckless enthusiasm, her bottom lip between her teeth and hair sweat-stuck to her face, just when you think she's going to catapult the pair of you clean off the bed, Holly smiles in that way, says 'brace yourself' and bounces even harder.

But, as much fun as a fumble with Holly undoubtedly is, it has to stop. In the four months since Christmas, I have slept with one colleague, one colleague of a friend, one friend of a friend, one friend of a friend's wife, two Sues, one jogger, one supermarket cashier, and one pregnant lady whom I helped home with her shopping. It is roughly ten weeks until C-day, and I'm still six away from one hundred. So if I'm going to sleep with the wrong person, I owe it to myself to make it someone new.

'Everything okay?' asks Holly.

'Sure, why?'

'You're biting your thumb.'

'Bad habit,' I say.

Holly takes hold of my thumb and runs her finger over the indented teeth marks. She kisses it better and I trace the forefinger of my free hand along the under-curve of her thigh.

'We'll have to be quick,' Holly says.

'Shouldn't be a problem.'

Holly pushes me flat and straddles my hips in one fluid motion. 'Brace yourself.'

Chapter Six

The Blank Slate office is an open-plan, warehouse-style space on the top floor of a four-storey slab just off Tottenham Court Road. The walls are bare brick hung with classic movie posters, and beside Holly's reception desk stands a glass cabinet containing minuscule film canisters, scaled-down director's chairs, dinky cameras on tripods, and other trinkets of industry recognition.

The most recent addition to this collection is a silver clapperboard bearing the name Ben Nicholson, awarded in the category of best director for a food commercial under thirty seconds with a budget under one hundred thousand pounds. It's probably unprofessional to have a favourite director, but I do and his name begins with 'B'. Ben and I have known each other since we were both runners, and this was his first award. It's not the Cannes Grand Prix, but the way we celebrated that night, it might as well have been. Although, in retrospect, this may have been a mistake. In the six weeks since, we've been offered a range of scripts. *Slightly* bigger budgets, *slightly* bigger brands, but Ben – an award-winning director now – is holding out for something he can be 'proud of'. Problem is, this is advertising, and those scripts don't come around all that often, and when they do, they tend to go to the guy who won the Cannes Grand Prix. Meanwhile, we all have bills to pay. It's my job – not only as Ben's producer, but as his friend – to snap him the fuck out of it. For one thing, I'm afraid of his wife. Sophie is currently on maternity leave from a big American bank; she earns more than Ben and me put together and is on full pay for a year. Ben sees this as a licence to procrastinate and demur. Sophie sees that as an affront to everything she has worked for. And she is holding me responsible.

I have four scripts in my bag that will pay him more than he's earned in the past six months added together, and I'm not going home until he agrees to shoot them.

'Hey, Tom,' says Holly as I walk through the door, as if she wasn't singing in my shower just three hours ago. 'And how are you today?' As if she hadn't been bouncing on my lap fit to break the bedsprings.

'I'm very well, Holly. Bright-tailed and bushy-eyed.'

'Hungover, then?' Ben says, typing at his keyboard.

'And a good day to you too, Benjamin.'

Rob, a junior director straight out of film school, looks up from a magazine. 'Tomster,' he says, making me grind my teeth. 'How's the head? Mine is *min*-ging.'

'Clear as a bell,' I lie.

'What time were you out till?' Ben asks, still not deigning to look at me.

'I'm not sure, Daddy. Did you wait up?'

Holly snorts.

'You were still there when I left,' says Rob helpfully. 'Weren't you, Tom? You and Holly.'

Now Ben looks at me.

Holly does a 'naughty me' face: *Aren't I crazy?*

'Really?' I say. 'You left before us, did you?'

'You were well pissed,' says Rob.

I frown with incredulity.

'You were,' Rob persists. 'Well wrecked.'

Holly mimes downing a pint and pulls cross-eyes.

It's not fair to hate Rob for this apparent whistle-blowing; he isn't criticising me, he's lauding me. No, I hate him for his boundless exuberance. What with him and Holly, this place should have a wicker basket and a rubber bone in the corner.

'Ben,' I say, holding my bag aloft, 'ready for a little tête-à-tête, or did you just come in to watch cat videos?'

'Five minutes,' says Ben.

'Fine,' I say. 'I'll be in the Fishbone.'

Ben's grumpiness is part of his charm, and he has a six-month-old baby at home who is apparently allergic to sleep. But he seems particularly curmudgeonly today. He's said little more than half a dozen words in ten minutes, and three of those were 'pie and chips'. Which means I've been looking at the top of his head for five minutes now as he hunkers down over his steak and kidney. It's a vaguely mesmerising view. Not long into his thirties, Ben is losing his hair the way a drunk loses his temper – rapidly and with a mixture of contempt, denial and defiance. Ben has updated the tradition of the comb-over by styling his hair upwards and inwards into a precarious, hollow quiff. The result is something like a bonfire built during a tree shortage, and I'd be doing him a favour if I struck a match and set the whole thing alight – it would be a brief and unspectacular blaze. As a friend, I should say something, but I've been hoping Sophie will spare me the embarrassment – after all, she's the one who has to sleep next to it, she's the one who vowed 'for better or worse'.

'How's the pie?' I ask.

Ben barely takes his eyes off his lunch. 'What happened with Holly last night?'

'Nothing.' I fork battered cod into my mouth.

'Nothing nothing, or shagged her again nothing?'

Everyone knows about me and Holly in January. Ben knows about me and Holly in February and March. But, as far as I'd hoped, only me and Holly know about me and Holly last night. Electing to brazen this challenge out, I shake my head in a way intended to convey righteous indignation.

'Well?'

'Well nothing,' I say. 'We left before closing, I gave Holly a lift in my taxi, end of story.'

All of which, if you think about it from the right angle, is true. We did share a taxi, and I don't intend expanding on events.

'Anyway,' I say, 'I thought we were meant to be talking about the pitch.'

'Have you called Flo?'

'*Jesus*, Ben.'

Ben puts his knife and fork down, all business. 'So that's a no, is it?'

'Yes, Ben. It's a no. No, I haven't called Flo.'

'And that's that, is it?'

'If you're so concerned,' I say, 'why don't you call her?'

'Because *I* didn't shag her?'

Flo is a college friend of Sophie's. And it was Sophie's idea to set us up on a date.

It was raining and I was early, so I found a table inside the designated bar and ordered a bottle of ostentatiously expensive red wine. Flo arrived half a glass later.

I stood to greet her, we shook hands, pecked cheeks. I filled Flo's glass while she collapsed her umbrella, placed it on the table, shook the raindrops from her coat and draped it across the back of her chair. As Flo took her seat I picked up her umbrella and levelled it at her chest. 'Stick 'em up,' I said, thinking it would be a funny icebreaker. But in the process of aiming Flo's umbrella, I must have clicked the trigger. The brolly telescoped towards Flo, unfolding and expanding in dreadful slow motion. I watched helplessly as the polka-dot canopy knocked the bottle from the table and the glass from Flo's hand. To give Flo her due, she maintained some degree of composure, but it didn't change the fact that her cream shirt (possibly new) was now soaked in Californian Pinot Noir.

If it had been deliberate I'd be a genius.

Flo needed to change so we took a cab back to her flat. And within fifteen minutes of walking through the front door we were naked on her sofa. From whence it progressed swiftly downhill – the sex was awkward, the post-sex conversation stilted and the takeaway pizza chewy. I didn't stay the night, and in the cab home I was under no illusions about ever making the return journey. Nevertheless, I'd felt it was a touch too soon to call Flo and apprise her of my decision at that precise moment, just one hundred and sixty-eight minutes post-coitus. Ditto Sunday – who wants that kind of conversation on a day of rest? And if there's one thing I learned from my relationship with Sadie, it's that women do not appreciate being dumped by email while at work on a Monday morning. Not that it should even qualify as a dumping; that would imply we were in a relationship. And we weren't. We never even made it into a bed.

Flo called on the Wednesday, and I explained I had plans that weekend. And, sorry, the weekend after, too. You'd think that would be the end of it. Short of spelling it out – *Listen, I know we had sex on your sofa and everything, but something about you just irritated the hell out of me* – I couldn't have been more explicit. And, hey, call me a bounder, but sometimes honesty is not the best policy.

I set down my own cutlery. 'Listen, Ben, what happened happened, and it's not going to happen again. I haven't spoken to Flo for two weeks and I reckon she's got the message by now. So why are you being so slow on the uptake?'

'Maybe it's because she was crying on the frigging phone to Sophie for an hour last night while I was trying to watch the footy.'

I can't help but smirk. 'So now we get down to it. You're in a big Hugh Huffner because Sophie gave you an earful about that awful friend of yours. Right?'

'And that if you're such a shit, maybe I am too,' says Ben.

'A shit?'

Ben shrugs and starts in again on his pie.

'Mate,' I say. 'I'm no psychologist—'

My friend laughs a staccato and mirthless 'Ha!' at this manifest truth.

'*But*,' I persist, 'if Flo was crying on the phone last night, it was because of something bigger and deeper than me. We barely spent five hours together – during which time she bemoaned her job, her flat, London, her ex-boyfriend, her sister's children and the sodding pizza we were eating. I'm the absolute least of her problems. And me calling her now isn't going to change any of that. If anything, it'll make matters worse.'

The corner of Ben's mouth tightens in an expression of reluctant agreement.

'Mate,' I say, 'I'm sorry if Sophie's giving you a hard time. But Flo's . . . you know . . .'

Ben nods. 'Hard graft.'

'Exactly. And you and Soph set me up with her. If anyone has the right to be in a strop, it's me.'

'Thought you might like her,' Ben says petulantly.

'Why? What exactly did you think I'd warm to? Her boundless optimism? Her wacky sense of humour? Her *joie de* sodding *vivre*?'

Ben smiles apologetically and mimes a pair of gigantic breasts.

'They were pretty spectacular,' I agree.

'Tell me about it,' says Ben, laughing.

'So' – I indicate my cooling fish and chips – 'can I eat my lunch now?'

'Sorry, mate; I'm exhausted. Sammy was up at two and again at four, and then I had Soph going on about private-school fees until five in the frigging morning. He's not even six months. Do you know how much it costs to put a nipper through private primary school?'

I shrug. 'Grand a month?'

'Hah! Try three.'

'Well,' I say, sensing my opening and reaching for my bag, 'this little lot will get him though the best part of three years.'

I place the scripts on the table between us. Collectively, the campaign is called Little Horrors – four scripts in which children behave like brats, are given sweets and settle down.

Ben puts his head in his hands, leaves it there for a second, then – with the look of a man cornered – peers at me from between his fingers.

'Have you read them yet?'

Ben nods. 'Bit derivative, aren't they?'

'I don't think so.'

'There was a campaign just like it last year. Little Devils, I think.'

I act like this means nothing to me.

'For Maltesers,' says Ben.

'Well, there you go; these are Skittles, entirely different. And anyway, who cares? Six months from now, no one will remember them anyway.'

'Is that supposed to motivate me?'

'Look, of course it's been done before, and it will be done again. And again. Like Shakespeare, but you don't hear Branagh going, "*Hamlet*? Sorry, love; it's been done", do you? No, we embrace the challenge and imbue it with our unique artistic vision.'

Ben shakes his head, but despite himself, he's smiling. Of course he doesn't buy my shtick, and if he did, I'd be disappointed. But his defences, I can tell, are weakening.

'Ben, they asked for you specifically. Big agency, big brand. One thing leads to another, right? Make some money now, win some awards later. I can call Kaz right this second' – I pick up my phone – 'and you can buy a bottle of champagne on the way home. Who knows, maybe Sophie'll be up for an early night.'

'Well, let's not count our . . . you know.'

'You'll be fine,' I say. 'Buy her some flowers. Chocolates too, go the whole nine yards.'

'That's not what I mean,' Ben says. 'What I mean is, I'm not necessarily one hundred per cent sure that I want to do them.'

'What are you on about? How necessarily sure are you? Ninety per cent?'

Ben screws up half of his face in a deliberative wince.

'Eighty?' I try.

'It's hard to be mathematically precise.'

'Seventy? For God's sake, it's got to be at least seventy.'

'Ish. Maybe.'

'Jesus, Ben, you're set to make more here than a junior doctor makes in a year. What the fuck is there to be *ish* about?'

'Well, it's the scripts, isn't it?'

'From where I'm sitting that's the good thing,' I say. 'There's four of the buggers.'

'I know, but they're not very . . . *good* buggers.'

'I'll let you in on a secret, shall I?'

'Spare me the lecture, Tom.'

'No can do. You see this isn't art, love. This is ads. This is a job. And you haven't earned a penny in nearly three months.'

'Something will come up.'

'Hello,' I say, rapping the scripts with my knuckles. 'It already has. *Four* scripts with a sodding great budget.'

'But the budget doesn't make the scripts any better, does it? You can't polish a turd.'

'No, you can't. But you can sprinkle glitter on it. And you can get paid a fortune to do it.'

'Let me sleep on it.'

'You don't get any sleep, remember? On account of your son, who is going to languish in a crappy state school if you don't earn some money fast.'

'I'd hardly say la—'

'If the poor boy learns anything at all it'll be how to climb drain-pipes and pick locks. He'll probably end up on drugs, and when he does you'll look back on this day and kick yourself hard. And if you don't, I will.'

'You're hysterical.'

I pour salt into my palm and sprinkle it across the table. 'Bit of glitter, yes? Little bit of Ben's fairy dust?'

Ben throws his hands in the air. 'Fine.'

'Get paid lots of lovely money? Yes? Little bit of cash?'

'Okay, you can stop now.'

'Make some dosh, chunk of change, fat stacks, big slice of cheddar, filthy lu—'

'I'll do it! I'll do it! Just please stop, before I change my mind.'

'You're sure? I'd hate to pressure you.'

'Fuck off.'

'Nice one. I'll let 'em know. Now, have you met the agency producer before? Kaz?'

'Once or twice.'

'Great. There's a party tonight in the N—'

'No way. I shoot the films, you kiss the arse. And be nice, yeah?'

'Nice is my middle name. You cheeky bastard.'

Chapter Seven

The party is in the basement of a private members' bar in the middle of Soho; it's cramped and dingy and any space not filled with bodies is filled with noise. The sun is still out above ground, but down here it could be midnight. Ben took the liberty of inviting Rob along on my behalf, saying it would be good for him to network. But I suspect he was actually hoping our junior director would function as a kind of unwitting chaperone.

Rob meets someone he knows at the bar, and I smile and nod and excuse myself to the toilets. I can't have been gone more than four minutes, but when I return there are twice as many people crowding the bar and there is a corresponding increase in noise and decrease in available oxygen. Whether or not Rob and my drink are still at the bar is impossible to tell from this vantage point, and I'd require a crowbar and a flashlight to get close enough to find out. I have neither, so I weave a reconnaissance circuit, following the path of least resistance through the tangle of bodies, but I see no sign of Kaz – the person I'm supposed to be schmoozing and the only reason I'm here instead of at home, catching up on much needed sleep. All at once, last night catches up with me like a punch in the back of the head and if I don't leave soon I might just pass out on the spot. Hauling myself forward like a thing undead, eyes locked onto the oblong of yellow light at the far end of the room, I have almost reached the exit when someone pinches me on the backside.

Kaz, the agency producer on Little Horrors, emerges from a shadow. And this must be how that guy felt in *The Great Escape*.

'Tom,' she says, inclining her cheek upwards. 'It's been ages.'

I catch a strong whiff of wine as I lean in to kiss the proffered cheek. 'Too long,' I say. 'But you'll be sick of the sight of me after the shoot.'

'So glad Ben's up for it. I've had my eye on him for a while, you know.' Kaz flutters a little wink.

'I'll let him know,' I tell her. 'And he loves the scripts, by the way. Loves them.'

Kaz flaps her hand dismissively. 'I think they're a bit derivative, TBH, and the creative is a twerp. But what's new?' She's not exactly slurring her words, but she is running them dangerously close together.

'Ben here?'

'New baby,' I say. 'He's gone home to try and get some sleep.'

Kaz drifts into my personal airspace. 'And what about you?' she says, taking hold of my left hand and inspecting the fingers. 'Is there a Mrs Tom?'

Kaz and I know each other in the same way that most of Ad-Land knows each other. Superficially – via industry parties, mutual acquaintances and dubious gossip. I don't know the word on me, but the word on Kaz is she's a good producer and a terrible flirt.

I shake my head. 'Single.'

'Not even a girlfriend?'

'No one'll have me,' I say.

'You're sweet,' says Kaz, taking a sip of her wine. She blinks lazily as if the booze has gone straight to her eyelids. 'Have to see if I can fix you up with one of my friends,' she says. 'I'm sure we can find someone for a good-looking boy like you.'

I laugh modestly.

'Seriously,' says Kaz. 'I'd definitely fix you up.'

Kaz looks like there's something Asian in her recent ancestry: sharp eyes, ink-black hair hanging to her shoulders. She looks like she gets great value out of her gym membership, and if it's true that birds of a feather flock together, then it's a good bet Kaz has some very sexy friends. But before my smirk spreads too wide, I flash back to my earlier conversation with Ben in the Fishbone café. I don't exactly have a great track record with friends of friends, or friends of anyone for that matter. A date with a friend of Kaz could be disastrous professionally.

'That's very kind,' I say. 'But I wouldn't wish me on any of your friends.'

'Confirmed bachelor?' says Kaz.

'Not at all,' I say with faux-defensiveness. 'Just haven't met the right girl yet.'

'Are you flirting with me, Thomas Ferguson?' She squeezes my hand and stares at me for maybe half a second too long – just long enough to be unnerving.

'No. God no.'

Kaz scowls, feigning offence.

'Not that I wou— I mean . . . I was just . . . you know, saying.'

'*Joking*,' she says, widening her eyes to make the point. 'I envy you. Being single.'

'God knows why.'

'Thrill of the chase,' she says, and still she is holding my hand. 'When you meet some cute guy in a bar . . . and you're not quite sure which way it's going to go?'

Kaz looks up at me from under her fringe, a hint of a pout on her lips. There are flecks of glitter on her cheekbones; cracks in her lipstick.

And then, over the top of her head, I spot Rob grinning like a ventriloquist's dummy. He gives me two thumbs up.

'You know what I mean?' says Kaz, tugging on my hand.

'Sure,' I say, and when I look up again, Rob has vanished. 'I know exactly what you mean.'

Kaz nods, slowly and sincerely, as if we're old friends sharing a deep insight into the ways of the world. 'You know what you are, Tom? You're a nice bloke.'

'Some people might debate that,' I say. 'But it's nice of you to say so.'

'I'd pull you,' says Kaz. 'If I was single.' Her thigh is flush against mine now, and my cock pulses reflexively.

'Story of my life,' I say. 'A day late and a dollar shor—'

'Hold on a second.' Kaz takes her hand from mine, slides it into her jeans pocket and produces a ringing phone. 'Hold that thought,' she says to me before answering the call.

What the *fuck* am I doing? From Holly to Kaz within the space of a dozen hours. Shitting on one's doorstep is inadvisable enough, and here am I, attempting to dump in the back garden while the mess on my front porch is still steaming.

Kaz twirls a lock of black hair around her index finger. Into her phone, half under her breath, she says, 'Do you now?' She smiles at me; I smile back: *Hello*. 'Tell me more,' Kaz says to her caller. 'Uh huh . . . mm hmm . . . *yes*, you know I do.' Kaz angles her body away from me, breaking eye contact, making me look even more like a six-foot-three-and-a-half-inch lemon. I sip my beer but it's lost its fizz.

'Where are you now?' Kaz says. I tap her on the shoulder, gesture towards the door, wave and mouth the words *Got to go*. She places her hand on my wrist, grips it, says into the phone: 'What? Oh, nothing . . . mm hmm . . . love you too. Kiss kiss. I'll get a taxi.' And she hangs up.

'Wrong number?' I ask.

Kaz punches me on the arm. 'Kidder.'

I widen my eyes, pull a jolly face.

'Well, I must fly,' says Kaz. 'Nice bumping into you, Tom.'

'Likewise,' I say. 'And I'm looking forward to working together.'

Kaz tiptoes up and pecks me once on each cheek. 'You bet,' she says. 'Give my love to Ben.'

I give Kaz a three-minute head start, then take myself and my wilted hard-on into the fading evening to find a taxi.

***

Fridays aren't what they used to be.

Usurped by Thursdays as the default night for a drink with your colleagues and a chance of getting one of them into bed, Fridays are now days of painful mornings, protracted lunches and early exits. The office is quiet as the remaining staff watch the clock, watch online videos and try to stay awake long enough to go home. Ben has already gone and I'd go myself but Kaz is keeping me busy, firing off a succession of brusque businesslike emails challenging every line on the budget for Little Horrors. A far cry from her flirty demeanour of nineteen hours ago; as if, in fact, she is punishing me for it. She is butchering our margin and asphyxiating the schedule. Faster, cheaper, thank you very much. She tried to cut Ben's fee by five grand, but I threatened to pull out. Kaz didn't reply for over an hour, and I was beginning to think she'd called my bluff. But we're still on, albeit on rather frosty terms. Up until now Kaz was at least signing off her emails with a pair of kisses, but these, like so much of our budget, have now vanished. But hey, it's not like I have anything better to do.

'Coffee,' says Holly, appearing at my side.

'Thanks, but I'm fine.'

Holly glances at my left hand. Written on the web of flesh between my thumb and index finger are the words *Call Sadie*.

It's been over four months since Sadie walked out, and in that time our jointly owned car has clocked up hundreds of miles doing little more than crossing the Thames as it shuttles between my flat in south

London and Sadie's in the north. In addition to the inconvenience of it all, Sadie has racked up a couple of hundred pounds in parking fines, and as the car is registered in my name at my address, the buggers end up hanging out of my letter box. We had agreed to figure out what to do with the Mini 'once the dust has settled'. Whether it has or not, I'm not sure, but another sixty-quid fine settled on the doormat yesterday, and the situation needs resolving before I get another.

I cross my arms, tucking my hand and Sadie's name beneath my armpit. 'Got anything left to do?' I ask Holly.

Holly shrugs, shakes her head.

'Why don't you head off?' I tell her.

'You sure?'

Holly's natural exuberance makes her hard to read, and I can't tell if she wants to go home or if she's hoping I'll suggest we go for a drink. I'd much rather have someone to hang around with than go home to an empty flat, but, slow learner that I am, I know it's a lousy idea.

'Yeah,' I say. 'Start the weekend early.'

'Cool, okay then. Well, you have a . . . you know, great weekend.' Holly turns to leave, stops, goes to kiss me on the cheek but lands it on my ear, then walks off to collect her things.

With Holly gone, the office is almost empty, so I go into one of the meeting rooms, close the door and call Sadie. It's the seventh time I've tried today, so I'm a little surprised when she answers immediately.

'Tom, what a pleasant and unexpected surprise.'

'As opposed to an expected surprise?' I counter.

One exchange in and my softly-nicely game plan's already out the window. I backtrack into the silence. 'So, how are you?'

'Busy.'

'Work?'

'Yes, work. It's what normal people do at four thirty on a Friday afternoon.'

'Right, yeah. Still, better than being bored, I suppose.'

'I'll take your word for it.'

'And how's everything else?'

'Listen, Tom, I'm up to my eyes in it. If I'm lucky I'll get home before midnight. So, much as I'd *love* to chat, could we move it along?'

'I've got another parking ticket.'

Intake of breath. Pause. Sigh.

'Highbury Terrace,' I say. 'Islington.'

'How much?'

'The usual. But if it's not paid in the next two weeks it goes up to a hundred and tw—'

'I'll send you a cheque for sixty quid, okay?'

'I thought if I gave you the number you could ca—'

'And I thought you were bored.'

'Well, yeah, sort of, but it's not my ticket, is it?'

'The reason I'm using parking meters in Islington, Tom, is because that's where I live. But the bloody car only has a bloody permit for where you live.'

'Right, I hadn't th—'

'It's a huge pain in the arse.'

'Sure.'

'And I've spent considerably more than sixty pounds parking my own car outside my own flat for the last four months.'

'Actually, it's *our* car.'

'. . .'

This line of reasoning is too ridiculous to pursue. A custody battle for a car. Visitation rights. Will the car develop a complex?

'Listen,' I say, 'forget the fine, I'll pay it. I mean, it's only sixty quid, right?'

'Great. Thank you.'

'No, no, it's nothing, I'm sorry for bugging you, it's just, you know . . . awkward.'

'Listen, I really do have to get on, so unless there's anything else.'

'Well, actually, it's just . . . maybe if you could let me know when you're planning on taking the car.'

'Oh for God's sake.'

'Or even just let me know *when* you've taken it?'

'Fine, I'll let you know. Shall I write, or call? Maybe we'll draw up a rota?'

'A text would be fine.'

'Fine,' says Sadie. 'I'll text.'

'Great, thanks. Well, it was good talking to y—'

Click.

So much for settled dust.

Chapter Eight

'That puts you on . . . exactly ninety,' says Doug. 'You're only eleven behind, lad. There's still time.'

I'd let Douglas win, if I was better than him. But the old bugger doesn't need the help. His clubs are older than I am, scuffed and with worn grips, but it doesn't seem to prevent them from driving a golf ball two hundred and fifty metres in a straight line. My downstairs neighbour will be seventy-two on his next birthday, but he's as healthy as a goat, and rotates smoothly about hip and shoulder as he tees off on the fifteenth hole. I'm beginning to flag, but Doug looks like he could keep this up all day long.

'Ach, dipped a bit early,' he says in his pleasant Ulster burr as the ball rolls onto the edge of the green.

'Shot,' I tell him as I line up my own ball.

'Wee flutter on the side?' he says.

'Sod off, Doug, if I lose another I'll have to give you my car keys.'

'Fat lot o' use they'd be when the motor's never here.'

'Thanks for driving, by the way. Do I owe you for petrol?'

'I may be a pensioner but I'm no . . . Ah, will you look at that,' Doug says as my ball swerves off into the trees. 'Hooked it again.'

'Bastard clubs.'

'A bad workman . . .' says Doug, and we set off to find my ball and sink his.

'So you and that wee lassie courting now?'

'Holly? No, we're just . . . you know.'

Doug laughs. 'Aye, reckon I do, Thomas. I dunny ken when they invented sound proofing, but I'd hazard a guess it was after they built our flats, wouldn't you say?'

'Sorry.'

'I was a weetchil once too, you know.'

'A what?'

'A youngster, lad. Chasing the girls and up to tae herry.'

I file *herry* away for later enquiry. 'So,' I ask him, 'how's Eileen?'

'A gentleman never tells,' says Doug.

'Good, then?'

'Wants me to take her away for the bank holiday weekend,' he says. 'Lyme Regis.'

'You old devil.'

'Not so much of the auld,' he says, winking.

Doug was widowed around five years ago, about two years before I moved in. There were many photographs of Doug's wife, Mary, in his flat, and after introducing myself to my new neighbour it took me less than five minutes – 'I see you're married' – to lodge my foot in my mouth. Philosophical and unabashed in his grief, Doug put the kettle on and brought out a big tin of biscuits. Recently retired, he and Mary had barely crossed off half a dozen items from the long list of things planned for their twilight years when Mary was diagnosed with late-stage leukaemia. Her prognosis was good, however, and she was responding well to therapy. And then one Wednesday morning in November, Doug came home from the butcher's to find Mary dead in her bed, her glasses still on her nose and an unfinished book splayed open on her chest. I told him about Mum's breast cancer, and Doug brought out the whisky. In the years since, we have become firm friends, and while the photos of Mary remain on his walls and shelves, Douglas has moved on, joining a senior citizens' cinema club, a bridge club, a salsa class and an allotment collective. He gets out more than I do.

'Went in here, didn't it?' says Doug, hacking at the undergrowth with a five iron.

'You've better eyes than me, if it did.'

'Now look at this,' says Doug, plucking a delicate yellow flower. 'Primrose.' And he bites the head off the flower and chews.

'Have you lost your marbles?'

''s a herb,' he says, chewing a leaf. 'Try it.'

'I'll pass. Are you sure?'

'Aye. Look, there's bings o' the stuff,' he says, pulling up great handfuls of the yellow plant. 'Makes guid tea. Can use it in salads too.'

'Give over.'

Doug laughs. 'You've nae sense of adventure, lad. What you doing thenicht?'

'Nothing.'

'Eileen's popping over tae watch *Strictly*. Double bill, apparently. She always asks after you. Come down and say hello. I'll make you a primrose omelette.'

Doug's had several 'girlfriends' in the last few years, but Eileen has been a steady feature for the past few months. She's glamorous, funny and has a good line in limericks.

'I might just do that,' I say in response to Doug's invitation.

And the sad thing is, I probably will.

I see my hairdresser for thirty minutes about once every three weeks. In what must amount to a three- or four-hour conversation in instalments, we have discussed my break-up with Sadie and subsequent lack of romantic progress, plus Alyson's on-off relationship with a 'body artist' called Bambi, who it took me three haircuts to ascertain was a human male.

'Out tonight?' asks Alyson's reflection.

'Might watch *Strictly* with the old man that lives downstairs,' I say, and Alyson laughs. 'How about you?'

Alyson shakes her head. 'Saving up for Ibiza.'

'You and Bambi?'

She gives me a thumbs down, shakes her head. 'Girls' holiday.'

Alyson is more interesting than pretty. Her blonde hair is cut in an asymmetric bob with dyed-black tips that accentuate her sharp features; she has a silver stud in her top lip, one in her tongue, another in her belly button. There are Celtic swirlings at the small of her back, a tattooed twist of thorns around her right ankle, a daisy on the inside of her left wrist. And I can't help imagining how much more ink and jewellery she might reveal on the beach in Ibiza.

Bianca wants to go on holiday with her friends this summer – to some party island made notorious in a TV reality show called *Sun, Sex and Suspicious Parents*. Needless to say, Dad is having none of it, and I have found myself – once again – in the middle of an explosive father-and-daughter battle of wills. I swear my phone feels an ounce heavier under the weight of accumulated text messages and voicemails. Bianca's texts tend to be pithy, expletive-laden assessments of Dad's character, judgement and parentage. Dad's voicemails are rambling re-enactments and analyses of the latest flare-up. I'm conflicted. Bianca is seventeen now, old enough to smoke, drive a car, start a family. Although it would be a tragedy if she exercised this last option on the island of Kavos with a scaffolder from Margate with more tattoos than IQ points. And then there's the drink; she'll be consuming plenty of it this summer whether she's home or abroad, but while she's within a taxi drive of Dad, it feels – illusory or not – as if my baby sister is less likely to come to serious harm. But, as Bianca continues to point out in a relentless barrage of SMSs, she is not a baby anymore. In her position, I'd take her side. And in Dad's I'd take his – but, and here's the rub, I think I'd be wrong. Bianca is smarter than she likes to admit, she works hard and she deserves a holiday. Let her make some mistakes, laugh about them and learn from them. I'm going home in a couple of weeks for Dad's birthday, and I'll do my best to make Bianca's case. I'm looking forward to getting between Bea and Dad about as much as I'm looking forward to losing my hair. But all of these things are in my blood, so I guess it's unavoidable.

'You going anywhere this summer?' Alyson asks.

I shake my head. Last summer I went to Palma with Sadie, and look where that got me. This summer, I'm going nowhere with no one. It makes me wonder, not for the first – or the ninth – time, about the wisdom of this whole bet I have with El. Not that I don't enjoy spending time in the company of attractive ladies, and not that there's anything wrong with enjoying a degree of sexual freedom. But you can have too much of a good thing, as they say, and too much freedom can get pretty damn lonely.

A shampoo and haircut costs thirty-five quid, and I tell Alyson to keep the change from two twenties.

'For the holiday fund,' I say, and inwardly cringe at how patronising I sound. 'Or you could blow it on a bottle of wine,' I add, attempting to smooth over the clumsy gambit.

'Maybe a nice rosé?' says Alyson with a small laugh. She takes a five from the till and folds it into her apron. 'Cheers.'

I almost turn to the door, but there's a coyness to Alyson's demeanour today that stops me. Encourages me. It's been a long week, it's Saturday night, and in the absence of someone to hold hands with, I'll take any company I can get.

'You know,' I say, 'seeing as how we're neither of us doing much tonight . . .'

Alyson bites her lip and her eyes widen ever so slightly. An expression of dread maybe.

'I thought maybe we could . . .' My cheeks begin to redden, but there's no turning back. I'm slow-motion skidding towards a brick wall and my wheels are locked.

'. . . have that bottle of rosé . . .'

Alyson's expression becomes the next best thing to a wince. Braced for impact.

'. . . together?'

Bang.

Behind me, someone coughs.

Alyson glances past my right shoulder. I follow her gaze to where another girl is sweeping the floor. She smiles at me and averts her eyes towards the hair clippings at her feet.

I turn back to Alyson, who looks like she's contemplating a particularly complex mathematical problem – eyebrows pulled together, mouth twisted to one side, fingers fidgeting with the pocket of her apron.

'There's a new bar in Clapham North?' I say. 'They do cocktails.'

The sweeper coughs again, not really disguising a snigger.

'If you like, I could swing by here arou—'

'I think maybe I'll just stay in,' says Alyson.

'Sure, fine, okay then,' I say, taking a sidestep towards the door. 'Cool.'

'Save up,' says Alyson.

''course,' I say, reaching for the door handle. 'Ibiza.'

'Yeah.'

'Nice one. No worries. Have a good . . . you know, night. See you soon.'

The doorbell ding-a-ling-a-lings behind me, but not loud enough to cover the sound of laughter.

'Now that,' says Eileen, 'is a well-made man.'

We're sitting three abreast on the sofa, eating off our knees in front of *Strictly*. A TV weather girl, visibly awkward in her split-to-the-hip ballgown, stands beside the male professional – a Portuguese hunk with perfect teeth, hair like midnight and a ridged torso of dark skin and sharp angles.

'Aye,' says Doug, flicking a glance in my direction.

We've had variations on the theme with every dance: Eileen appraising the various male dancers' legs, chests, bums, rhythm. I interject the occasional comment on the ladies, just to redress the balance, but when it comes to objectifying the opposite sex, I'm not in the same league as Eileen.

'Do you suppose he shaves his chest?' she says, before devouring a forkful of primrose omelette. 'Call me old-fashioned, but I like a bit of hair on a man. Something to run my fingers through. Mind you, I'm not complaining; that is a very well-made man.'

Doug has never been particularly garrulous, but he seems particularly coy tonight. In a strange kind of generational role reversal, I feel like a parent in the company of a couple of teenage sweethearts. Eileen has to lean forwards in order to look around me and wink at Doug or, on a couple of occasions, squeeze his knee.

'Oh, they're doing a tango,' she says, leaning forwards again. 'I do love a good tango.' And here she raises her eyebrows at Douglas. 'The dance of passion.'

'Lovely omelette,' I say to Doug.

'Aye,' says Doug.

On screen the lights rise, picking out a set styled after an old-fashioned piano bar. The two dancers take their positions, the music starts and the weather girl pirouettes into the professional's arms.

'Oh, take me away,' coos Eileen.

I'm thinking the same thing.

The dancers finish their routine, face the judges and receive their scores – two sixes and an extravagant seven from the excitable camp one. Next up are a former footballer and an Eastern European pro with legs like a sprinter and eyes like a killer. In their video montage, the couple tell us they will be performing the salsa, and we see them go through the standard rigmarole of training, falling over, arguing and so on.

'Don't you do a salsa class?' I say to Doug.

'He does,' says Eileen, snapping her fingers like castanets. 'And he's got very agile hips.'

Doug clears his throat.

'Is this true?' I ask. 'Douglas McSnakehips?'

'I'll Douglas McKick your backside in a minute, lad.'

Eileen laughs as if Doug is joking.

The dancers take to the stage. Her dressed like a prostitute; him too, for that matter.

'Good grief,' says Eileen. 'Those trousers don't leave much to the imagination, do they?'

I check my watch and see that we're a little over thirty minutes into a two-hour double bill. Doug and I reach for the wine simultaneously, our hands touch and recoil from each other, again with perfect synchronicity.

'Cha-cha-cha!' says Eileen.

The wine is practically empty, so I squeeze myself out from between Doug and Eileen.

'I'll go and open another bottle,' I tell him.

'Aye,' says Doug.

Chapter Nine

'Nothn in two weeks!'

It's the last day of May, four weeks since my close encounter with Kaz. And while it's been a busy month in the office, things have slowed down considerably in the bedroom. Just over a fortnight ago, there was a thing with Emma, the script supervisor on a Toilet Duck commercial, which delighted El ('Toilet Fuck!') when I told him. Today, though, I have nothing to report.

My recollection of my most recent conquest, however, makes me cringe, and not simply on account of the product that brought us together. Lying in bed in the small hours, Emma asked about my plans for the approaching summer – an innocent enquiry probably, but I answered evasively and not entirely honestly. Emma's job, however, is to spot continuity errors, and the look on her face when she spotted mine made me feel about two feet tall.

At least I didn't sleep with Holly again. I know this isn't something for which I deserve a certificate of achievement or a medal of abstention, but you take your consolations where you find them. Holly was the runner on the Toilet Duck shoot, and while she maintained a professional distance throughout the day, she closed that gap at the wrap party. It had been two weeks since our last encounter, and I'd gone out of my way to be, well, out of the way. The third or fourth time Holly sidled up to me, standing close enough that I could feel the heat of her breast pressed against my arm, I felt my resolve weakening and took defensive measures. I flirted with Emma. Short of being brutally explicit, it was the least awkward way I could conceive of to reinforce a point already made. Getting Emma into bed was not my objective, but merely a fortuitous side effect. My intentions were true. Noble, even. 'Enjoy your summer,' Emma said when she left the following morning, but when I went to kiss her goodbye, she twisted her face to the side.

'Not a single soltry fuck. You're fuckig slipping, mate,' says El at a volume that might be acceptable in a noisy pub, but is a touch unnecessary for a quiet restaurant.

From where I'm sitting, with my back to the kitchen, I can't see Jiang – but I can sense him wincing.

'Try some of this,' I say, spooning Szechuan chicken onto El's plate.

In the five months since Christmas – since El's bet – my friend's tics have grown more frequent and more pronounced. His legs bounce constantly as if he's tapping his feet to music, and the motion, transmitted through his trunk, makes his head wobble. His limbs spasm and jerk with increased regularity. Walking is awkward, shaving perilous, eating and drinking messy. Some weeks back, I gave Jiang a stack of plastic pint glasses for our beer. El holds his with two hands.

'More thn'anythin, it disappoints me. I live vica. . . varoious. . . whassa word?'

'Vicariously?'

So far tonight we've drunk less than a half a glass of beer each, but El's speech is slurred nevertheless – simply one more symptom of his progressing Huntington's.

'Yeah, through you,' says El. 'So where's the fun for me in you not fuckig? No fucks no fun. No fuckig fun whatsever.'

'Well, I'm sorry to disap—'

El turns around in his chair and shouts across the restaurant. 'Jiang! Jiang, have you got a' – his fingers dance over an invisible keyboard – 'calclator?'

Jiang walks up to our table. 'Is everything okay?' he asks, looking at our half-finished food. 'You want the bill?'

'No, a . . . a calcalator,' says El. 'Fr'addin up.'

'The bill?'

'I want to see how shit Tom is.'

Jiang looks to me for clarification, and I can only shrug apologetically.

'How far away's C-Day?' asks El after Jiang has supplied him with a calculator the size of a sandwich.

'I honestly don't know.'

'You've go a calendar on y' phone, right? Come on ch. . . ch. . . chop chop.'

I open up my calendar app and count backwards from July the nineteenth. 'Seven weeks. Exactly.'

'And you've fucked how many?'

'Jesus, El,' I say, miming a volume switch being turned down to somewhere below level nine.

'Keep yr knickers on,' says El in a stage whisper barely an increment quieter than his previous outburst. 'I was only asking how many birds you've—'

'You know how many,' I tell him, dropping my voice to a whisper. 'Ninety-five.'

'One hundred minus niney-five is' – El taps the digits into his calculator – 'five. Five fucks.'

'El, what are you—'

'Patience. I'll lose my place. Seven weeks is' – tap tap tap – 'forty-nine days. Forty-nine divided by five is . . . nine-poin-eight.' El shows me this number on the calculator. 'Nine-poin-eight DPF.'

'I'm sorry? DP what?'

'F,' says El. 'Days – per – fuck.'

'Do you have to?'

'Yes I do. 'swhat you need to get yr hunred for C-Day.'

I try burying my head in my hands.

'I'm juss tryin to help,' says El. 'Give you a target. Small 'ch. . . 'chievable goals.'

'Well, thank you for your concern,' I say from behind my hands.

'Well, you're very welcome.'

We eat for a while. El vibrates in his seat, bouncing his heels, listening to music on invisible headphones. It takes him two, three, four attempts to load rice onto his fork. He fumbles a piece of prawn toast, so I hand one to him before he knocks the table over.

'Hope you've washed yr hans,' says El.

'Ingrate.'

'Like one of those dancin' puppets, aren' I?' he says. 'Like you see blokes sellin out'f suitcases.'

'Here,' I say, handing him the bread.

El sighs. 'Guess when I lass had sex?'

'Mate, I haven't got a clue.'

'Me either. I tried to remember, but I juss carn.' He says this quietly, almost apologetically. 'Maybe not since Christmas – we must've done it at Christmas.'

'It's okay,' I say. 'Phil understands.'

'Some people like me, with this' – El presents his arms as if they were evidence – 'they go sex mad. Turn into fuckig nymphos.'

'I didn't know that.'

'I haven got that. Lucky I s'pose. I mean, s'ardly very sexy, is it?'

'Phil understands.'

'Yeah, y'already said.'

I sip my beer.

'I wan him to get a new boyfren,' says El.

'What the hell are you talking about?'

'You know what dysphagia is?'

I shake my head.

'Trouble swallowing. You cn breathe liquid into your lungs and drown on your beer. They give you powder to thicken y'drinks.' El takes a two-handed gulp of lager. 'Lager milkshakes.'

'Yummy.'

'Yeah, well, I've got that to look forward to – lager jelly. No wonder we kill ourselves.'

'Oh, knock it off.'

'Just saying, aren I? Lager soup.'

'What's that got to do with Phil finding a new boyfriend?' I ask.

'Best snario, I've got fifteen years, ten.'

'Fifteen years is a long time, El. Fift—'

'Thass my point,' El says. 'I'm only going downhill from here, aren I? Won't be able to eat, wash, read, shit outside of my fuckig pants . . . Fifteen years is *worst*-case snario.'

'El, come on—'

'Full-time care.'

'If you need help, Phil'll get help.'

'In ten years Phil'll be in his fifties. I wan him t'ave some'un now, before he's too old t'enjoy it.'

'Maybe he doesn—'

'*I'd* want somen else. Wouldn you? Fuckig . . . look at me,' says El, and his eyes are full of tears. He drops his napkin, so I reach across the table and wipe his cheeks with mine.

'Very fuckig gallant,' says El.

'Yeah,' I tell him, 'you're very fuckig welcome.'

El smiles and takes a sip of his beer. 'I juss want Phil to be happy.'

'I understand that,' I say.

El brightens by a shade. 'Really?'

'Of course.'

'Thass good. I dumped him.'

'You what?!'

'I'm movin out,' he says, nodding emphatically.

'Wh— Oh you daft bastard. Where to?'

El looks at me like I know the answer full well.

'Piss off. No. Forget it.'

El smiles sweetly.

'Do you know what a Gilligan Cut is?' I ask him.

'Never heard of him.'

'There's an old American sitcom called *Gilligan's Island*, about this shipwrecked family. And the guy, Gilligan, would say something like, "No way am I getting on that raft!" and then they'd *cut to* . . . ?'

'Gillingham on a raft?' says El, a sparkle of hope in his eyes.

'Exactly,' I say. 'And this isn't one of those. You are not getting on my raft.'

'Fine,' says El. 'I'll sleep rough.'

'Oh shut up.' I wave at Jiang and indicate that I want the bill. 'Drink up, we're going.'

If you had to guess, you'd guess Phil was gay. His head is small and tidily angular, with evenly cropped, half-grey half-dark hair. He is always clean-shaven and precisely ironed. He wears tight T-shirts, usually white, that show off his toned yoga arms and neat wine-drinker's paunch. He is neat in every respect apart from his fingernails, which are bitten back to the pulp.

'If it isn't my ex-boyfriend,' he says as we enter the living room. He's curled up on the sofa, tinkering with his laptop, something acoustic on the stereo, a glass and a bottle of wine on a lacquered occasional table. Chez Phil is all wallpaper and antique furniture, like your parents' house if they had good taste. He glares at El. 'Didn't drop dead over dinner then?'

El walks through the room and into the adjoining kitchen; he flicks two fingers at Phil en route.

'Hey, Phil,' I say. 'El just told me.'

'*Just?* He told me he was moving in with you.'

'Yeah, he just told me that, too. Phil, I had no idea.'

'Little bugger.'

'I'm bigger'n you,' El says, re-entering the room with two wine glasses.

'Only in height,' says Phil. 'When you're gone I'll move in a Samoan lodger with a cock like a rounders bat. I'll take inches in lieu of rent.'

I inspect the embroidery on the cushion clutched to my lap.

'You woudn know what t'do with it,' says El, reaching for the wine.

Phil snatches the bottle away. 'I'll pour. How much has he had, Tom?'

'Two pints of Tsingtao.'

'Lager porridge,' says El, lowering himself with some difficulty onto the sofa beside Phil.

'Porridge?' asks Phil.

'Old joke,' I say.

Phil elects to let it drop, pours a splash of wine into El's glass, crosses the room and fills mine to within a finger of the rim.

'Sure y'could spare it?' says El.

Phil turns to me. 'So, plans for the bank holiday?'

It's a question I've been asking myself for the last seven days, since I realised I was staring down the barrel of a three-day weekend.

I was with Sadie for a little over a year, but in that time I appear to have lost the knack of weekends – those glorious two days that used to sparkle like an oasis at the far end of the working week. Single friends have found partners; hitched friends have produced children. Sadie and I did nothing special between Friday night and Monday morning, but there was always someone to do it with – cinema, wine bar, restaurant. Things you don't do on your own. Or cooking a nice meal, a long bath, an afternoon on the sofa – they are different propositions in an empty flat. Weekends are now an exercise in making time pass rather than making it last. I churn out thousands of metres on my stationary rower, killing minutes but going nowhere. I read, I walk, I can make a trip to the supermarket last two hours. There is barely a speck of dust in the flat and I can see my reflection on the inside of the oven. A regular weekend is long enough; a three-day weekend gives me palpitations. Everyone has something to do. Ben is visiting his in-laws, Phil and El are weekending in the Cotswolds, Doug has his dirty weekend with Eileen.

I was almost tempted to visit Dad and Bianca, but my nerves haven't fully recovered from my last visit two weeks ago. I was barely through the door on Friday evening when Bianca began with *Will you tell him; He's not listening; It's not fair.* Before I'd had a chance to put my bag down, Dad was firing back with *You're still a child; You're my responsibility,* and, the perennial favourite: *Just because everyone is doing it doesn't make it right.* They hectored me while I made supper, harangued me while I ate it. Doors were slammed, threats made, names called. The campaign continued over breakfast the next morning without missing a beat; it followed us from room to room to the garden, shouted though walls and up and down the stairs. I attempted to interject equanimity and reason into the gaps, but the gaps were small and filled with reverb from the latest salvos of accusation and counter-accusation.

On Sunday there was a brief suspension of hostilities as we gave Dad his birthday presents, played The Minister's Cat and ate birthday cake. 'The minister's cat is a stuffed cat,' Bianca said, taking a final forkful of cake and pushing aside her plate. 'The minister's cat is a taxidermist's cat,' Dad said without missing a beat, and Bianca – briefly forgetting she was at war with her father – snorted with laughter and came close to choking on her chocolate sponge.

It was a lousy way in, but I was running out of time and the mood was the lightest it was likely to get before I had to head back to London. 'The, er, minister's cat understands everyone's side of the argument?' I tried.

The laughter stopped abruptly. No one spoke, but I could see both Bianca and my father preparing to launch either an attack or a defence.

'The thing is,' I went on, 'the minister's c— I mean the daughter, the Bianca, is going to university in a year or so.'

Dad cocked an eyebrow.

'The minister's cat *will be* a varsity cat,' said Bianca.

'Right,' I went on. 'And once Bianca's there sh—'

'A year is a long time from now, Thomas. And—'

'But,' I went on, sensing a tiny opening, 'a week in Kavos . . . isn't a long time at all.'

'But they're going for *two* weeks,' Bianca said.

I shushed her with my eyes and my sister took the hint.

'If anything,' I went on, 'it might prepare her for uni.'

'What, by going out and drinking?'

'Well, kind of, yes. The ones who've never been away are the worst. Like hounds off the leash.'

'You hadn't been away,' Dad said.

'Exactly.'

Dad took a sip of his whisky, held it in his mouth. He nodded, although to such a subtle extent I doubt he knew he was doing it. 'A week,' he said.

Bianca took a preparatory breath . . .

'A week,' I interjected, my eyes again warning her not to disturb this delicate compromise.

Dad went to speak but this time Bianca beat him to it: 'I'll call every night. And if you find out I've been acting like those idiots on the telly, I'm grounded.'

'You said it,' Dad told her. And I got the very clear impression Bea would consider a grounding small price to pay for behaving like those idiots off the telly. And in her position, I would think exactly the same way.

But even though the temperature has dropped at Dad's house, Bianca is halfway through her AS levels and there's more than enough potential for another uprising.

So it looks like I'll be spending the long weekend rowing nowhere and cleaning the fluff from between the floorboards.

'Just chilling out,' I say in answer to Phil's question.

'Billy no mates,' says El.

'Sorry, I wasn't too conversational earlier,' Phil says. 'I'm afraid it's been' – he glances at El – 'one of those days.'

I've hardly touched my wine, but Phil tops up my glass nevertheless, before topping up his own.

'Ah-he-he-hem!' El holds his empty glass aloft.

'You've probably had enough, darling.'

'I pr. . . prolly f. . . fucking havn't!'

Phil slumps onto the sofa beside El. 'I'm only thinking of you,' he says.

'Well, you won't have to after tonight, will you? You can listen to y'own music, drink y'own wine, stick your legs behind your head and suck y'own fuckig dick.'

'Fine,' says Phil, pouring a dribble of wine into El's glass. 'Now stop showing off.'

'You won be able to talk to your Samoan cock monster like that. He'd bash in your little head with his rounders bat.'

'Nice wine,' I say.

'Chianti,' says Phil.

El burps.

'So, Tom, what do you make of Laurence's plan to abandon me?'

'He thinks iss brilliant,' says El. 'Someone to keep him compny, hey, Tom? I'll finish my Chanti then go an pack.'

'Laurence,' says Phil, 'you are not bloody well going anywhere.'

El turns to me. 'Tom, would you, or would you not, like to see Uncle Phil happy for once?'

'Oh hon,' says Phil, shifting along and placing his hand on El's knee. 'Of course this whole . . . *thing*, it breaks my bloody heart. But you moving out isn't going to make you any better or make me any happier.'

I drink my wine and try to look sympathetic but at the same time inconspicuous; I study the carpet.

'You're getting fat,' says El, prodding a finger into Phil's belly.

'I know what you're trying to do, you awful little bugger. And it won't work. I don't want another boyfriend and you're not moving out. No one else would put up with you, Elly – or with me for that matter. Get used to it, we're stuck with each other.'

'Wha'bout sex?'

'God!' Phil throws me an exasperated glance. 'To be perfectly honest, I could do without it. I don't mean to flatten your puny ego, darling, but really, there's more to life.'

El pouts.

'Tom, will you tell him?' says Phil.

'Why y'askin him?' says El. 'Tom's a slut.'

'Nice one, El,' I say, raising my wine. 'Cheers.'

'Don't insult the guests, Laurence. Even if they are morally dubious.'

El chuckles, Phil hugs him, and El hugs him back.

'Up yours,' I say to the pair of them.

Phil pulls an ironed handkerchief from his pocket and carefully blots tears from his eyes and cheeks. 'Oh God,' he says, fanning his face with his hand, 'how bloody camp.' He kisses El on the cheek. 'I love you, Elly, you do know that?'

'Fine,' says El. 'I'll stay. But yr still dumped.'

JUNE

Chapter Ten

It's a little after lunchtime and the long weekend starts now.

The contracts are signed for the Little Horrors shoot, the crew is assembled, and after the bank holiday we begin on pre-production: casting, location scouting, set design, make-up tests, and more meetings than you can shake a croissant at. But for now, tools are down, the company credit card is behind the bar and everyone is making good use of it before they head off on their various bank holiday diversions. The long weekend is late this year, coinciding with the first weekend in June, a fact that seems to heighten the sense of expectation and release. Everyone has something to or somewhere to go to: family, friends, a festival, a wedding, a reunion. Ben, however, is clinging to an air of peevishness, as if it were a matter of principle. I thought he'd made his peace with the scripts, but he's been almost deliberately surly for the last two weeks. Maybe he's tired.

'*I am the Anti-Christ*,' says Marlon. '*You got me in a vendetta kind of mood.*'

Marlon is the production assistant on our upcoming shoot, and far from being evil incarnate, he's a charming and affable chap with a soft Welsh accent that clashes with his malevolent declaration. We're playing the quote game, and in honour of the Little Horrors production, we're giving it a loose horror theme.

'Good one,' says Rob. 'What's that one with Micky Rourke? *Angel Heart!*'

Rob will be working as assistant director, and he's so excited it's almost unbearable.

'Too literal,' says Marlon. 'It's not a horror.'

'Any more?' asks Rob.

'*You never seen evil so singularly personified,*' continues Marlon in his Valleys lilt, '*as you did in the face of the man who killed you.*'

'Brilliant,' howls Holly. '*Scream.*'

Everyone screams.

Marlon shakes his head.

'It's not a horror,' I remind Holly.

'*Final Destination,*' she tries. '*The Exorcist, Saw, Saw Two, Saw Three, Hostel, Ho—*'

'What about *Saw Four*?' I say, and Marlon laughs.

'Don't be smug,' says Ben.

'Fine,' I say. '*True Romance.* Christopher Walken to Dennis Hopper.' And Ben gives me a patronising little theatre clap.

'Your turn,' says Holly, apparently oblivious to the congealing atmosphere.

On construction sites, in power plants and other high-risk environments they have signs – updated daily – declaring how long it's been since the last incident: '21 DAYS WITHOUT AN ACCIDENT', '674 DAYS WITHOUT A MELTDOWN'. The last time I slept with Holly was four weeks ago yesterday. '29 DAYS WITHOUT AN INCIDENT'. Holly is too nice to bear a grudge, but there is awkwardness between us that wasn't there before. She still flirts, but less frequently and with less conviction. And behind it all I sense an undercurrent of disappointment or maybe disenchantment. I feel that I should address the whole thing, but the longer we go without incident, the more it feels like I might be tempting fate or simply stating the obvious.

Girl 99

'Take it for me,' I say to Holly. 'I'm going to the bar. Same again all round?'

'Same again,' everyone choruses.

'Okay,' says Holly as I walk away from the table. '*You've got red on you.*'

In the furore that ensues, I go to the bar to order another round of drinks. The new barmaid is serving a customer, so I hang back under the pretence of checking something on my phone. Over the last two weeks, I have casually ascertained that she is Brazilian – a nationality that conjures images like no other – and her name is Christina. Whether or not she is single remains to be discovered. If she is, it won't be for lack of attention. Long dark hair, tanned skin dusted with freckles, sinfully pneumatic and a smile that says she knows it; Christina would be a wonderful way to spend the long weekend. She hands the change to her customer – who tips her – and I step smartly up to the bar.

'*Boa noite,*' I say, flashing my suavest smile.

The barmaid appears impressed. '*Você fala português?*'

I have a pretty good idea what I've just been asked, and, if I'm right, the answer is no. I googled the translation for 'good evening' twenty seconds ago, and it is the full extent of my Portuguese.

I shrug apologetically. 'No, but I'd like to learn. It's a lovely language.'

I cringe at my obviousness, but Christina, I sense, has developed an immunity to this kind of ham-fisted flirting. '*Obrigada.* So, drinks?'

I reel off the order, and Christina sets about opening bottles and pulling pints.

'Christina, isn't it?' I say.

'I surprise you remember,' says Christina, and she doesn't need the accent to be sexy but it doesn't do any harm either.

I act offended. 'Of course I do. Why wouldn't I?'

Christina raises her thick eyebrows as she places a glass of wine in front of me, as if it holds the answer to my question. 'I'm Tom,' I say.

91

Several feet behind me, Holly squeals.

'Celebrating,' I tell Christina.

The barmaid nods as if this is self-evident.

'I produce TV commercials.'

She fetches Rob's cider.

'Yeah,' I go on, 'just got a big job. Shooting four scripts.'

And Ben's bitter.

'For Skittles,' I say.

Christina rotates Holly's wine glass. 'Skittles?'

'Sweets. Candy.'

Christina shakes her head and turns out her bottom lip in an expression of incomprehension.

'They're very English,' I tell her. 'I'll get you some.'

'Bad for me,' says Christina, holding her hands against her round hips.

'Or . . . we could just go for a drink?'

'More?' Christina indicates the glasses in front of me.

'Somewhere else?' I say, and I can feel my cheeks beginning to warm.

'*Aye ya!*' Christina claps her hands together and then wags her finger left and right. 'I don't think your girlfriend likes it.'

'What girlf— I don't have a girlfriend.'

Christina raises her eyebrows and I follow her gaze across the bar. Holly looks away; Ben shakes his head.

'We just work together,' I say to Christina, and force a laugh. 'She's not my girlfriend.'

'Just good friends,' says Christina.

'Exactly.'

She nods at the round of drinks. 'So is one for myself?'

'Stick it on the tab,' I say.

'*Muito obrigada*, Tom.'

It takes two trips to carry the drinks back to the table, and when I return to the bar for the second batch, Christina is flirting with a pock-marked customer in a shiny suit. She laughs at some joke and turns to fill a tumbler from the whisky optic. A barman I've never seen before – skinny jeans hanging off his flat backside, hair like an indie band guitarist – squeezes past Christina, and his hand trails from left hip to right. They make eye contact, and something unsaid is said.

Back at the table, Ben and Rob and Holly are leaning forwards on their seats, listening to Marlon.

'. . . and Paul Newman taps her on the shoulder and says, "Madam, it's in your handbag."'

Ben and Rob laugh. Holly's hand goes to her mouth. '*No.*'

Marlon nods. 'God's honest. Can you imagine?'

'Imagine what?' I say. 'What was in the handbag?'

'Ice cream,' explains Rob.

'In a handbag?'

Ben sighs. 'Yes, in a handbag. Would you like me to recap everything you missed?'

'Not if it's going to put you out, no. But here's an idea – next time, you can queue at the bar while I sit on my fat arse waiting for you to bring it to me.'

And just in case Ben doesn't pick up on the extent of my vexation, I glare at him defiantly.

'Works for me,' says Ben smugly. 'At least I'll get my drink while it's still cold.'

'Cheers,' says Rob, picking up his cider.

Marlon tilts his pint in my direction.

Holly smiles.

Ben grunts.

We all take a drink.

'Toilet,' says Holly, getting up from her stool and squeezing past our various knees.

'Thanks for squeezing me in on the shoot,' says Rob.

Ben huffs loudly, stands, pulls on his jacket.

'Not going to drink your drink I got for you?' I enquire, not unsarcastically.

'Had more than enough,' says Ben. 'Have a nice weekend, lads,' he says, looking at Marlon and Rob but not me.

The boys bid him farewell.

'And say goodbye to Holly for me,' says Ben, his eyes flicking in my direction.

I catch up with him on the pavement outside. 'Hoy. What was all that about?'

'All what?' says Ben. 'Nothing, I'm tired.'

'Sure. Blame it on that again.'

Ben shakes his head dismissively.

'It must be awful,' I say. 'Being so tired you can't even *pretend* to enjoy yourself.'

'It is,' Ben says. 'It really is. And here's the thing, Tom – watching you make a twat of yourself with the barmaid is less enjoyable than you might think.'

'A *twat*? And what's it to you if I chat up the barmaid?'

'Find 'em, fuck 'em, forget 'em, yeah?' Ben buddy-punches me on the shoulder. Only there's not much buddy on it. Fights have started over lesser blows.

'You know how you sound? You sound jealous, mate.'

Ben laughs dismissively. 'I'm really not.'

'How about instead of getting on my case, you get on top of your wife for five minutes?'

If I could take it back, I would. But it's too late for that and the muscles at the hinges of Ben's jaw are standing out like gobstoppers.

'Or maybe I should fuck a script supervisor,' he says.

'Been checking up on me?'

'It's a small business, Tom. And a smaller office.'

In the absence of a pithy comeback, I huff contempt and shake my head.

Ben takes a deep breath. 'Look, I'm not trying to be sanctimonious—'

I laugh. 'Really? Because you're doing a good fucking job of it.'

'Okay,' says Ben. 'You want to know what pisses me off?'

'Everything?'

'What pisses me well and truly off, Tom, is talking to the back of your head while you look around the room for someone else to fuck. It's boring.'

'Talk about the pot calling the . . . Do you have any idea how tedious it is listening to you banging on about nappies and milk and sleepless sodding nights? It's mind-numbing, Ben, it really is.'

'It's real life, is what it is. Mate.'

'Oh please, spare me.'

Ben sighs. 'Listen, do what you want. Whatever makes you happy.'

'Thanks for your permission.'

'But you might want to think about Holly's feelings.'

'Jesus! Are we still going on about that? Didn't I say nothing happened?'

'Yeah,' Ben says, 'you said. Just try a little tact. Don't rub the poor girl's face in it.'

'She's not a child, Ben.'

'And you're not a cunt. So why don't you stop acting like one?'

With an almost imperceptible shake of his head, Ben turns and walks away.

Chapter Eleven

Every action has a consequence. Every decision leads – inevitably – to an outcome, foreseen or otherwise. Like me, sitting here on a rainy Sunday evening, two days into my solitary bank holiday weekend.

The local cinema has a high balcony with a wonderful view of the local wildlife. Plus, they make good coffee and they serve it in big cups. In front of the cinema is an open square where the indigenous winos and nutters congregate. In summer, the local vagrants sleep on benches, beneath the bushes, or wherever the hell they fall. In the morning, walking to the tube station, you can see them sprawled and passed out on the other side of the iron railings. A human zoo.

An estate agent would call the area 'vibrant'. Which it is. But so is a lunatic asylum. The postcode has undergone significant regeneration in recent years, and house prices are doing what London house prices do. Even so, some original features remain. The backstreets within a half-mile radius of the tube station are crawling with junkies and dealers, pimps and hookers, touts and hasslers. I have witnessed a filthy, half-naked man hauled screaming into a police car; a woman pushed to the ground and her cash snatched at the hole-in-the-wall; a person on hands and knees in the shadow of a skip behind Nando's, trousers around calves, injecting God-knows-what into fuck-knows-where. Too much 'vibrant' can give you a headache, and maybe it's time I tried something more soothing.

It's raining this morning and the scene is less eclectic than usual. But despite the weather, a lone man paces erratic loops beneath the balcony. Phone pressed to his ear, a can and a smoking cigarette in the other hand, he gesticulates expansively as he speaks:

'You don't know nuffink. No, you might fink you kn— Shut it! Shut up and get it out of your head, Trace. You don't know nuffink.'

As theatre goes, it's a bit too slice-of-life for my taste, but it's got to be better than anything playing inside the cinema – there is a superhero movie starting in thirty minutes and a romcom in twenty but I'm yet to decide if I'll watch either.

The guy below the balcony is virtually shouting now.

'I don't care what you *fink* you know when I'm givin it to you, but . . . You. Don't. Know. Nuffink.'

The guy postures defiantly at passers-by. He inflates himself and juts his head left and right. But not up. He is as oblivious to me as I am tuned in to him. A waitress brings a second hat-sized mug of coffee, but I'm already jittery with caffeine and I only ordered it to occupy my hands.

'So facking what. Trace? Trace! So what! I don't give a rat's fucking fuck what your sister finks because she don't know nuffink neither.'

Does this guy love Trace? Does Trace love him? Will they kiss and make up this evening? Will he buy her flowers?

Will he fuck.

I'm not saying Ben was entirely right, but he did have a point. I have been insensitive towards Holly. More than that, probably, and I have no defence that doesn't require further justification. One thing leading to another to another to another. And I am embarrassed for telling Ben his new-dad rants have become tedious. Particularly because it's true and I'm sure Ben knows it.

And what would my friend think if he knew I was on a mission to sleep with one hundred women? What would my father or my sister think? What would anyone other than El with his neurodegenerative disease think? Not so much of the debauchery as the design. They wouldn't think much and, if I'm honest with myself, neither do I. After I left the pub on Friday night I went straight home, washed down an over-the-counter sleeping tablet with a pot of primrose tea and was in bed before ten o'clock.

I woke appallingly early and cracking with unwanted energy. By eight a.m., I'd cleaned every square centimetre of the bathroom, rowed twelve thousand metres along the River Nowhere. I showered and gave the bathroom an auxiliary wipe down. I bleached the mugs and cleaned the filters on the washing machine and dishwasher.

While Doug is away tending to Eileen, he's asked me to tend his herbs, so I popped downstairs to water the basil, mint, parsley and whatever else he's growing in his window box. He's a neat old gent, clean-shaven and well turned out, but his kitchen looked like it hadn't had a thorough clean since his wife passed away. So I wiped down the surfaces, descaled his kettle and cleaned the crumbs and peas and grains of rice from beneath the appliances.

Back in my own flat I was about to iron the curtains when I realised I was teetering on the lip of a steep and slippery slope. Where it led, I wasn't sure, but I sensed it involved cardigans, corduroy trousers and possibly cats, so I unplugged the iron and grabbed the car keys. My mind came alive with possibilities – I could drive to the coast, paddle in the sea and eat fish and chips out of the paper. Maybe drive to the New Forest, hire a bike and get with nature. Perhaps check into a B'n'B somewhere, talk to strangers, share stories and exchange jokes.

But it turned out that Sadie had put paid to that idea.

I couldn't be entirely positive, but I was pretty sure the car had been parked in front of the flat the evening before. And if it had been, then when did Sadie drive it away? While I was sipping primrose tea, sleeping, rowing, cleaning the fucking grout between the bathroom tiles? Yes, it's Sadie's car too, and she's as entitled to use it as I am, but is a little communication too much to ask? I mean, where does this stop?

Sadie travels the best part of an hour from Islington, maybe she needs to pee, and if she does then what's to stop her letting herself into *my* flat to use *my* toilet? I couldn't remember Sadie ever returning her keys, but I checked the glass bowl in the hallway nevertheless. No keys. And what if I were in bed with someone? How would that unfold? More than likely not into a threesome.

And one action leads to another.

The locksmith charged me £110 to replace the lock.

But he damaged the paintwork in the process so I took a bus to the DIY superstore and a taxi back along with four litres of Mocha emulsion, four Mountain White, four Tuscan Olive, and a party pack of brushes, rollers and sponges. Good bachelor colours. Sadie convinced me to repaint throughout in various yellows – Florida Sunrise, Lemon Cheesecake, Cold Custard. I didn't like them then and I should have repainted months ago.

By four thirty on Saturday I'd finished the bedroom and worked up a righteous thirst, so I picked up my new keys and popped out to the off-licence.

The off-licence is next door to an estate agent. They're coming to photograph the flat on Tuesday morning.

All the walls are now painted and I have blisters from holding a brush. I'd flake out on the sofa but the flat is thick with paint fumes and they were giving me a headache. So here I am, sipping a giant cup of coffee on the balcony of the cinema on a bank holiday Sunday.

'Trace,' says the pacing, gesticulating, bullying bastard beneath the balcony. 'Get it into your head, Trace. You know nuffink, and you *are* nuffink.'

And you think about the things you might do, could do, shouldn't have said and should have done.

I could tip my coffee on this idiot's head without rising from my seat.

So that's exactly what I do.

Have a nice facking day.

The romcom wasn't bad at all. I laughed in most of the right places and, if I'd allowed myself, I'm sure I could have shed a tear at the final act. Takeaway Indian for supper, another pot of primrose tea, another early night. And on bank holiday Monday, another day with paint in my hair – this time white gloss from repainting the architraves, skirting boards and dado rails. I was hoping the woodwork would take up the whole day, but it's a small flat and I'm all done by lunchtime. Which is probably just as well: the flat smells like a chemical spill and I'm beginning to hallucinate that the walls are closing in on me. Even an angry text from Bianca or a fretful message from Dad would be a welcome distraction but, thanks to me, they seem to be living in a bubble of rare harmony. That'll teach me to go interfering.

Doug isn't due back until tomorrow morning, so I gather my cleaning products and head downstairs to water his herbs and give the place a good spring clean.

'Wakey wakey, lad.'

'Doug?'

'Were y'expectin someone else?'

I remember sitting down in Doug's armchair, but surely that was only five minutes ago. The plan was to take a quick breather after cleaning the bathroom, then run the vacuum over the carpets. The sun has set and my neck is stiff.

'Is it Tuesday already?'

'Not quite. Ten to, in fact.'

'What are you doing back here?'

'Might ask you the same thing, lad, but I reckon I can make a pretty good guess,' he says, nodding at my yellow Marigolds.

'Right, sorry. Hope you don't mind – I was . . . Well, to tell the truth, Doug, I didn't have anything better to do.'

'Aye, well, thank you. It was good of ye all the same. It's been a while since this place has had a woman's touch.'

'Bit like myself,' I say. 'And by the way, that's sexist.'

Doug shakes his head. 'What's not? Honestly, I dinnae ken the world anymore. Was a time when you could hold a door for a lady and she'd say thank you.'

'Is everything okay? Where's Eileen?'

'I'll put the kettle on,' says Doug. 'Unless you think you've earned a brandy.'

Doug fetches a couple of brandy balloons and a bottle from the kitchen. 'You must have been bored,' he says, holding up the glasses to the light.

'Idle hands,' I tell him, pulling off my Marigolds.

Doug pours two generous snifters and passes one to me. 'Good health.'

'Good health. So . . . why are you back so soon? Eileen tire you out?'

Doug sighs. 'Did you water the herbs?'

'Of course,' I tell him. 'What kind of woman do you take me for?'

Doug laughs gently, tilts his glass towards mine. 'Thank you,' he says. 'They were Mary's.'

'The herbs?'

Doug nods and sips his brandy. 'Aye, it started with a few pots o' herbs, then the allotment. Cabbages, tomatoes, courgettes. Strawberries some years but not for a guid bit now.'

'I always thought the allotment was your thing.'

'That's sexist,' says Doug, smiling.

'Touché, sir.'

Another tip of the brandy balloon. 'She had a proper green thumb,' he says. 'Always wanted a big garden. We thought one day we might retire to the countryside, but . . .' Doug shrugs, tops up his brandy and my own.

'My mum always said she'd retire by the sea,' I say. 'Her grandfather was a fisherman in Cork. Seawater in her blood, she liked to say.'

'Aye,' says Doug. 'You never ken the day.'

'Can I ask you something, Doug?'

Doug turns to fully face me and rests his glass on the arm of his chair.

'Is that . . .' I nod at the pots of herbs ranged across the kitchen surfaces. 'Mary . . .' I say. 'Is that why . . . why you and Eileen are, you know . . . why you're here with me and not there with her?'

Doug smiles at me with something like paternal affection, lifts his glass and takes a drink. 'No,' he says after a while. 'See the chilli plant?'

'I've cooked with them.'

'Aye, of course you have. Mary planted that. All the others, they died a while back – the others are just replacements. But that little bugger, though, that's hers, still going strong.' Doug swirls his brandy in the bottom of his glass, but doesn't drink. 'Mary was irreplaceable,' he says. 'So I'm not trying to replace her. Eileen is . . . she's different. She's Eileen.' He smiles fondly. 'If that makes any sense.'

'I think I follow,' I tell him.

Doug nods. 'Aye, you will,' he says. 'One day you will.'

Chapter Twelve

Before cameras roll there is the pre-production meeting. And before the pre-production meeting is the pre-pre-production meeting. Ben says he knows a guy that once attended a pre-pre-pre-production meeting, but that's just silly.

The receptionist at Splash Advertising informs me that my colleague is waiting for me, and escorts me to a meeting room called Bob. Whether this is a reference to a famous Robert, or simply what passes for irony in an advertising agency, she doesn't say.

Ben is alone in the room, facing a corner, mobile phone pressed to his head. He turns and nods; I return the gesture and Ben turns back to the corner. The chairs, upholstered in orange and brown stripes, are arranged around a solid wood table the size of a trampoline. I take a seat facing the wall-mounted clock and watch three minutes tick by before Ben hangs up his call. He walks up to the table and has to stretch onto tiptoes to reach the silver coffee pot in the centre.

'Coffee?'

It's the first word he's spoken to me since Friday night.

'Cheers.'

Ben pours two cups of coffee. 'Good weekend?'

'Quiet,' I say. 'You?'

'Nothing much. Just a bunch of boring baby shit.'

'Right,' I say. 'Sorry about that. I was, you know . . .'

Ben adds milk to my coffee. 'Yeah, well, likewise.'

'I didn't mean it,' I say.

'About me being tedious, or me needing to' – he searches his memory for the phrase – 'climb on top of my wife for five minutes?'

'The first one,' I say behind a laugh.

'Fair enough.' Ben takes a step back from the table and spreads his arms wide. 'Come here.'

'What?'

'Come to Ben.'

'Don't be soft.'

'I'll be gentle,' he says.

'They'll be here in a second.'

Ben beckons with his outstretched fingers.

'Fine.'

My friend wraps his arms around me, pats my back twice and says into my ear: 'I'm sorry I called you a cunt.'

'Even if I am?'

'Even if you are.'

'Oops,' says a female voice from somewhere behind me. 'Not interrupting anything, am I?'

'Verity,' says Ben, releasing me from his embrace. 'How've you been?'

Ben kisses Verity on one cheek and then the other.

'Been good, thanks,' says Verity. 'Busy busy. But good, yeah.'

Verity is wearing a satin bomber jacket over a pink vest top, and denim shorts. And at the bottom of a pair of pretty fantastic legs – lithely muscular, showing shadows of definition as she bounces lightly on her toes – a pair of pretty fantastic stripy socks. There's a lot going on and it could almost distract you from her hair, but not quite. Parted dead centre, and flowing east and west in wild blonde waves, Verity's hair brings to mind the American heroines of '70s TV; women with deadly hands and powerful hairdryers. It's not so much that she looks bad (she looks great, in fact), but that she's in the wrong decade. Ben doesn't comment on Verity's get-up, so I assume this is our production designer's default look. She'll be overseeing the art department, including everything from set design to hair and make-up, so a certain amount of creative eccentricity is no bad thing. I know Ben and Verity worked together years before, but I've never had the pleasure.

'You haven't met Tom, have you?' says Ben.

'Haven't had the pleasure,' says Verity. 'Pleased to meet you, Tom.'

I offer Verity my hand at the same moment she reaches up on tiptoes for a kiss on the cheek. I withdraw my hand and go for the kiss, but Verity has withdrawn her cheek and stuck out her hand.

Verity throws both hands in the air. 'Awkward!'

'Who's awkward?' says Kaz, walking into the room with a guy who – chin beard, checked shirt, thick-framed glasses, Converse – I assume is the creative behind the Little Horrors scripts.

'That would be me,' says Verity. 'Verity.'

Kaz introduces herself and the creative. 'Like the look,' she says, taking in Verity's outfit.

'Thank you. Bit mad, though, isn't it?' she says.

'Little bit,' says Ben.

'Date night,' says Verity, and Kaz flicks me the very briefest of glances. 'Bloody roller disco! And I can't even roll.'

'Can you disco?' I ask.

Verity laughs. 'He's a dry one, isn't he?'

And I have to wonder what kind of guy takes his girlfriend to a roller disco on a Tuesday night. The sort of guy who dates the sort of girl who'd go, I suppose.

'Honestly,' says Verity. 'I felt like a right wally on the tube, but I'm going straight from here so . . . get in character, hey.'

Ben, standing behind Verity, grins and crosses his eyes to indicate, I assume, *Bonkers*.

'And how are you, trouble?' Kaz presses herself close to my side as she kisses my cheek.

'Oh, you know me,' I say, and I make a stupid duck and dive gesture.

'I certainly do,' says Kaz. 'Right, shall we talk Little Monsters?'

'*Horrors*,' says the creative, whose name I can't seem to retain.

'Whatevs,' says Kaz.

At this stage, my role is largely that of an observer and arbitrator. This is Ben's meeting, where he presents his treatment for the four commercials to the agency. Production design, in particular hair and make-up, will be important on the shoot, and so Ben has invited Verity to present some initial concepts.

Doug and I stayed up a little too late drinking brandy last night, and I've had a particularly busy morning, so while Ben goes through a mood board of reference material, I zone out and doodle a pair of roller skates on my notepad. I'm just adding a pair of lightning bolts to the sides when my mobile vibrates with an incoming text message.

I slip my phone from my pocket and read the message under cover of the tabletop.

Thinking naughty thoughts xxx Yvette.

Yvette: a stranger to me four hours ago, now my estate agent, now sending me suggestive texts.

I write the number *96* on my pad, fattening out the digits and turning them into three-dimensional figures extending backwards along a line of perspective.

Three days ago I texted Sadie:

> Got shoot, need car. Can I collect today? Hope work easing off. T.

Next week I'll have to scout up to a dozen locations all over London, and I'd like to do it in my own car. Otherwise, what's the bloody point in having one, right? I tried again on Sunday morning. And Sunday afternoon. And Sunday suppertime.

Nothing, nothing, up yours, Tom.

She calls at ten thirty Sunday bedtime.

'I'm on hands-free,' says Sadie, 'so I'll have to be quick.'

'Where are you?'

'M25.'

'Been away?'

'No, Tom, I'm driving around the M25 at ten thirty-three on a Sunday night for the fun of it.'

'Well, whatever turns you on.'

Sadie coughs, only it doesn't sound like Sadie. It sounds more . . . *male*? Some album I've never heard is playing in the background.

'Good weekend?' I try.

'Yes, thank you very much,' says Sadie, and she sounds more than a little smug about it.

'Nice weather?'

'I'll leave the car on Highbury Terrace,' says Sadie.

I collected the car at eight this morning. The paintwork was mud-spattered in brown plumes around each wheel arch. Sods of earth in the alloys. Muddy smears on the velour floor mats, both sides. The discarded wrappers from a packet of six mini pork pies, a mouthful of Coke in a two-litre bottle, thirty-four individual Opal Fruit wrappers like fat confetti, Silk Cut cigarette ends in the ashtray. I didn't even know Sadie smoked. A Mars bar wrapper, a Twix wrapper, a single

Scotch egg wrapper. Flecks of chocolate matted into the upholstery. A greasy white paper bag from Debbie's bakery. The car smelled like the inside of a pub. A footprint above the glovebox. A big one. Pastry flakes on the floor. Grease of unknown origin on the leather fucking gear knob.

Two hours later, I'm standing on the pavement outside my flat, elbow-deep in suds, when a Foxtons Mini Cooper parks in the space directly in front.

'Yvette,' I say as the estate agent climbs out of her car. 'Thanks for coming over.'

'That's my job,' she says. Her legs are slim and bare beneath a narrow skirt. Barely a head taller than the Mini, Yvette is diminutive in every regard other than her smile.

I dry my hand on my jeans and offer it to Yvette.

'Snap,' she says, nodding at the Mini. 'Dirty weekend?'

'Ahh . . . something like that.' I motion towards the flat. 'Shall we?'

There is no deliberate seduction, no obvious play. We walk from room to room, Yvette asking questions, me answering. *What do you do for a living? Do you meet lots of famous people? Does it pay well?* In a wine bar, I'd say she was hitting on me, but we're drinking water and this is simple professional courtesy. In a nightclub we'd talk movies, jobs, music. Yvette asks about plumbing, cupboards, floorboards. She comments on the colour scheme. *Do you live alone? Why are you selling? Did she break your heart?* She touches my arm. I have nothing to lose. *Is this the bedroom?*

The small talk as we hunt for socks and underwear is more stilted.

Neither of us smoke, so I make coffee. Yvette asks what music I'm into. I ask if she likes her job. She laughs, 'Today I do.' And then she bursts into tears. *What must you think? I'm an idiot. I could lose my job.* It doesn't appear to be an act, and I give all the appropriate reassurances. It feels as if it would be rude – callous, in fact – not to retain her services in a professional capacity. We're grown-ups, I tell her, and if she's as good with buyers as she is with sellers, she'll have an offer by the end of the day. The latter, obviously, being entirely the wrong thing to say. And then I'm backtracking through more tears:

Of course I don't think you're a slut. What would that say about me? Of course I think you're pretty. But, no, I'm not ready for a relationship just now. I'm still getting over Sadie. I'm very busy with work. Perhaps it's best if, for now at least, we keep this professional. It's not you, it's me.

I give Yvette the option to decline the job, but she doesn't take the bait and I give her a set of keys to the flat instead.

I'm a good lover. I think.

I have nothing to compare me to, but I read magazines, watch chat shows, talk to people. I know how a woman's body is put together; I'm attentive, unselfish, intrepid. My stamina is good, my equipment sound. I enjoy sex; I get involved. The women I sleep with have, generally, as far as I can tell, a good experience. Didn't I put a smile on Yvette's face? Didn't she buck and thrash and scratch and octave forward and back through the vowels? Didn't I brighten her otherwise mundane Tuesday morning?

I wish someone would brighten my mundane Tuesday afternoon.

The Little Horrors pre-prod is still a long way from halfway finished. Kaz distributes copies of a timing plan.

Set out in calendar format, it begins last Friday with *Approve Budget*, and concludes six weeks later with *Deliver finished films*. In today's square I write the number *96*. Counting the squares forwards it is now forty-four days to what El calls Cherry Day. Forty-four days to score four more cherries. That's a DPF of exactly eleven . . .

'Tom?'

'Uh, sorry?'

'And he's back in the room,' says Kaz.

'Sorry, just . . . checking the . . . the dates.'

'And do they meet with your approval?'

The four shoot days are spread over two weeks: a Thursday and Friday followed by a Monday and Wednesday.

'Yes, they look f—' I begin, but then I focus on the dates, on 24 June in particular, and my stomach folds in on itself. 'I can't do the Monday,' I say.

'Something more important?' says Kaz.

'Family stuff.'

The Sunday before the Monday in question I'll be at Dad's, commemorating the anniversary of my mum's death, and I have no intention of leaving early to drive back to London. For a start, I won't be sober enough.

'Sorry,' I say, 'it's . . .' I look at Ben, and he knows.

'We can shift everything back a day or two,' he says, sparing me from having to explain myself any further. But perhaps Kaz is more perceptive than I might have given her credit for.

'Sure,' she says, smiling in my direction. 'Not a problem.'

Kaz is a tricky one to figure out; occasionally caught up in her perceived self-importance, but not without a sense of humour. Alternately cold then flirtatious, antagonistic and gregarious, she's a riddle for sure. Not someone I'd want as a girlfriend – even if she were single – but after this small moment of understanding, she's definitely on my Christmas card list.

'Okay,' she says, turning to Verity. 'Prod design.'

'Right,' says Verity, clapping her hands together. 'Can I just start by saying, I think these are such good scripts.'

They're really not, but the creative takes the compliment at face value.

'I've always loved horror films,' says Verity. 'Not that torture nonsense, but zombies, vampires and all that lot. There's such a rich tradition, so many visual tropes and conventions, we're spoiled for choice.'

Again the creative nods, and you get the sense that Verity could lead him anywhere now.

'I've talked to Ben, and my instinct is go goofy. I don't mean toothy goofy, I mean daft goofy, you know. After all, we're not trying to scare anyone, just give 'em a giggle and send them down to the shops for a packet of Skittles, right? Keep it light. Wonky fangs, big hair, a couple of warts and maybe a pair of coloured contacts. The last thing you want is for the make-up to overshadow the performances. Less is more and all that. In fact, the more I think about it, the more I think the trick here is in the casting, not the make-up. Same with set design – locations first, moody lighting, Dutch the camera a bit. But be sparing with the cobwebs and whatnot – keep the camera on the kiddies, right? God, listen to me going on. I'm talking myself out of a job here, aren't I?'

'Not at all,' says Kaz.

'Spot on,' says the creative, looking like he's fallen a little in love with our production designer.

'Why don't you show them the sketches, Vee?' says Ben.

Verity opens up a small portfolio case and sets out four A3 boards on the table, one for each of the scripts.

'Did you draw these?' asks Kaz.

Verity nods modestly.

'Bloody hell,' says the creative, 'you could flog these.'

And he's right. Rendered in a variety of styles from graphic-noir vampire to cross-hatched Frankenstein's monster, to Japan-pop were-wolf and movie-poster zombies, every single one is good enough to hang on a wall.

'Keep 'em,' says Verity, as if she were giving away a doodle on a napkin.

I look down at my own notepad, the clumsy sketch of roller skates, the ridiculous number *96*. And I feel all of a sudden very tired and thoroughly deflated.

It takes a further fifty-seven minutes to tick off the remaining items on the agenda, and I'm cross-eyed and brain-limp when we get to the handshakes and goodbyes. The creative asks if any of us are going to some production company's summer party on Thursday – although it's clear he's asking Verity, even if she does have a boyfriend who takes her to roller discos on a Tuesday night.

'Maybe,' she says. 'Have to check my busy diary. Anyone else going?'

I open my mouth to answer – affirmative or negative, I haven't decided, but Kaz saves me the effort of choosing.

'No,' she says. 'The boys have got a busy week, haven't you, boys?'

Verity catches my expression and, out of Kaz's eyeline, grits her teeth and lashes an invisible whip. She has fantastic teeth.

Chapter Thirteen

Anything is ripe for a double entendre, if you put your mind to it. You can pick up a nice birdie in golf, sneak into the double top in darts and, of course, apply a delicate kiss on the pink in snooker.

But when I point out that Douglas has just done the latter, he doesn't guffaw like usual. Of course it isn't funny, but it's a traditional aspect of the game, and if I had any doubts at all, now I'm certain Doug is brooding about something.

I lean over the table to take my shot: an easy red in the corner pocket.

'One,' intones Doug as the ball drops.

I'm a little high for the black, so I walk around the table to take the blue. 'Casting tomorrow,' I say.

'Aye,' says Doug. 'The monsters.'

'A whole graveyard full of them. You got any plans?'

'Six,' says Doug, with regards to my score, rather than his plans.

'Salsa tomorrow, isn't it?'

'Think I'll gie it a miss,' he says. 'Talking of which . . .'

I underhit the red, leaving it hovering over the pocket. Doug chalks up his cue and puts the ball away.

'One,' I say, noting Doug's score. 'Won't Eileen be disappointed?'

Doug slams in a black with way more force than necessary. 'Ye'd have to ask Eileen,' he says.

'Eight. Have you two fallen out?'

Doug isn't given to profanity or crudity, but when he misses his next red and pots the white he lets go with a belter.

'Right,' I say.

'Four to you,' says Doug.

We continue to knock the balls around the table, occasionally dropping one or two in the pocket, in relative silence for the next fifteen minutes or so. It's not as much fun as a roller disco, that's for sure.

We're down to the last five colours, and Doug rattles the green in the jaws of the top-left corner pocket.

'Get to the allotment today?' I ask.

I return the favour and knock the green off three cushions, but nowhere near a pocket.

'Stayed in,' says Doug.

'Catching up on sleep, I expect.'

Doug gives me a sideways glance. 'Aye, well, bit noisy for that.'

Yvette.

'Sorry,' I say, 'it just sort of happened.'

'Just sort of happens affen, doesn't it?' Doug trickles the green into the middle pocket, and sets himself up nicely for the brown. 'That girl from work again?'

'Three points,' I say. 'No, she was . . . an estate agent.'

Doug laughs. 'Thorough lass,' he says.

'You could say that. Shot. Seven points.'

'So, you're moving?'

'Dunno, Doug. Maybe. Just thought I'd see what's . . . you know, out there.'

'You'll still visit?'

'Not a chance.'

'Ach, well, that's all right then.'

Doug chalks his cue, and flicks me a look before bending down to line up his shot.

'Are you sensible, Thomas?'

There are several ways to answer Doug's enquiry, but I elect for the most straightforward and tell him that I am.

'Well,' he says. 'Boys will be boys. I suppose.'

He drops the blue and the white ball rolls up to the pink, nudging it off the cushion and into play.

'Twelve,' I say. 'With a . . .'

'Aye,' says Doug. 'With a nice wee kiss on the pink.'

***

We play one more frame and drink one more pint of beer. I ask again if Doug would be seeing Eileen any time soon, but Doug mutters an ambivalent and non-sequiturial answer involving the words *dunny*, *canny*, *wouldny*, *bother* and *bugger*. So I take the hint and we walk home in relative silence. We shake hands and say goodnight on the doorstep of our empty flats, then Doug lays his hand on my shoulder, gives it a gentle squeeze and tells me, 'Look after yourself, lad.' His hand feels heavy, as if transmitting the weight of his loneliness. Or maybe it's simply pushing against the weight of my own.

After Doug lets himself into his flat, I spot a brown envelope lying on the doormat inside the communal porch.

Stamped on the front in red letters are the words *Penalty Charge Notice*. Sixty sodding quid for parking illegally in a restricted zone on Highbury fucking Terrace, Islington. What I want is a stiff drink, but after screaming silent expletives in every room of the flat, I text Sadie a sarcastic thank you, make a pot of calming primrose tea and settle down to watch a little TV before bed.

Beside the remote control, however, is a packet of candy Love Hearts – standing upright on my coffee table like a stick of pastel dynamite. And only a rabbit boiling in my Le Creuset stockpot could induce more dread than the sight of this dreadful love token from my estate agent.

Between Sadie and Yvette, it's getting so I'm afraid to be in my own home. I deadbolt the door, turn off my phone and pour myself what Doug would call a 'good glug' of whisky.

Chapter Fourteen

Casting is fun maybe the first two or three times you do it. After that it's a bad case of déjà vu. Imagine watching looped repeats of the same commercial again and again and again, only each time with a different actor. That's casting. We're looking for actors that fit the scripts and can take direction; someone Ben can work with over a long day under hot lights. I'm here to take notes, liaise with the casting director and make sure everyone has the right kind of coffee. Some castings – those involving lingerie models, for example – are more bearable than others – those involving howling, screaming, yowling children pretending to be monsters, for example.

Groaaaaan.

'Next.'

Mneaaaaarrr.

'Next.'

You're looking for that little something extra.

Arghhhhhhh.

A spark.

Vvvvrrrrr.

Personality.

Brrrrraiiiiiiiiiinnnnnnsssssss.

Someone like Alice. As well as an eerie undulating quality to her 'brains', nine-year-old Alice has a great zombie walk – rhythmic, rickety and dislocated, like an undead body-popper. Plus, Alice has unfortunate bug eyes which she can cross one at a time or both together. We've found our first zombie.

Verity is passing the time by sketching caricatures. So far today, she has drawn a vampire Holly, a werewolf Tom and a Verity with a bolt through her neck. Right now she is outlining a zombie Ben that doesn't look too dissimilar to the one beside me, drinking his fourth espresso of the morning.

Ben yawns expansively, and I watch as Verity captures the gesture in pencil.

'You've captured his eyes beautifully,' I say.

Verity smiles as she opens up a cavity in the side of zombie Ben's neck.

'Wait till you have kids,' says Ben. 'See how funny it is then.'

Ben's yawn is contagious and, fight as I might, I can't suppress one of my own.

'Your baby got a cold, too?' says Verity.

'No baby, no cold,' I say. 'Stayed up late watching a movie.'

'Anything good?'

'*Total Recall*,' I say, feeling myself flush.

'*Get your ass to Mars.*' This from Ben.

'Dick,' Verity mutters under her breath.

Ben double-takes as if he's misheard. 'Excuse me?'

Verity laughs. 'Sorry, I think out loud when I draw, apparently. Philip K. Dick. Wrote the short story *Total Recall*'s based on. Only it's called something else.'

'There you go,' says Ben. 'That's our something new for the day.'

'And he wrote *Blade Runner*,' says Verity. 'But that one was called *Do Androids Dream of Electric Sheep?*'

'You into sci-fi?' I ask.

'Not exactly,' says Verity. 'But I am a bit of a book nerd. And I've got a big brother.'

Holly escorts our next actor into the room and Ben orders another coffee.

Garrrrrrrr.

'Next.'

Uurrgggghhh.

'Next.'

Oooooooooooo.

Next. Next. Next. Next. Next. Next.

Uuuurmphhh . . .

George has definitely got 'something'. Although not a something you'd want in your own child, or nephew, or kid next door.

His hands hang limp at his sides, he rolls his eyes back into his skull and fixes you with a boiled-egg stare, then he shuffles slowly – inexorably, you feel – forward. From the depths of his belly, George dredges up a sound that lies beyond our alphabet, and a gob of spittle spills from his slack mouth.

'Thank you, George,' says Ben.

But George keeps on coming.

'Okay, George,' I say. 'That's great.'

Relentless.

'Cut!'

When George stops two paces in front of our table, I'm leaning away from him to the extent that I'm bruising my vertebrae against the chair's backrest.

'How was that?' he asks as his eyes swivel back into place.

I take a breath and lower my shoulders from up around my ears. 'Truly disturbing,' I say.

'Thank you very much,' says George. 'Can I go now?'

As fast as your creepy little feet can carry you.

Horrible kid, great zombie.

Frankenstein's monsters are a little thinner on the ground. The role requires a degree of physical presence that your average nine-to-thirteen-year-old doesn't possess. A square head would also be handy; but this, too, is unusual in schoolchildren.

'Maybe we'll *dig up* something after lunch,' says Ben.

'Let's hope so.'

'Get it?' says Ben. '*Dig up . . .*'

'Ah,' says Verity. 'That would be one of those dad jokes.'

'Fine,' says Ben. 'I'm going to find a table to sleep under.' And he does exactly that.

'Sunshine?' whispers Verity.

'Excuse me?'

'There's a balcony on top of the building,' she says. 'Views all over Soho.'

'It's raining,' I tell her.

Verity produces a purple telescopic umbrella from her bag. 'Stick 'em up,' she says, levelling the thing at my chest.

I flash back to my date with Flo: me doing the same thing Verity is doing now – pointing Flo's polka-dot umbrella at her across a table. That night went the way it did, and it occurs to me how much of our lives come down to luck and timing. Right person, right place, right time is what you're looking for, but my judgement stinks and my timing is lousy. Even so, I feel an instinctive sense of Verity's 'rightness'. It's not about lust – despite her smile and her eyes and her quite fantastic legs – it's about something less easy to pinpoint. There's a wavelength, I think. Like being the kind of person who holds up another person with a telescopic umbrella.

And yeah, her legs really are wonderful.

'Don't look so alarmed,' Verity says, swinging the umbrella under her arm. 'It's not loaded.'

'Come on then. Show me this balcony.'

The streets are black and shining with rain, and the tourists and lunchtime workers sprint from awning to doorway, oblivious to Verity and me peering down on them from the sixth floor of this dirty Soho building. Verity's umbrella has a narrow radius, so we are squashed close together as we spy on the hoi polloi.

Verity looks different today, and if you were to walk past her in the street you could be forgiven for not recognising her. Although I think I would. Her hair is styled in a tight French plait. Or maybe it's a Dutch braid, I always confuse the two. In stark contrast to the rollergirl get-up, Verity has something of a sailor vibe going on this afternoon: Breton top, sharply ironed culottes and open-toed sandals. Maybe she has another date tonight. Something on a yacht, perhaps. A very expensive one.

'Are your feet not cold?' I ask her.

'Freezing,' she says. 'But I've got wicked blisters from those pigging roller skates.'

'Ouch. Still, it's good to try new things.'

'Verity is the spice of life.' She says it with such deadpan delivery that I glance sideways, unsure whether or not I misheard. 'It always comes up sooner or later,' Verity says.

'Funny.'

'Yeah, I suppose. The first ninety-nine times, anyway.'

Verity's whole demeanour is calmer and more measured today. The nervous energy has given way to a more laidback and natural disposition.

'So, no more roller discos?' I say.

'No more Geoffrey,' she says, twirling her umbrella and sending out a scatter of raindrops.

'Your boyfriend?'

Verity laughs. 'My date. We never progressed to the boyfriend stage. First date, last date,' she says.

I take care not to sound too interested in this development. 'I see. It's just with you saying "date night", I assumed it was a regular . . . you know, fixture.'

'Oh, it is,' Verity says. 'I'm a serial dater. Tuesday nights are date nights whenever I can make it.'

'A serial dater?'

'You know what they say about kissing frogs.'

'That you need to kiss a lot of 'em?'

'Well, there you go.'

'But no prince, I take it.'

'They're harder to find than you might think. Have you heard about that experiment?'

'Haven't there been a few?'

Verity inclines the umbrella away from me for a second, briefly exposing me to the cold rain. 'Hey!'

'No brolly for smart alecs. It's the rules.'

'Right,' I say. 'No. I haven't heard about *the* experiment.'

'So they got forty volunteers. Twenty men, twenty women. And they stuck a number – from one to twenty – on everyone's back, so they couldn't see it but everyone else in the room could.'

'Based on how they looked?' I'm a little appalled at the idea.

'No, arbitrarily. Like a substitute for real-world attractiveness. You might have a big fat guy with BO and pimples, but if he's a Twenty, then he's the most desirable guy in the room.'

'Got you. I think.'

'So you've got a guy One and a girl One, a guy Two and a girl Two. All the way up to . . . ?'

'Guy Twenty and girl Twenty.'

'Okay. And they told everyone to go and pair up with the highest number they could. But remember, they have no idea what their own value is.'

'Interesting.'

'I know! So guess what happens.'

'Everyone tries to pull the Twenties?'

'Get you, well done. The Twenties are surrounded by guys or girls wanting to hook up with them. So they quickly realise they're high value. All that interest, you see. So they reject the Ones and Twos and all the low numbers. And the low numbers, well, no one's interested in them, so they realise they are low value and start buzzing about the place trying to hook up with anyone who'll have 'em. Like the drunk kid at ten to two in any nightclub in the world.'

'Proving?'

'Well, at the end of the experiment – within a number or two – all the high numbers paired off with the high numbers and the low numbers with the low numbers.'

'Like beautiful couples and—'

'Not-so-beautiful couples. Exactly. Well, kind of – you see mismatches, don't you? Something else compensating, like talent or personality or—'

'Money.'

'That too. Proving . . . I dunno, that—'

'It's a numbers game?'

Verity sighs. 'Maybe. I was going to say that there's someone for everyone. But, yeah, you've gotta find 'em first. Got to keep kissing those frogs.'

We have been gazing across the rooftops as we've talked, and watching the rain and the traffic and the scurrying figures below. Not looking at each other, so it's hard to tell if this silence is awkward or not. It doesn't feel awkward. I chance a sideways glance at Verity, who seems temporarily lost in her thoughts.

My phone rings in my pocket. I take it out to check the caller and wince.

'Work?' asks Verity.

'Estate agent,' I tell her. 'I'd better . . . you know.'

Verity inclines the brolly away from me. 'See you for the werewolves,' she says.

'Hello,' I say into the phone, with as much formality as I can muster. 'Tom Ferguson.'

'Hello, lover boy,' a voice whispers.

I wait until I'm in the stairwell and the door has closed behind me before I answer.

'Hello,' says the voice again. 'It's Yvette. From Foxtons. Haven't forgotten me already, have you?'

'Yvette, hi. Sorry, I was . . . we're casting.'

'So glamorous,' Yvette says, and it's clear that she means it. 'I called yesterday but couldn't get you.'

Five times!

'Sorry. No phones allowed on location.'

'I measured and photographed the flat . . .'

Yvette says this as if it's loaded with subtext. As if she's describing her underwear, perhaps.

'Great.'

'Did you get my pressie?'

My stomach clenches. 'Right . . . the sweets.'

'*Love Hearts*,' Yvette corrects in a put-out baby voice.

'Yeah, of course, Love Hearts.' My voice echoes in the stairwell, and I check behind me as I trot down to the ground floor.

'Around five?' Yvette says, and I realise she is waiting for an answer to a question I haven't registered.

'Five?'

'Saturday.'

'Excuse me?'

'For the viewing.'

'A viewing,' I say, finally picking up the thread. 'Someone wants to see the flat?'

'I was thinking' – Yvette's voice drops to a whisper – 'maybe afterwards, seeing as it's a Saturday, maybe we could go for a drink . . .'

Shit.

'. . . or something?'

The foot of the stairs is busy with people coming in and out of the building, so I dash through the rain to a doorway across the street.

'Actually, Yvette, it's not a great time for me.'

'Or Sunday,' says Yvette. 'I could do Sunday.'

'I mean in general. I mean, I'd love to and everything, I'm just incredibly busy. With this shoot and . . . stuff.'

'Right, yes, of course. I didn't mean anything heavy, just . . . you know . . .'

'I'll be working all weekend,' I say. 'In fact, I'll be non-stop for the rest of the summer.' I glance up to the roof of the casting studio, but if Verity is still up there, I can't see her.

'I understand,' Yvette says, her tone cold.

'Are you sure?' I say, attempting to sound soothing.

'Really, it's not a problem. So are we okay for the viewing?'

'I'll make sure I've cleaned away all my dirty laundry,' I say.

'Fine,' says Yvette. 'I'll be there at five.'

Fine. I won't be.

You just know when someone's right.

Friends, girlfriends, werewolves.

Elijah the werewolf is ten and ten-twelfths, can eat a Mars bar sideways, and his wolf howl makes the hairs in my ears stand on end. Verity sketches a slightly disturbing picture of the boy howling at a heavy moon, strings of saliva dripping from his fangs, his brow wrinkled in rage and hunger. Almost as if he can't comprehend his own nature. Or maybe I'm reading too much into a ten-minute doodle.

'Goosebumpers,' says Holly, leaning over her shoulder. 'Ready for the Frankensteins?' she says to Ben and me.

'Wheel 'em in,' says Ben.

As she turns to leave, Holly's eyes flick to Verity and then back to me. She smiles, but it doesn't quite reach her eyes. The raised eyebrow and the hint of a wink that used to characterise a smile from Holly have gone now. Instead there's a layer of something else and it tugs at my conscience.

We can't choose who or what we're attracted to. Any more than you can change your nature. Verity is kissing frogs, and Lord knows I fit the description. But a prince? I don't think so – ask Sadie, ask Flo, ask Holly, ask Emma, ask Yvette. I can't see the number on my back, but if it's higher than a two I'll be very surprised.

We audition the Frankensteins two at a time, and Albert is teamed up with Hugo, a cocky stage-school brat who recently 'starred' in a commercial for air fresheners.

'Okay then,' I say. 'Who wants to be Frankenstein first?'

'If you mean Frankenstein's *monster*,' says Hugo, 'then I'll go first.'

Ben gets Hugo to lie on a table while Albert plays the role of Doctor Frankenstein. A broom propped against the table represents the master switch. It's not a scene we'll use in the commercial, but it gives us a chance to see if the kids can act and take direction.

Hugo makes a bit of a fuss about getting himself set on the table. Ben calls 'Action'.

Albert twiddles an invisible dial, but something is wrong. He turns more dials, flicks switches, clenches his fists and stares towards the darkening sky. His eyes widen at an inner revelation. He lopes across the lab, connects two lengths of heavy cable, calibrates a bank of instruments. Now he's ready. Every muscle in his body is tense and his knuckles are white on the master switch as he watches the sky for lightning. And when it comes, something broken flashes in the doctor's eyes. He heaves on the lever.

Hugo sits upright, his arms float upwards in front of him. He turns to Doctor Frankenstein, who has fallen to his knees and seems only now to appreciate the horror, the wonder, the dreadful truth of what he has done. '*Garrrr*,' says Hugo, swinging his legs from the table and hopping to the floor. '*Eurgggh*,' he says, striding stiff-leggedly across the room and blocking my view of the cursed doctor, who is now beseeching God above for forgiveness.

'Cut,' shouts Ben. 'Abso-blooming-lutely brilliant.'

Hugo cocks his head immodestly, demonstrating a capacity for self-delusion that far outstrips his acting talents.

We reverse the roles – Hugo as mad scientist, Albert as his creation – and when Ben calls 'Action', Hugo, the ham, completely plagiarises Albert's earlier improvisation. But there is no thunderstorm, no lightning; there are no dials, switches or levers – just a wooden broom and a table. Hugo pulls the broom, drops to his knees, and shakes his fists at the fluorescent lights. When the monster doesn't move, Hugo looks irritatedly at Albert and goes to give the broom another yank.

The monster howls in anguish.

Hugo drops the broom and yelps.

Again a pitiful sound from the creature, clearly in pain as it struggles to a seated position. One arm hangs useless as the opposite hand clutches at his throat, fingering the scars there. The monster looks at his hand and doesn't recognise it. And his expression is the saddest thing in the world.

Hugo is frozen; one hand outstretched protectively, the other clutched in an awkward fist at his side.

The monster's mouth works silently, the effort of opening his dead jaws is excruciating and his eyes are wet with pain and incomprehension.

'Wh . . . w . . .' He heaves air into collapsed lungs, and when the dry words come, his voice is heartbreak. 'Why?'

Hugo shakes his head, looks to me for help, doesn't get any, and shakes his head once again in the face of the awful monster.

'WHY?' The monster half climbs, half falls from the gurney. 'WHY!!!'

Ben nudges me, whispers in my ear, 'Shall we cut now, or wait until Hugo actually shits his cords?'

'I dunno,' I whisper, as Albert's monster advances on Hugo. 'What do you reckon?'

Ben waggles his hand, fifty-fifty.

Me? It's not just that Hugo's predicament is amusing – which it is, utterly – but I could watch Albert all day long. If I'd paid forty-five quid to see this at the theatre I'd consider it a bargain and urge my friends to go and see it too. He might be the most gifted actor I've ever seen; and I'm going to slap green make-up on him and feed him sweets. The horror.

Ben calls 'Cut' a moment before Hugo throws himself out of the window.

Before we leave, Verity gives Holly, Ben and myself the sketches she drew of us during the long day. In mine, I'm holding a purple umbrella.

Chapter Fifteen

There are four Little Horrors scripts. Little Werewolf and Little Zombies are set in domestic situations, so we'll film them in a studio. Little Vampire involves a wedding, so we'll need a church, preferably one with high arches, gargoyles, stained glass and so on; and Frankenstein's Little Monster is based around a school trip to a castle, so I'm looking for something with towers, dungeons, manacles, ravens. We spent the morning at the Tower of London, taking snaps of me lurching past Traitors' Gate, Ben looming over battlements, me rattling chains. This afternoon we've visited three churches, and we're driving to our fourth.

'Are you sure you haven't been smoking in here?' says Ben.

'I still don't smoke.'

'Well, it still smells of cigarettes.'

This is a conversation I don't want to have, so I lower Ben's window and cross my fingers that he'll take the hint and let it go.

'Has somebody been dating?' he asks, elbowing me playfully.

'*Somebody* may well have been,' I say. 'But it wasn't me.'

'Who then?' says Ben.

'Who do you think?'

'I don't know, do I? If I knew I wouldn't a— Ahh.' A penny drops and clangs heavily.

'Yes,' I say. '*Ahh.*'

'Sadie?'

'Looks like it.'

Of course Sadie has been dating, and I wish nothing less for her. I want her to find a good guy, be happy, have fun. But, call me precious, I don't necessarily need to know about it, and I don't particularly want her doing it in my car.

'Where now?' I ask Ben.

Ben consults the map on his lap. 'Right here, third left onto . . . Morningside Road.'

I nudge the nose of the Mini into the oncoming traffic. A woman in a Land Rover honks unnecessarily and I give her a very necessary hand gesture.

In the following silence, Karen Carpenter croons the lyrics to 'Solitaire'. Neither Ben nor I acknowledge the irony of this. Although it's hardly a coincidence. *Gold* is an album to overdose to: 'Goodbye to Love', 'Rainy Days and Mondays', 'I Won't Last a Day Without You', 'I Need to Be in Love', 'This Masquerade', 'Only Yesterday' . . . 'Ticket to Ride', for Christ's sake.

'Got anything else?' says Ben, tapping the CD player. 'I hate the Carpenters.'

'Help yourself,' I say, and an old gent in a Mercedes waves me through.

Ben pops open the glovebox and rummages through its contents.

'Queen, Stones, ABBA, it's a right mess in h— Opal Fruits! Want one?'

'I'm fine.'

'There's red, yellow . . . looks like some tosser's eaten all the green ones. Purple, want a purple one?' Ben holds a sweet towards me.

'You have it. Have the bag.'

'Sure?'

'Positive.'

'Nice one.' Ben stuffs the sweet into his mouth and the pack in his pocket. 'Right . . . Elton John, Elvis, *Eighties Pop Anthems* . . . How about Elvis?'

'Yeah, whatev—'

I spot my turning too late and hit the brakes too hard.

'Bollocks!' Ben says, spilling a handful of CDs onto the floor between his feet.

'Sorry. You okay?'

'Fine,' says Ben, rubbing the top of his head. 'Gave me a bit of a fright, that's all. Watch the road, you tosser.'

I reverse back to the turning and set off down a double-parked residential street. 'Sure you're all right?'

'Fine,' says Ben, holding up a shattered CD case. 'But I think I've killed Elton John.'

Maybe I'm a little wired on adrenalin, but I laugh harder than the quip warrants.

'Never liked him either,' Ben says, picking up the debris and stuffing it back into the glovebox. 'I'll never get all this shit back in here.'

'Leave it,' I say. 'We'll sort it out later.'

'Just need to make some space.' Ben starts removing various items. 'Torn map, hairbrush, plastic bag, pen, two pens, two batteries, what the hell is . . .'

In the corner of my vision Ben holds up something that might be a handkerchief. With a lace trim.

Ben glances at me furtively and bundles the glovebox junk into the plastic bag. 'Straight to the end, left, and it's about a hundred y—'

'What was that?' I say, jerking my thumb at the bag.

'Eh?'

'What you just put in the bag.'

'Just . . . you know, shit.'

'That last thing,' I say.

Ben rummages in the bag and removes a battery. 'Battery,' he says with contrived offhandedness.

'After that,' I say.

'Pen,' Ben says, producing a capless red biro.

'It looked like a . . . a rag?'

'Yeah,' says Ben. 'A rag.'

'Show me.'

'What?'

I hit the brakes. 'The fucking knickers, Ben.'

Ben smiles apologetically and hands over the plastic bag.

I remove a pair of silk, rose-petal pink, La Perla pants. The thigh holes are bordered with butterflies trapped in inch-wide lace; the front panel is a delicate mesh, fine enough to show a shadow of pubic hair; at the back, below the waistband, is a small slit closed off with a knotted bow. Exactly like the pair I bought for £120 on Valentine's Day last year. Presumably Sadie still has the matching bra.

My instinct is to ram the Mini into the nearest lamp post, but I've done enough damage to Ben already. I drive a few yards further up the road until I find a parking space.

'You okay?' asks Ben.

I gather up my notes, phone and camera, climb out of the Mini, walk round to Ben's side and open his door for him.

Ben gets out, looking slightly confused. 'Are we walking?'

'Have you got everything?' I ask him.

Ben pats his pockets and the Opal Fruits rustle. 'Think so.'

'Phone, wallet, keys?'

Ben nod, nod, nods.

'Jolly good.' I close his door, kick it, lock the car and set off towards the main road, scanning the pavement until I see what I'm looking for.

Ben catches up just as I drop the car keys. 'The church is the oth—'

The keys bounce off the iron grate and drop into the drain with a satisfying *plip*.

Ben points at the drain, then at the Mini, then at me. I'm smiling.

'What about the church?'

'I thought you liked the Anglican place in Shepherd's Bush,' I say. 'I loved it.'

'Good. We'll go with the Anglicans, then.'

'Okay,' says Ben, staring into the drain. 'The Anglicans. Great.'

'Right, I need a drink.'

Chapter Sixteen

!

This is the first thought to lance through my brain on Friday morning.

A sharp, stark exclamation point.

!

Some people call them screamers.

Whereas the horrors of the previous night sometimes take a moment to dawn, this morning mine are already awake and waiting for me. I've never been a professional-standard drinker, but that didn't stop me trying last night. Images of myself, shouting too loud, saying too much, trying too hard. I've got the booze paranoia with great big rusty bells on. And it's the least of my worries. It feels like I'm sick with some tropical disease. One that eats away at your brain flesh from the inside. Where larvae hatch and writhe in the pit of your belly. One that leaves you panting with nausea and anxiety. There's a dried-out sponge that I use to clean the toilet, and right now I'd rather have that inside my mouth than the sticky, foul-tasting lump of flesh that is my own tongue.

My first hangover was the morning after I lost my virginity to Trudi Roberts. I don't remember the extent of my symptoms – only that they were subdued by an elation no headache or stomach pain could compete with. This morning, though, there is no elation to do battle with my hangover. Despair and remorse have joined my physical symptoms and they're all fighting on the same side against me.

My mind flashes scenes of me making an imbecile of myself in the Stuffed Goose, downing shots, ruining jokes, mangling philosophical nonsense. At least by that point no one was paying very much attention. Ben had left an hour previously; Marlon our cameraman was largely unresponsive (only opening his mouth to drink, only opening his eyes to locate his pint); and Holly said less than a dozen words to me all night.

I remembered the creative mentioning a party, and Kaz asserting that I couldn't go because I had a 'busy week'. Well, she was right about that busy part.

The next time Holly took a toilet break I sidled up to Rob and asked if he fancied sneaking off to a party, but Rob had plans of his own so I left Marlon to his dreams and Rob to his own devices.

If anything, Kaz was more drunk, and correspondingly more flirtatious than the night she pinched my arse in the basement of the King George on Dean Street.

'Surprised to see you here,' she said, mock-reproval in her voice. 'Haven't you got make-up tests tomorrow?'

'Well, Ben and Verity do. I'm a mere observer, Kaz.'

'Yes,' she says. 'Aren't you just?'

'And what's that supposed to mean?'

'Meaning,' Kaz said, her hand finding mine, 'I'm going now. And if you were to leave exactly two minutes later, you'd probably find me outside getting into a cab.'

'What about your boyfriend?'

'Two minutes,' she repeated and was gone.

Hardly subtle and hardly a seduction. If I had to put a number between one and twenty on Kaz's back it would be a fourteen or a fifteen. Higher than mine, I'd say. Begging the question: what's my compensating feature? Talent, personality and money are the ones Verity and I mentioned on the balcony in the rain, but there are others too. Availability, proximity, ego, ease. Not being the boyfriend you're bored with, the girlfriend you're angry or disenchanted with. I can't begin to decode Kaz, and I have no intention of trying. I don't even understand myself.

After I slept with Trudi Roberts, I told my friends. Trudi told her friends; our friends told theirs. It's good gossip and it goes around. My credibility grew, my popularity received a boost and I felt pretty bloody good about myself. So I did it again: same result, this time with a little notoriety thrown in – and notoriety is cool, particularly when you're a fifteen-year-old boy. But this? This bet, this mission, quest, debacle, call it what you will? Kaz was my ninety-seventh lover, and if for one second I imagined I would feel ninety-seven times taller than I did on the day I lost my virginity . . . well, I'd have been an idiot. What I feel this morning is sore, sordid and depressed.

An aggressive but otherwise dispassionate lover, Kaz fucked me like I owed her money. Like I owed her every penny of the budget and every pound we had bickered over. Savage and methodical, she transitioned through all the positions, made all the appropriate noises and said all the dirty words.

When I was thirteen or fourteen, I briefly took karate classes. The plan was to get a black belt then kick the shit out of Declan Chambers and his crew of wankers. We learned kata – drills of kicks and blocks and punches against imagined opponents. One two punch; three four turn; five six kick; seven eight thrust; sex with Kaz; nine ten scream. An approximation of the real deal.

Trimmed into a tapering strip, Kaz's pubic hair glistened like black ink. Like an exclamation mark.

!

Like a screamer.

!

Fuck!

Fucking hell!

Fucking hell squared!

She left nearly five hours ago, and the small snatches of sleep I've had since have been fretful, haunted and, if anything, more tiring than no sleep at all. I roll onto my side as a preparatory manoeuvre for disembarking the bed, swing my legs off the side, and recoil as my foot touches something cold and yielding. Lying on the carpet, like a pair of obese worms, are two dry, hair-stuck condoms knotted full with last night's semen. My stomach rides up my throat and I fall back onto the bed with a hand clamped over my mouth.

It's forty-one days to the anniversary of the day I lost my virginity, and I'm one notch closer to taking a thousand pounds off my terminally ill best friend. There is a bite mark on my shoulder and my testicles ache like they've been sat on.

I'd imagined a more frivolous affair with Kaz. Jokes about close-ups, reveals . . . *And action!* At some time after three thirty in the morning, she called a cab, showered and dressed. She said it had been 'fun' and told me she loved her boyfriend, saying the latter in a tone that defied contradiction and implied – contrary to the evidence of the past several hours – this was information that should go without saying. We hugged stiffly on my doorstep, and only a handshake would have been more perfunctory.

On the way out of the flat to the make-up tests, I bump into Douglas on the doorstep.

'Morning, Doug,' I say sheepishly.

'You're going then,' he says, pointing at the 'FOR SALE' sign that's been nailed to the gatepost.

'I don't know. I just . . . I don't know. You off out?'

'Bridge.'

'Is Eileen going?'

'Expect so. I was going to put this through your letter box.' Doug hands me a fat brown envelope. 'But as you're here.'

'What is it?' I ask, taking the small package.

'Starflower,' says Doug. 'Supposed to be good for hangovers. So Mary used to say, anyway.'

'Right, thanks. Listen,' I say, indicating where I keep my watch, 'I should be off.'

'Is it making you happy, Thomas? All this running around.'

'No,' I say. 'Not particularly.'

Doug nods. 'A didnae think so, lad.' He holds my eyes, waiting for an answer, or at least an acknowledgement that I've heard and understood him.

I nod and put the envelope of herbs into my bag.

'Starflower's all well and guid,' says Doug. 'But I've always sworn by bacon and eggs. Come on, I'll buy you breakfast.'

Chapter Seventeen

The make-up tests are in the same place that we did the casting, and I'm the last person to arrive – tired, hungover and reeking of apathy. Ben, Holly and Verity are gathered around a table, laughing at something in Verity's sketchbook. Also present is our make-up artist, Laura, and the creative – and although I checked before he got here, I still can't recall his name.

'Shut up!' says another person, obscured from view at the back of this huddle. 'I do not look at all like that.'

'Beg to differ,' says Ben.

Kaz stands up from the table. 'Tom,' she says, as if I were the last person she was expecting to walk through the door. 'Blimey, talk about the living dead. Late night, babes?'

Verity twists her face into a lopsided smile and mimes zombie hands. Today she is wearing a sleeveless cotton dress, red with white polka dots and evocative of the '50s or '60s. Her hair is tied in a tight wide bun on the top of her head. Vintage, you might call it, but I could be wrong. I remember her joking that 'Verity is the spice of life', but I'm beginning to think it may be more of a personal mantra than an offhand quip.

'Er . . . a few . . . you know, drinks,' I say, wishing there was a rail nearby I could grab on to.

'Verity's done me as a vampire, look,' says Kaz, walking towards me and opening her arms for a hug. 'I don't look like a vampire, do I?'

With her back to the room, Kaz scowls at me: *Not a word.*

'Vampire?' I manage.

'Blimey,' says Kaz, 'looks like someone needs mucho coffee. Tell you what, I'll pop to Starbucks. Anyone else?'

Everyone shouts their orders to Kaz. She looks like she slept nine hours on a feather mattress, woke early, swam twenty lengths and had a high-protein low-fat breakfast.

Kaz kisses me on the cheek on the way out. 'Say anything to anyone,' she whispers in my ear, 'and I'll fucking murder you.'

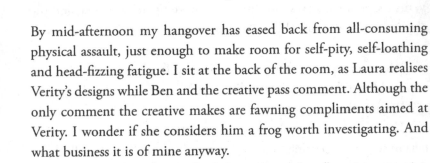

By mid-afternoon my hangover has eased back from all-consuming physical assault, just enough to make room for self-pity, self-loathing and head-fizzing fatigue. I sit at the back of the room, as Laura realises Verity's designs while Ben and the creative pass comment. Although the only comment the creative makes are fawning compliments aimed at Verity. I wonder if she considers him a frog worth investigating. And what business it is of mine anyway.

Over breakfast, Doug talked about the weekend's various sporting fixtures. He didn't want me to ask about Eileen, and neither did I want to talk about the sorry mess of my own affairs. Nothing was said to this effect, but it was clearly communicated nevertheless. True to his promise, Doug paid for my breakfast, and before we went our separate ways, he squeezed me tight around the bicep and told me I'd be all right. 'Get some rest,' he said, holding my eyes with his. As on the doorstep an hour earlier, the gesture said: *Understand?* And I nodded silently back that I did.

If I was hesitant on Tuesday, I am resolute today that I can't be anything more than a professional acquaintance of our funny, cool, very attractive, slightly bonkers production designer. If I am anything at all, it's a toad, and nothing good comes from kissing a toad.

Kaz went back to the agency after we'd completed the first test on Ruth the vampire, and I'm pretty sure the only reason she came at all was to threaten me with murder. She could have saved herself a trip and delivered this information when we hugged like mannequins on my doorstep twelve hours ago, but maybe she thought it would ruin the moment.

After Kaz left we moved on to Frankenstein's Albert and, guided by Verity's artwork, Laura made him over as a blue monster with spiked green hair. She used strips of tape to hold his eyes shocked-wide open, and it occurred to me that I'd never before seen a version of the iconic monster that looked as if he really had conducted one million volts through his temples. Instead of the traditional scar, Verity had specified a zipper running across Albert's forehead, and the effect was every bit as funny as it was disturbing.

The sun is out today, so Holly went to Pret and everyone ate their lunch on the rooftop balcony. I was experiencing a late-onset relapse, so I shuffled off to the chemists for Alka-Seltzer and a bottle of water. Besides, I didn't feel like particularly good company, and three hours later, I still don't.

While the vampire and monster tests progressed quickly, the zombies – as they are wont to do – are dragging. George and Alice will play brother and sister in the commercials, so are having their make-up tests together. Ben and I observe at a discreet distance as Laura alternates between the children, layering on blue foundation, pink eyeliner and dark shadow. At eleven, George is two years older than Alice, a big deal at that age and something he points out at every opportunity. An awkward boy, he sits stiffly in his chair, interrogating Laura, questioning every choice, and undermining Alice by tutting derisively at any expression of her excitement until he has all but snuffed it out. It doesn't bode well for the shoot. Verity, however, has been patient and playful, indulging George, distracting Alice and doing everything she can to keep the energy alive. But after an hour with the little bugger, I sense she too is losing her spark.

'Perhaps we should have flesh hanging off,' says George. 'After all, the zombies would be decomposing in all likelihood. You could use bacon.'

Verity laughs. 'I'd rather have it on a sandwich,' she says.

My mind flashes to the breakfast I ate with Doug this morning: the slightly undercooked eggs, the greasy sausages, the fatty bacon. And – like so much else in my life – I'm not sure it was an entirely sensible idea. I take a deep breath and my stomach desists in its revolt. The regret and self-reproach, however, are as troublesome as they've been all day long.

'Do you know what decomposing means?' he asks Alice.

Alice shakes her head.

Verity says, 'I don't think we need to get into that n—'

'It's when dead people's skin rots off their bones,' George says. 'Isn't it?'

And another deep breath.

Alice looks appalled, and stares at Verity as if beseeching her to deny this dreadful notion.

'Okay, zombies,' says Verity, 'you are just about done. Shall we put some more blue on their lips?' she asks the room in general.

'Good idea,' says the creative. 'Great idea.'

'Pout your lips like you're about to whistle,' says Laura the make-up artist.

'I can whistle,' says Alice, and she does just that – jamming two fingers into either side of her mouth and whistling so loud it sets my hangover back by about three hours.

'Whatever,' says George.

'Wow,' says Verity.

'We've got a dog,' says Alice. 'He's a labradood—'

'A dog on the news bit a little girl,' says George. 'And they had to kill it.'

'That's sad,' says Verity.

'Once they taste blood, you have to kill them,' says George.

'I bit my brother once,' says Alice. 'He drew glasses and a beard on my best dolly, so I bit him on the finger and blood came out.'

Ben laughs out loud. 'Blimey,' he says. 'Bitten by a zombie! You're not going to bite any of us, are you?'

Alice shakes her head emphatically.

'You sure?' I say. 'We can't have you turning the cameraman into a zombie, can we?'

Alice giggles at this.

'How do you stop zombies?' says Ben.

'You have to destroy the brain,' says George.

'Right,' says Verity, 'I'll have to bring my big scissors.' And she snips her fingers at Alice's, making her shriek and duck away.

'I won't bite anyone,' says Alice. 'I promise.'

'And how about you, George?' says Verity, ruffling his hair.

George looks at her as if to say, *Do you really expect me to dignify that with a response?* So Verity shrugs and ruffles his hair again.

Our final make-up session is Elijah the werewolf, and Elijah is so taken with his new look – monobrow, snaggle-fangs, hairy ears – that he asks if he can wear it home to frighten his sister. It's a nice end to a long day, and there's an air of positivity in the room as Ben lays out Polaroids of our little horrors.

'Good day,' he says. 'Really good.'

'Amazing,' says the creative. 'Top job, Vee.'

Vee?

'Yeah,' I say. 'They look great. Particularly Zipperhead.' Verity laughs, and I resist an impulse to poke my tongue at the agency twerp. 'I'm not sure about George, though.'

'Looks okay to me,' says Ben, squaring off the photo.

'Not the make-up. The make-up's great,' I say, smiling at Verity. 'I'm not sure about the kid.'

Ben nods. 'Doesn't exactly ooze charisma, does he?'

'Not exactly, no. What do you think?' I ask Verity.

'Well, it's not really my call, is it?'

'You're part of the team now,' says Ben. 'Like it or not.'

Verity picks up George's Polaroid. 'I feel quite sorry for him,' she says.

'Me too,' says the twerp.

'I mean,' continues Verity, 'something's a bit . . . well, off, isn't it?'

We all nod.

'But,' she adds, 'he can do that rolling-his-eyes-back-in-his-head thing.'

'True,' I say. 'Which does go well with Alice's eye-crossing thing.'

'*And*,' says Verity, 'I'm pretty sure zombies hunt in packs. I mean, you never get just the one, do you?'

'True again,' I say. 'All right then. We'll give him a go. If he ruins everything we blame Ben.'

'Sounds like a plan,' says Ben. 'Well, I don't know about you lot, but I am parched. Goose?'

'It's a pub,' I say in response to Verity's baffled expression.

'Can we tempt you to a drink, Verity?' Ben asks.

'Yeah,' says Verity. 'Why not?'

'Nice one,' says the idiot.

Ben turns to me, rubbing his hands together. 'Ready, Tom?'

I have the gut-knotting sensation of being ambushed. If we go to the Goose, we'll inevitably be joined by Rob and Marlon and Holly. Add Christina the flirty barmaid. Add alcohol. Add me. It would be a rotten idea even if I weren't hungover and exhausted.

It's been a long and shitty week, and all I want to do is go home. My sofa, takeaway curry and bed, a quiet weekend and a lot of sleep.

'I'd love to,' I say, 'but . . . I'll pass.'

The fool from the agency smiles a little at this and I nearly change my mind. But only nearly. 'I'll see you all next week,' I say, shaking hands with Ben and the moron.

Verity pretends to go for the shake, then kisses me on the cheek, and this time it's not at all uncomfortable.

'Sorry to be a bore,' I say. 'Another time.'

Verity smiles. 'Definitely.'

Definitely.

I'm eating a microwave spaghetti Bolognese for one in front of *Rocky* when I receive a text from Bea:

Dad is such a dick!

I message back asking what he's done, but Bea's response – Just being a dick – does little to clarify the situation.

Twenty minutes later I get a message from Dad:

Are you still coming home for Mum's anniversary?

I tell him of course I am, and Dad replies: Good. We need to talk about your sister. I'm tempted to ask what's going on, but I've had enough drama for one week without getting between Dad and Bianca.

On screen a fearful Rocky Balboa kneels in front of the sink in his dressing room and prays that God will help him through the ordeal to come.

Mum's anniversary is in two weeks' time and, impertinent atheist that I am, I offer up a little prayer that whatever's going on between Dad and Bea, it will have blown over in the next fourteen days.

Chapter Eighteen

Sadie and I are sitting at a table for two in the window of a north London pub, a short walk from where I abandoned the car three days ago. My snowboard is propped against the wall behind Sadie, but so far neither of us has mentioned it. It's just looming in the background like a mute witness. I called Sadie yesterday, and following predictably uncordial preliminaries she agreed to meet me for Sunday lunch. I don't know if a bottle of pink Zinfandel and a bowl of olives constitute 'lunch', but that's what we're having.

'I looked it up on the Internet,' says Sadie.

'Oh really?' I say, raising my eyebrows as if this is a great idea but one that had not occurred to me.

'Yes, really,' says Sadie. She might smile, but she is rolling an olive around her mouth so it's difficult to tell. 'Guess.'

I blow air out, thinking. 'It was what, eighteen grand new?'

Sadie gives nothing away. All I told her yesterday was that I was sick of the car share and custody needed to be resolved 'one way or the other'. Sadie agreed and here we are.

'And I imagine it will have depreciated by' – I roll out my bottom lip, shrug – 'three . . . four grand? God, I dunno, five maybe?'

'Two.' Showing me said amount of fingers for clarity.

'Only two? Blimey.'

'Good olives,' says Sadie, nudging the bowl towards me.

'Two grand,' I say, shaking my head and jabbing a cocktail stick into a black olive. 'Who'd have thought?'

'Try a green one,' says Sadie. 'You *can* tell the difference, can't you?' she says, her tone somewhere between playful and confrontational.

In the interest of harmony, I play along, spear a green olive and present it as proof of competency.

'I mean,' says Sadie, 'I'm not green, am I?' She plucks the olive from my cocktail stick and holds it beside her head for comparison. 'I don't look green, do I, Tom?'

I make a show of deliberation, before nodding and conceding the point: *No, you don't look green.*

Sadie places the olive between her teeth and bites it in two. 'Sixteen grand, the car's worth. And I hope you're a better producer than you are an actor.'

I open my bag, remove a black zip-up wallet containing the Mini's documents and place it on the table between us.

Sadie looks at it and laughs. 'I didn't say I was going to buy it, Tom. This was your idea, remember?'

I slide the documents towards Sadie. 'Just fill in your details and it's yours. I've already signed.'

'I haven't got . . . eight grand just lying around, Tom.'

'Who mentioned eight grand?'

'Half of sixteen is eight grand, okay? And who said I even want the Mini?'

I empty my glass, refill it, top up Sadie's. 'Well, do you?'

'What? Do I what, Tom?'

'Want the car, Sadie.'

Sadie regards her wine, stabs one, two, three olives, and glares at me while she chews.

'Don't you?' she asks.

'Don't I what?'

'Oh, fuck off, smart-arse,' she says, only slightly infuriated. 'Christ, can you imagine what this must be like with a kid?'

'I'd rather not,' I say.

Sadie traces the grain of our table with the tip of a cocktail stick. 'Are you seeing anyone?'

'No.' I shake my head. 'Not really.'

Sadie contemplates this, takes a drink. 'What about that girl? The one . . .' She gestures at us, the table, the bowl of olives, this whole thing, I suppose. 'The one you got off with.'

'*Kissed.*'

Sadie nods. 'What was her name?'

'Holly.'

'You didn't . . . get together?'

'She's not my type. Never was.'

Sadie holds her glass up to the light and it glows like a gaudy lamp. She looks me in the eye. 'But did you fuck her?'

I shake my head, not in the negative, but to demonstrate my disapproval at this line of questioning. 'Why is that important?'

'Was she eighty-six?'

'Sadie. Please.'

Sadie's eyes are wet and angry. 'Do you know how that made me feel?'

'I'm sorry, really, it was . . . you weren't meant to see it.'

'Yeah, well, I did, didn't I?'

Yes, because you let yourself into the flat to steal my bloody snowboard for your new fucking boyfriend! Did he wait outside, in the car? Or did you bring him in and make him a cup of tea?

I sip my Zinfandel.

'You told me twenty-five,' Sadie says, shaking her head in an expression that's part disappointment, part exasperation.

I glance at the snowboard behind Sadie.

We were on a skiing trip in Tignes. We'd only been dating a couple of months, and, pleasantly drunk on mulled wine, sitting in front of an open fire, we were having one of those conversations that you have round about that time in a new relationship. As far as I can remember, we started off in the harmless territory of first kisses, first girlfriends and boyfriends, then gathered momentum along the slippery slopes of first gropes and first shags, before veering off-piste into the treacherous *How many people have you slept with?* region. I didn't know the precise answer then but I could have guessed, give or take fifteen notches, and still that number would have been too big to laugh off in front of a roaring log fire. So I picked my birthday – a palatable, easy-to-remember lie.

'Well, I couldn't have said . . . you know . . .'

'What?' says Sadie. 'Eighty-five?'

Hearing the figure (obsolete as it is) out loud makes me wince. 'It would have been a bit of a moment-ruiner, don't you think?'

Sadie shrugs. 'Some moment.' She uses her cocktail stick to dig something from under one of her fingernails, then sets it aside. 'I lied too.'

'You lied? Which way? More or less?'

Sadie takes a tiny sip of wine, barely enough to wet her lips. 'Does it matter?'

'I told *you*.'

Sadie shakes her head. 'Nuh-uh. I found out. *Big* difference.'

'But . . .'

But what?

I put my hand on Sadie's. 'I'm sorry. About everything.'

'Yeah, well . . . I'm sorry too. About the whole, you know—'

'I know,' I say, shuddering at the memory.

It's raining outside, again, and the exiled smokers flatten themselves against the wall to keep their cigarettes dry. At this specific point in time I envy them their inconvenient habit.

I take a gulp of wine. 'So, how's it going with . . . Connor, is it?'

Sadie shakes her head. 'Connor was a dickhead. Didn't last past January.'

'Right,' I say, the satisfaction of discovering that Connor is a dickhead somewhat diluted by the realisation that Sadie has replaced me not once, but twice. At least. 'So who is it going well with?'

Sadie sighs, shakes her head.

'What?'

'Let's just say I seem to be drawn to dickheads.'

'I messed it all up, didn't I?'

Sadie strokes my hand. 'Do you miss me?'

'Of course. Sometimes. Some things.'

Sadie smiles and wipes the corners of her eyes with a paper napkin. And then she punches me on the shoulder, picks up her wine and drains the glass. She reaches for the bottle.

'You know,' I say, 'you might want to take it easy. I mean, if you're planning on driving.'

'Car's not going anywhere,' she says.

'I wouldn't bet on it. It's been parked without a permit since Thursday.'

'Where?'

'About five minutes from here. Maybe ten.'

Sadie tilts her empty glass and lets a pink drop run towards the rim. She rotates the stem between her fingers, watching the drop gradually diminish as it rolls across the inside circumference of the glass.

'So,' she says, 'what's the plan?'

'I want you to take it.'

'Tom, I can't afford it.'

'What can you afford?'

'Fuck all.'

'Can you afford four?'

'I still owe my dad four grand from when we bought it the first time.'

'Which you'll never have to pay him,' I say.

'Which isn't the point. And why four?'

'Rent and depreciation.'

Sadie looks at me as if I'm speaking a foreign language. 'What? Rent?'

'Rent. Rent you paid while you were living with me.'

'Tom, what are you talking about?'

'Well, it was never meant to be rent, was it? The way I saw it, we were sharing the mortgage. It was never meant to be a business proposition.'

'I lived there for six months, Tom.'

'Exactly.'

Sadie rubs her temples as if her head hurts. 'That doesn't make any sense.'

'So what else do we do? The car share isn't working, you don't have eight grand, I don't want the sodding car.'

'Why don't you?'

'How long have you got?' I say.

Sadie picks up a clean cocktail stick, harpoons olives – green, black, green – and eats them sequentially.

'Surely you can afford four grand,' I say.

'Tom, I don't know.'

'Plus sixty quid. For the last fine.'

Sadie nods. 'Sorry about that.'

'Pay it then.'

'It feels wrong.'

'Why?'

'Because,' says Sadie, 'it's worth more.'

'Not to me it's not. I haven't even got a key.'

And I explain to Sadie about the knickers in the glovebox and the car keys down the drain. And yes, I do derive some pleasure from her discomfort.

'I'm so, so sorry,' she says. 'That must have been . . . *God!* It can't have been very nice.'

I shake my head and then nod towards the documents sitting between us. 'And you pay any fines I've accumulated in the last four days. Could be a few quid.'

Sadie sighs. She tucks the documents into her handbag then produces a bunch of keys. 'I suppose you should have these,' she says.

They're the keys to my flat. I consider telling Sadie that I've had the lock changed, but it might sound ungracious – or stupid – so I mutter a thank you and slip the keys into my bag.

'Oh,' says Sadie, 'and I brought your snowboard.'

I act surprised, pointing over her shoulder at the two-metre board in a padded silver carry bag. 'Is that what that is?'

'Do you think we'll stay friends?' Sadie asks.

'Why wouldn't we?' I say.

Sadie huffs a tiny laugh behind closed, half-smiling lips. 'Find yourself someone nice,' she says. 'Everyone deserves someone nice. Even you.' And she punches me again.

Chapter Nineteen

'Well,' says El, 'are you gonna tell me, or do I have to throw a tantrum?'

After El's performance the last time we met, I rearranged tonight's meal for six thirty – an hour earlier than usual. Accordingly, El and I are the Lucky Dragon's sole diners. It's a little light on atmosphere, but my friend can curse and shout and twitch and drop things with impunity.

El slaps the table. 'How many!'

'Ninety-seven,' I say, unable to suppress a guilty smile.

'Fuck off.'

I nod.

'Wha was it lass time? Lass time we were here.'

'Ninety-five,' I tell him.

'So thass . . .' Dr Laurence Christopher's brow furrows as he wrestles with the mathematics. 'Two. Two in two weeks.'

'Uh-huh. Two in three days actually, but who's counting?'

'Bullshit.'

I shake my head. 'Worried you're going to lose your bet?'

Jiang arrives with a trolley bearing enough food for four rugby players.

'Careful, Jiang,' says El. 'Tom's in season.'

'Thank you, sir,' says Jiang. He cleans scattered fragments of prawn cracker from El's side of the table and arranges our various dishes. 'Do you need anything else?' he asks without irony.

'Two more beers,' says El.

'One more,' I say.

El scowls as Jiang retreats to the kitchen. 'You're worse'n Phil.'

'How is he?'

El shrugs. 'Who're these women then?'

'Someone I work with—'

'"Brace yourself?" She doesn't count.'

'Someone else.'

'You'd think they'd've learned by now. D'they have a club? Secret hanshake?' El mimes a masturbating hand.

'Yes, very clever.'

An image of Verity pops into my head, and I feel pretty bloody puerile. I'm tempted to mention her to El, but in this context, and with him in this mood, it feels neither appropriate nor well advised. It would have been nice to have a drink with Verity the other night, and I could have made time for one, but the opportunities for me to make a good impression were far outweighed by their opposite number. And I have only myself to blame. And maybe El – this bet was, after all, his idea.

Jiang returns with a bottle of Tsingtao. I pour a third of it into El's plastic glass, and the rest into my own.

El downs half of his drink in one go. 'Who else?'

'Who what?'

'Who else d'you fuck?'

'My estate agent,' I say, sighing.

'I thought that only happened in wank mags.' Something dawns on El. He drops his fork and levels a finger at me. 'You're movin'ouse?'

'Thinking about it.'

'Why?'

'Just . . . you know, seemed like a good idea.'

'Where to?'

'Haven't decided.'

El shakes his head. 'So what you gonna do? Sleep in your car?'

'I sold it.'

'The Mini?'

I nod.

'Nice car, that,' says El.

'I know.'

'So why'd you sell it?'

I take a long pull on my beer. 'It's complicated.'

'You've got issues,' says El. 'You do know that?'

'Yup. I do.'

When I drop El at home he's exhausted, so I stay just long enough to drink a cup of tea. Nevertheless, he is asleep in his armchair before I've finished it.

On the doorstep, Phil asks how El was this evening.

'The usual,' I tell him. 'Loud and embarrassing.'

Phil hesitates, goes to bite a thumbnail then stops himself, puts his hands in his pockets.

'What?'

'He hit me, Tom.'

'He bloody what!'

Phil nods.

'Do you want me to have a word?'

Phil shakes his head. 'It's not him, it's that awful disease.'

'Where did he hit you?'

Phil sniffs. 'God, it's pathetic.' He shakes his head and is overcome by laughter.

'What? What did he do?'

'Slapped me.' Phil holds a hand to his cheek. 'Maybe it was my own fault.'

'What happened?'

'God. You know how he is when he's got an idea in his head. He's been driving me to distraction, suggesting people I could date, bars I should go to, speed-dating, online dating. Honestly, he's relentless.'

It's easy to imagine and, tragic as it is, wrong as it is, I laugh.

'Oh, Tom, you must think I sound pathetic.'

'Not at all. I know exactly what you mean. It's just . . . funny.'

Phil smiles. 'I know it is. And I know it's not his fault. It's just wearing me down.'

I make a gesture indicating I wouldn't be too quick to absolve El of all responsibility for his behaviour. 'So,' I say, 'what happened?'

Phil takes a deep breath and sighs. 'I flipped. Shouted at him, told him his disease wasn't an excuse to behave like a brat.'

'Ouch.'

'Maybe I deserved it,' says Phil.

I shake my head. 'Personally, I think you're a saint.'

'Bloody hell, Tom. Very far from it. But thank you, it's very sweet of you.'

'Well, you're looking after my best friend for me,' I say.

Phil hugs me, and we stand that way for more than a short time.

'The neighbours'll talk,' I say after a while.

'Repressed middle-class heterosexuals,' says Phil. 'No offence.'

'Er . . . thanks.'

'Oh, you're all right,' he says, and laughs to himself. 'Some of my best friends are heterosexuals. So, what do you think I should do?'

'About El?'

'No,' he says, and glances downwards as if he's admitting some terrible secret. 'About me.'

I stare dumbly back.

'Do you think I should, you know, meet other people?'

'God, Phil, I don't think it's any of my . . . I mean, *Christ*.'

'Oh God, Tom, I'm sorry. He's your best friend, and here I am talking about . . . I don't know.'

'You're my friend too, Phil.'

Phil chews at what's left of a thumbnail.

'I don't think you shouldn't,' I say.

Chapter Twenty

I've been thinking.

After the mess and chaos of the last two weeks, of the last couple of months, of the whole sodding year when you get right down to it, I've had a lot to think about. And since walking out of the make-up tests six days ago, I've done little else.

I thought about Phil and El, the humour and compassion and empathy that will outlast the passion and romance. How Phil's love for El will survive El himself, and whether he can, should or will find a new person to curl up with on cold nights while his partner of ten years slowly slips away.

I thought about Doug and Eileen and his dead wife Mary. When I cleaned Doug's flat, I took a duster to the photographs of Mary and found the glass was already spotless. What is now going on with my neighbour and Eileen, I don't know, but if Doug was going to talk about it, he'd have done so by now.

Perhaps he's like my father, unable or unwilling to move on after being left behind.

I thought about the things Ben said about being a father and being, I suppose, a man.

I thought about Sadie saying everyone deserves someone nice. Even me.

I thought about Verity saying there is someone for everyone.

I thought about Verity kissing frogs.

I thought about Verity.

'Doing anything tonight?' asks Ben, trying to sound casual.

I shake my head.

'What you smiling about?' he asks.

'Nothing.'

'Well, stop it, it's unnerving.'

When I woke up this morning I was smiling, and I couldn't remember the last time I had come out of sleep this way. This whole bet, challenge, mission, folly, fucking around – well, fuck all of that. I don't need it and I don't want it. If there is someone for everyone, then I'm not going to find it like this. Maybe the one for me looks a lot like Verity. Maybe not, but I won't know if I don't find out.

I've met Verity three times now, but I know almost nothing about her. With the exception of thirty minutes under her umbrella, we have always been in the company of other people. And I find myself resenting them for it; wishing I could click my fingers and send them all away. People gravitate to Verity; they stand next to her, sit beside her, turn their attention towards her, asking, talking, telling and generally getting in my way. She's interested and interesting. She's somehow naive and knowing. She's different. Not just the shifting style, but the girl underneath. For the last five months I've been looking at women the way a starving cartoon character looks at the dog, cat or duck next to him – as if they're meat. But as gorgeous as Verity is, she provokes something different in me. She's confident but ever so slightly shy. If you were to ask her what number she wears on her back, I suspect Verity would guess at a number in the low to mid-teens – an immodest fourteen, perhaps. But from where I'm standing, she's out by around half a dozen. She's funny and smart and talented, and more than getting her into bed, my overriding thought is that I know almost nothing about her, but I want to know an awful lot more.

We have the final pre-production meeting for Little Horrors in half an hour, but I wanted to grab a quick coffee with Ben first. Ostensibly to make sure we're on the same page about the shoot. To check if he has any doubts or concerns. I don't intend asking Verity to accompany me to a roller disco, a restaurant or even a balcony until the shoot is over. My life is complicated enough as it is. And when I do decide to do something, I certainly don't need Ben's approval. But it would probably be better for our friendship if he understood where I'm coming from.

'So,' I say, 'how was the Goose last week?'

'Same as it always is, overpriced and overcrowded.'

'I mean, did you . . . was it . . . ?' Ben raises his eyebrows: *What?* 'Did you have a nice time?'

'You mean how was Verity?' He's smiling, though.

'Not specifically, but . . .'

'That plonker from the agency hit on her.'

'He what?'

Ben takes a sip of coffee. He takes his time savouring it. 'Have to admire the kid's balls, though.'

'His balls?'

'We're all having a drink. Me, Holly, Marlon, Verity and whatshisface. And whatshisface says to Verity how he's got a spare ticket for a gig – some band I've never heard of – and would she like to go. Right in front of everyone.'

'Oh. Fancy . . . that.'

'Is this Ethiopian?' says Ben before taking another sip of coffee.

'Oh shut up.'

All innocence: 'What?'

'Fine. Did Verity accept plonker's ticket?'

'Of course not; he's a divvy. Give the girl some credit.' And he says this last with a slightly pointed look.

'Cool. I mean . . . you know, good.'

'Don't be too pleased with yourself, though,' says Ben.

'I'm not pleas— Why, what do you mean?'

'Saw her yesterday to finalise the sets.'

'And?'

Ben's face softens. 'You've missed the boat, mate.'

'What are you on about?'

'Had a date on Tuesday. Cocktail-making course with a joiner – huh, there's a joke in that, somewhere – anyway . . . rugged, charming, good with his hands, blah blah blah, second date next Tuesday.'

'Oh. I mean . . . good for her, right?'

Ben pats me on the shoulder. 'Yes, mate. Good for her. Come on, we don't want to be late – Kaz has been spiky as a porcupine all sodding week.'

A joiner? I'll bet he's got a beard, muscular arms, smells of wood shavings. He sounds like a bit of a dick to me, but that's Verity's problem now. And what's it to me, anyway?

I've met her three times and I know next to nothing about her – except that she's smart, funny, unpredictable, can't roller skate and looks fantastic in a pair of denim shorts.

According to the leopard-print wall clock, we've been sitting here for one hour, twenty-seven minutes and . . . thirty-six seconds. Every time I pass comment, Kaz pulls a face, makes a noise or just outright contradicts me. So I've stopped trying. I zone in briefly when the discussion turns to make-up. Everyone loves the Polaroids of Verity's monsters. And why wouldn't they? I zone out again.

When I started dating Sadie, she was seeing somebody else. So it does happen. People meet new people, leave old people. But where does that end? Pretty soon the new people are old people and it's time to move on and give a co-worker a hand job. It's almost definitely a good thing that nothing is going to happen between me and Verity.

I don't know what the hell is going on in this meeting, but everyone is laughing.

I imagine the joiner is called Chris – a manly, no-nonsense name. I bet Chris rides a single-speed bike, he probably plays football on Sundays, I wonder if he can cook. I bet he can cook. If they buy a house together, Chris will fit new bookshelves, construct built-in wardrobes, a rocking chair. Maybe he'll make a cot. Maybe the bastard will slip with his chisel and take his sodding thumb off.

As the meeting draws to a conclusion, talk turns – as it invariably does – to everyone's plans for the weekend. Ben moans about having to attend a wedding, the creative is going to a festival, Kaz's boyfriend is taking her to Paris. Verity isn't here today, and for the first time since I met her, I'm glad – she's probably going on a hot date with Chris the carpenter and if she is, I certainly don't want to hear about it.

It's Ben's birthday on Sunday but he thinks we've all forgotten. And as our taxi approaches the office, he's getting agitated. The weekend starts in ten minutes, and Ben is becoming increasingly concerned he'll have to go home sober. His pride won't allow him to mention his birthday but he's been dropping hints all week. On Wednesday he asked Holly how old she was, then Rob, then Marlon. Everybody's been briefed and nobody took the bait. Yesterday he read his horoscope out loud, but we all feigned indifference. This afternoon he suggested a few pints tonight, but the reaction ranged from lukewarm to non-committal. It's cruel but hugely entertaining.

'Swifty?' he says offhandedly.

'To be honest, mate, I'm knackered.'

Ben's bottom lip rolls out like a sulky child's. 'What's up with you?'

'Nothing's up with me,' I say.

'Sulking about Verity?'

Ouch.

'Fine,' I say. 'But just a swifty. And I've got to pick up some stuff from the office first.'

Ben checks his watch. 'I'll see if there's anyone still there.'

He calls the office, but no one answers.

'Lazy fuckers,' he says, snapping his phone closed.

The Blank Slate offices are on the third floor and I take the stairs two at a time while Ben waits for the lift. As I pass them, I hit the call buttons on every floor.

I texted ahead, and Holly, Rob and Marlon are standing by.

'Light the candles,' I say as soon as I'm through the door.

On Ben's desk are a birthday cake, a bottle of champagne and a row of glasses. I grab the champagne and aim it at the ceiling above the door.

Ben arrives approximately thirty seconds later. And about three seconds after that he realises what he's just walked into.

'Happy Birthday,' shouts Holly as the cork pings off the ceiling.

'Bastards,' says Ben, and his smile is childlike and absolute.

───※───

'T.G.T.B.A.T.U.,' says Holly.

Marlon puts his hand up.

'One round handicap,' Ben warns, pointing his glass at Marlon.

We moved on to the Goose several pints, one tequila and one sambuca ago. No one has work tomorrow, and we're all making the most of it.

'Say again?' asks Rob.

Holly has made an effort for the occasion. Instead of the usual jeans and T-shirt, she is wearing a new skirt and a thin silk top that shows the outline of her bra and the protrusion of her nipples. She has retouched her make-up at least twice over the course of the evening. You could do a whole lot worse.

'T.G.,' she says, pausing, 'T.B.' – another pause – 'A.T.U.'

'Which one am I?' I ask, smiling.

Holly pouts. 'I thought that would take ages.'

'Hello?' says Ben.

'*The Good, the Bad and the Ugly,*' I tell him.

'Well, you're the ugly, obviously,' he says.

'Harsh,' says Holly.

'Good one, Holly,' says Rob, 'I'd never have got it,' and Holly flashes him a coy smile.

The weekend is looming at the end of the night, and yet again I have nothing to do and no one to do it with. So Verity isn't The One. But what if The One was under my nose all this time but I was too distracted to notice?

'Okay,' I say, glancing at Holly and holding eye contact for a second. 'N.A.A.H.W.'

'Saucy,' says Marlon.

'I've got a better one,' says Ben. 'T.I.Y.R.'

He picks up his glass, drains the remaining half-pint in one swallow and lowers the glass to the table, all without breaking eye contact with me.

'N.A.A.H.W.' I try again, apparently to no one.

'T.I.Y.R.,' Ben presses, his eyes boring into me. 'Anyone? Tom?'

'Haven't got a clue,' I say.

Ben taps his empty glass, 'Tom . . . It's . . . Your . . . Round.'

Everyone except me laughs.

'Same again?' I say to the table.

'Same again!' Ben slams the flat of his hand on the table. 'And a round of tequilas.'

An hour later, Ben is sick in the Gents and we send him home in a cab. Two rounds after that, Marlon is passed out in the corner, Rob is in the toilets, and, for a couple of minutes, it's just me and Holly. This could be awkward but I'm too drunk to care; also, Rob will be back any moment so I haven't the time to be embarrassed.

'God, I'm pissed,' I say. 'I should probably head off.'

'Me too,' says Holly. 'I mean . . . you know,' as she mimes downing a drink.

'Listen,' I say, putting my hand on her back. 'Do you fancy sharing a cab?'

'Ah thanks, Tom. But I'll be okay on the tube.'

'Well, I was sort of thinking we might . . . you know. I've got a bottle of wine in the fridge.'

Holly fidgets and takes a sip of her wine. 'Actually, Tom, I'm . . .' She removes my hand from her back, holds it in hers. 'I'm going with Rob.'

'Why? He doesn't live anywhere near you. He's in north Londo— Oh.'

Holly gives my hand a squeeze. 'I should have said something sooner, but I didn't want to embarrass you.'

'No, no,' I say, retrieving my hand. 'No worries. It's fine. Good. Absolutely for the best.'

'I think so,' says Holly. 'Will you be okay?'

I nearly fall over the table as I try to stand and put my jacket on at the same time. 'Don't you worry about me,' I say, 'I'm great. No, this is good. Give my love to Rob. I mean . . . you know what I mean.' I back out of the door, waving.

The Goose has a midnight licence, and it's not far off that as I veer through the backstreets towards Oxford Circus tube station. Goodge Street is closer but from Oxford Circus it's a direct train home, and, considering the amount of beer and silly spirits I've consumed, the less time I spend in an enclosed space the better for everyone.

The tube is packed with returning theatregoers, workaholics and a party pack of boozed-up boys and girls. During daylight hours most commuters wouldn't talk to you if you sat in their lap, but on the Pisshead Express everyone's best friends – hanging off the overhead bars, singing, flirting and holding shouted cross-carriage conversations. There's a woman passed out asleep in the next compartment along. Her head is rested against the glass partition, her curly hair flattened into a brown smear that obscures her face. A cheeky chappy caresses the glass so it looks like he's stroking her hair, and a few people laugh.

It's less than twenty minutes to the end of the line, and the last few drinks have caught up with me. When the train jolts to a stop, my stomach trips over and I already have the beginnings of what promises to be a spectacular hangover. The carriage empties out, but the curly-haired girl is still asleep and has folded in on herself so that her head hovers an inch above her lap.

'It's the end of the line,' I say, tapping on the glass partition.

The girl doesn't respond, and I'm apprehensive about touching her in case she wakes up and thinks she's being molested.

I kick her on the foot.

'Wh. . . ?' Her hair is stuck to the side of her face, some of it in her mouth.

'End of the line,' I say.

'Who, wha . . . ? What time is it?'

'Twelve . . . thirty, almost,' I say after some initial difficulty resolving my watch face into only two hands and twelve numbers.

A guard appears in the carriage doorway. 'Everybody off.'

'Not going back out?' the girl asks.

'Not for another five hours and fifteen minutes, love.'

'I've got to get to Clapham Common,' she says, as if the guard might change his mind and run her home.

'Plenty of buses on the high street,' says the guard with weary contempt, and he walks off up the platform looking for further stragglers.

'Come on,' I say, 'I'll point you in the right direction.'

She's steady enough on her feet, her speech is coherent, and she seems fully aware of where she is and where she's going. But once we get outside the station, it's raining and the LED information panel at the bus stop has been vandalised. The streets are relatively quiet but there are still enough dodgy lurkers to make it unsafe for a lone woman, particularly a drunk lone woman, to fall asleep at a bus stop – so I encourage this one to catch a cab.

We make small talk – her job, mine, where we've been, the cast of *Celebrity Big Brother* – while we wait. We're just touching on the business of the weather – wet for the time of year – when a battered Ford somethingorother pulls up to the kerb. A guy who looks like an escaped serial killer winds down his window and asks 'Verre to?' in a thick Eastern European accent. The woman (*Pamela? Penny?*) opens the back door and is halfway in before I snatch the collar of her suit jacket and persuade her to wait for a licensed cab. The serial killer gives me the finger and speeds off.

Maybe it's five minutes later, or maybe it's ten, when this girl decides that she's had enough and she's getting in the next vehicle that stops.

'You can call a cab from my place,' I say. 'It's only up the road, and it's dry. You can have a cup of tea while you wait.'

The flat can't be half a mile away, but at this hour, in this weather, it feels four times further and it's gone one when we clatter over the threshold. My guest doesn't want tea, so I pour two glasses of wine and call a local taxi firm. The controller says the cab will be about thirty minutes. Two minutes later, me and this woman are fumbling with each other's clothes. Five minutes later I cancel the cab. And six minutes later, sprawled half on and half off the sofa, clothes removed, unzipped, pulled aside, it's fairly apparent that this encounter is going the distance. Little Tom, however, is being a little slow on the uptake, so to buy myself time – and because, hey, I'm a gentleman – I get down on my knees and go down on this (*Petula?*) lady. And I don't know how long I'm down there before I fall asleep, but it's a heck of a fright when she knuckle-raps me on the forehead and I wake up with pubic hair in my mouth, in my eyes and up my nose. It's proper Mills and Boon stuff. My neck has seized, my mouth is cloyed and it tastes like vagina. The only liquid at hand is Chardonnay dregs, but the sight of it makes my gut juices curdle. I sway to my feet, apologising, muttering about water, and the room is on loose springs and my left leg is numb.

'Don't stop,' she says. 'Fuck me. Fuck my pussy.'

Ever the romantic, I extend my hand towards her. 'Let's go to the bedroom.'

How drunk are we? Not too drunk not to use a condom. But drunk enough that neither of us feels the sodding thing split open. I don't discover that little surprise until I withdraw my limp and dripping penis. And I feel, all of a sudden, pretty fucking sober.

'The condom broke,' I say to the woman spreadeagled across half of my bed.

She sits up and puts a hand to her mouth. 'I feel sick.'

And that's Number 98.

⁂

It's after two when the taxi honks its horn outside the flat. She's still in the bathroom, naked, half sitting, half lying in front of the toilet, one hand pushing her hair out of her face, the other draped nonchalantly around the bowl. There's something pre-Raphaelite about it. If the toilet were a fountain, and if she wasn't connected to it via a string of saliva, it might make a rather charming fresco.

The cab sounds its horn again. Three blasts. Risking stating the obvious, I inform my houseguest that her carriage has arrived, and go to the bedroom to gather as many of her clothes as I can find. When I return to the bathroom the still life is moving, her back arching, her buttocks clenching into dimples as she retches silently into the fountain. 'Cab's here,' I say, trying to imbue the two words with a sense of irresistible allure. My muse (*Priscilla? Paris? Pearl?*) waves me away with a glistening hand. She honks. The cab honks – three more blasts. I pull on a pair of jeans and go outside to tell the driver that his services will no longer be required. The Eastern European serial killer behind the wheel of the battered Ford doesn't see the funny side, and even though I hand the square-headed bastard a tenner, he gives me the finger for the second time and sounds his horn in a continuous fifteen-second blast as he accelerates out of Chaucer Road.

I wake at five thirty-eight a.m., and my hangover has a hangover. My headache starts in the middle of my back, arcs over and through my head and into my eyes. I am nauseous from my testicles through to my lungs. At some point during the earlier hours of the morning, the woman must have returned to my bed. If I noticed, I don't remember. She is snoring. Getting out of bed is a slow and agonising process; one thigh aches as if it's been drained of blood and my brain is too large for my skull.

The poster on my wall says: *Obstacles are what we see when we take our eyes off the goal.*

Probably I'm imagining it, but the water appears to undulate and I feel as if the floorboards are swaying beneath my feet. Bracing one hand against the wall, I creep through to the kitchen and drink half a litre of apple juice straight from the carton. Then immediately throw it back up into the sink.

It's too early to be awake but I can't face climbing back into bed next to Cinderella. The leather sofa is clammy beneath my bare torso, birds are tweeting, and a baseball bat-wide shaft of sunlight bludgeons me relentlessly across the side of my face.

When I was at university there was an infamous drinking game called Down 101, and El was adamant we were going to play. Some student with too much time on his hands had figured out that six cans of Special Brew broke down into 101 egg-cupfuls of nine per cent beer. The idea was to drink one a minute – six cans of extra-strength lager in one hour and forty-one minutes.

The first six are easy. You knock them back in a second and spend the next fifty-nine laughing and waiting for your next egg-cupful of fun. If anything, the pace feels too slow. Seven, eight, nine . . . ten. After only seventeen minutes you've consumed an entire can. And somewhere in the mid-twenties you begin to feel the effects. Your head is thickening, your belly bloats with gas and liquid, and the sickly taste coats your tongue. With a little over half an hour expired, you've finished two cans of nutter-strength booze and the next egg-cupful has become a thing of dread. By number fifty you've consumed the alcoholic equivalent of a bottle of sherry. You're properly drunk. And you're still only halfway there. It takes you maybe two or three sips now to finish each dose of Special Brew. The minutes are collapsing into each other and it's shot after gulp after mouthful of syrupy lager. If you need a piss, you take your can and your egg cup with you. Seventy shots, eighty. You can't watch a movie because all your focus is on that tick-tick-sip. You can't hold a conversation because it's interrupted every sixty seconds. Ninety minutes – an hour and half of your life – and all you have to show for it is blurred vision, a bad aftertaste and five empty tins on the table in front of you. The sight of them makes your guts twist. And you're still not done. You've almost an entire can left, and it's become very apparent that this was a very bad idea. But you're too close to the finish to quit. So you press on, you drink on and you finish your six cans of horrible lager. You become a bona fide member of the 101 Club, and you spend the rest of the evening kneeling in front of the toilet, dripping tears and snot and vomit. Funny, the things you remember.

I'm dozing fretfully when the toilet flushes, followed shortly by the sound of running water. I want to vanish down the back of the sofa with the dust and crumbs and lost pennies, but as hard as I press my head into the leather cleft, it refuses to swallow me up. And so, while my houseguest showers, I unpeel myself from the sticky sofa, pull on clean clothes over my dirty body and open every window in the flat. I'm emptying the remainder of last night's wine down the sink when she wanders into the kitchen, buttoning up her crumpled shirt.

'Any chance of a tea?'

'Yeah, sure,' I say. 'Sleep well?'

She sighs and perches on a stool at the breakfast bar. 'Have you got a cab number?'

'Clapham Common, right?'

She closes her eyes and nods, and I hit last-number redial and call the cab that should have been here seven hours ago.

I pick up Sadie's old cat mug to make this woman's tea, but it seems somehow sacrilegious and I swap it for a chipped old article from the back of the cupboard.

'How do you take it?' I ask.

She coughs out a dry laugh (*Pixie?*) and shakes her head. 'Just milk,' she says. 'Sweet enough already, aren't I?'

She sips her tea, while I look at mine.

'Listen,' I say, 'I probably should have asked last night, but . . . are you on the pill?'

'I thought we used a whatsit,' she says, frowning.

'It broke.'

The furrows deepen on this woman's forehead. 'But you . . . you stopped? Right?'

'Too late,' I say, wincing.

Her head lolls back onto her shoulders as she emits a long sigh towards the ceiling. 'Effing brilliant.'

'Sorry,' I say.

'That'll be me getting the morning-after pill then, won't it?'

'I suppose.'

I sincerely sodding hope!

'Thirty effing quid,' she says. 'Fan-effing-tastic.'

'Perhaps I could give you the money for the, you know, pill thing.'

'Fine,' she says. 'Got any Nurofen?'

We don't kiss goodbye on the doorstep, we don't hug and we don't shake hands. I just hand over thirty quid, and she (*Precious?*) doesn't even say thank you. And she doesn't ask for my phone number, which – while undeniably a relief – I do take as a bit of a slight.

I clean the toilet, strip the bed, and throw the sheets, pillowcases and duvet cover into the washing machine. I make a pot of tea using the small purple starflowers Doug gave me, but it does nothing for my hangover so I chew a handful of raw flowers and chase them down with a glass of milk and a banana. It doesn't help.

What I need more than anything else right now is deep and dreamless sleep, but Yvette is showing someone around the flat at ten, and I don't want to be within a mile of the place. So I lace up my trainers and trot off to the park. Maybe I can flush some of the toxins and despair out of my system.

The first five minutes are heavy and plodding, but when I hit the park – maybe it's the open space, the green, the sunshine, The Beatles on my iPod – I find a gear and kick to match the trip-along rhythm of 'Paperback Writer'. Halfway around the park, the path ascends steeply and abruptly. And as I haul my increasingly heavy self clockwise and upwards, the Fab Four start in on 'Helter Skelter'. And the effect is exactly that. The guitars are frantic, the drums aggressive, and it feels as if my brain has come free from its stem and is revolving inside my skull. The final minute of the track is a mess of screeching, smashing feedback, and I yank the headphones from my ears and veer towards a tree to spew for the second time this morning – a yellow froth flecked with purple scraps of chewed-up starflower that splashes over my trainers and up my shins.

It takes fifteen minutes for me to regain my balance, and another thirty to walk back to the flat.

Chapter Twenty-One

I'm in the shower when I hear a loud knock at the door. Yvette was due to show a potential buyer around at ten, but I didn't get back from my aborted run until after eleven.

The knock comes again, louder.

Maybe I got the time wrong. Maybe the viewer was late.

If it is Yvette, she's got a key, so I turn off the shower and wrap a towel around my waist. I'm looking around the flat for somewhere to hide when a female voice shouts through the downstairs letter box: 'Hello?'

It doesn't sound like Yvette, but I have water in my ears and the voice has travelled up thirteen steps and through the door to my flat, so it's difficult to be sure.

'Thomas!'

No one calls me Thomas except my dad and Douglas. And . . .

I open my door and shout down the stairs: 'Eileen?'

⁂

Eileen has been married and raised three sons, so she knows a hangover when she sees one. She sent me back to the bathroom to finish my shower, and after I'd towelled off and thrown on some clothes, I found her waiting for me at the living room table, steam rising from a bowl of chicken soup. A cup of tea, a plate of buttered bread.

I still don't know why she's here.

Eileen regards me as I try a spoonful of soup, and it seems we're both a little on edge while my guts decide what to do with it. It stays down, for the moment, and I reload the spoon.

'Friend's birthday,' I say plaintively.

'Boys will be boys,' says Eileen. 'Well, given half a chance.' She smiles, but it doesn't make it all the way to her eyes.

'So,' I say. 'This is a nice surprise. Were you looking for Doug?'

'If I was, I'd go to the allotments. The courgettes are out,' she adds somewhat wistfully.

I take another mouthful of soup, decide to risk a slice of bread; it slips down easily, settles, and a little life ebbs back into me.

'Have you two fallen out?' I ask.

'Not really. Sort of. No, well, it's complicated, love.'

'Is something wrong?'

Eileen regards me as if she's assessing some crucial aspect of my character. And then she nods. 'When I started courting Fred – my husband – I was twenty-two, he was nineteen. A boy really. Handsome as a matinee idol, but a boy, all the same.'

Eileen pauses, lifts her drawn-on eyebrows as if she's waiting for me to confirm that I'm keeping up. I'm not sure that I am, but I nod anyway.

'You have to understand, I'd had a few boyfriends.' Eileen leans forward conspiratorially. 'If you know what I mean.'

'O-*kay* . . .'

'Sex,' says Eileen.

'Listen, Eileen, I don't know what Dou—'

'Shush up and eat your soup. I'm trying to tell you something here, and it's hard enough without you interrupting me.'

'Sorry.' I tear the rest of the bread into pieces and float them on the surface of my soup.

Eileen takes a deep breath and continues: 'Fred had the biggest winkle I'd ever laid eyes on.' She holds her palms apart – and if she's not exaggerating, then Fred had a winkle roughly the size of a can of hairspray.

I hold up a hand.

'What?' says Eileen.

I realise I have nothing to say, so I lower my arm and mutter, 'Nothing.'

'Good. So as I was saying, Fred's thingummy—'

'His winkle?'

'Yes, love, his winkle. The thing was . . . as *big* as it was . . . poor Fred, he didn't have a clue what to do with it. But it was okay, see, because I'd been there before. I understood the situation and knew how to . . . guide him through it, if you will.'

Oh my God.

'That was forty-one years ago,' Eileen goes on. 'And we had a wonderful sex life. Right up until the end.'

'Brilliant,' I say, rising from my seat. 'I'm glad you thought you could tell me. It's good to . . . share . . . these things. Another cuppa?'

'But it wasn't always *easy*. You understand?'

I sit back down.

'As a man gets older his body gets older. Aching back, sore knees and whatnot. Things, *things* . . . aren't what they used to be.'

Eileen gives me a look – *Do you follow?* – and I nod that I do.

'But we'd known each other since we were kids. We'd been through it all together, so we went through this together. Went to the doctor's, got the Viagras, happy days are here again.'

Eileen reaches into her handbag and produces a box of Viagra. She puts them on the table between us.

'There's three left,' she says, tapping the box, once, twice, three times.

'Listen, Eileen, no offence, but I . . . I don't . . .'

'Not for you, Thomas. For Douglas.'

'Eileen, I'm not sure this is any of my . . . I don't understand.'

'I want you to give them to him, love.'

'Does he need them?'

Eileen sips her tea. 'I think so, sweetheart. We haven't actually . . . Did he tell you about Lyme Regis?'

I shake my head.

'Me and Doug have been together for six months. We've kissed and canoodled, of course, plenty of canoodling, but we haven't actually . . . you know.'

'I see.'

'Bonked.'

'Right.'

'Now, six months is a long time to wait. A person gets frustrated, Thomas. So I suggested Lyme Regis. I assumed Doug was either shy or just being a gentleman, but I thought a weekend away might, well, open the window, so to speak.'

'More tea?'

'I'm fine, love. Too much and I get cystitis.'

My soup's turned tepid and I've lost the little appetite I had. 'Is it hot in here?' I ask. 'I'll just open the w— Just let some air in.'

Eileen continues as I open the window and briefly contemplate jumping out of it and running away.

'So I booked the train, booked the B'n'B. Single room, double bed. Sit down, I can't talk to the back of your head, lovely as it is. Thank you. So, long story short, Douglas took a turn. Demanded the poor woman at the B'n'B put us in separate rooms, and I'm afraid that rather set the tone for the whole weekend. By Monday I was losing patience, so I asked Doug to help find a dropped earring in my room.'

'But you hadn't dropped an earring, had you?'

Eileen grins and shakes her head.

'You minx.'

'I have my moments. But this wasn't one of my best, I'm afraid.'

'He sussed?'

'Far from it. He found the earring I'd placed under the bed, so I said thank you and gave him a big kiss. A real smoocher. And Doug kissed me back. Things' – Eileen glances at the table, as if she has X-ray vision and is seeing through the wood and through my trousers – 'began to progress.'

I don't want to hear this or think about this, but I'm cornered and there's nothing to do but wait it out and try and block any unwelcome mental images.

'We closed the curtains – I mean, we'd only just had breakfast and my room overlooked the main road – and made our way onto and into the bed. You're gritting your teeth, love.'

'Headache,' I say.

'Well, that'll teach you. Where was I?'

'In bed, I think.'

'Right, and then, well . . .' Eileen smiles sadly, holds up her index finger and then lets it droop. 'I tried to tell him not to worry, but he didn't want to talk about it. I suggested a walk, but Doug said he had a headache and went back to his room. We were meant to be staying Monday night, but Doug said the bed was aggravating his shingles, and we caught the last train back to London. Hardly said a word the whole way back.'

'Have you talked to him since?'

'I've seen him at bridge, and he was a gentleman, of course. But it's awkward now, and there's been no canoodling whatsoever.'

'I'm so sorry to hear it, Eileen. I thought you two were good together.'

'We bloody well were, love. We are. And I'm not one for quitting.'

I try not to look at the Viagra, but their gravity is too strong to resist. *100mg film-coated Sildenafil tablets.*

'So you're going to . . .' I nod at the pills. 'Give him the . . .'

Eileen laughs. 'He won't hear it from me, love.' And she stares hard at me.

'Me? No, no way.'

'Well, there's no way I can give him my dead husband's leftover dicky pills, is there?'

Dicky pills?

'So what do you want me to do?'

'Tell him they're yours.'

'Mine?'

'Well, he knows what you get up to, love. He's heard all your comings and your goings. Drop it into conversation. Tell him you swear by the Viagras. Offer him a couple.'

There is nowhere to hide in my living room, no cupboard to climb into, no curtains to conceal me, no trapdoor; all I can do is hunch my shoulders around my ears, hide my face in my hands, and hope Eileen will get bored and let herself out.

'There's no need to blush,' says Eileen's voice. 'Blimey, love, do you need a glass of water?'

'Yes,' I say. 'Yes, I do.'

Eileen follows me through to the kitchen. 'Honestly,' she says. 'You'd think no one had ever done it before. So . . . will you help me, love?' And the way she looks at me is heartfelt and honest and it breaks my heart.

As hard as it's been for me listening to this, it must have been ten times harder for Eileen to tell it.

'Okay. I'll do it.'

'You're a good boy, really,' she says, kissing me on the cheek. 'Now, you'd better sneak me out – gawd knows what Doug would do he if found me up here with a lad of your reputation.'

According to the time on my mobile, it's one forty-one a.m. on Sunday morning when Kaz texts: If I find out you've told anyone, I'll ruin you.

I'm tempted to text back and say there's no need, I'm ruining myself, but I don't want to antagonise her any more than I already have.

Chapter Twenty-Two

Despite being mid-June, St Michael's Church is as cold as a meat locker at seven a.m. on Thursday morning. Location scouting notwithstanding, it's been a year almost to the day since I was last in a church. Today, though, I'll be the man telling everyone how to behave. *The Gospel According to Thomas Ferguson.*

The crew arrive first – dressing the sets, setting up the lighting, blocking off shots. Verity is friendly and relaxed; more than that, she seems particularly upbeat this morning – literally whistling while she works – and I can't help but wonder if this has something to do with her handsome carpenter. Joe said they'd arranged a second date, and judging by Verity's demeanour this morning, I'm guessing it went well. I come at it obliquely, asking if she had a good night with everyone at the Goose the other week; Verity says she did, but doesn't give anything else away.

Ruth the vampire arrives and goes straight into make-up while Rob and I set up for the first shot. At nine thirty the agency and the client arrive, and Ben and I go to brief them over pre-shoot bacon sandwiches.

The scene waiting for us on the catering bus – a converted double-decker fitted with tables and bench seats – is like something from a teen road movie. It's chaos, with maybe a dozen excited people crowded into a small area at the back. They're surrounding someone, and it's not until I get within a few feet of the melee that I see it's Kaz. Holly is holding her wrist, and my first thought is that Kaz has had some sort of accident. But the mood is too high, there's too much laughter and delighted squealing. And Kaz is wearing what looks like a bridal veil.

And then I see it, the source of all this clamour – a diamond ring.

Kaz's boyfriend Marcus, I am told by several people all at once, proposed on Saturday night. On the steps of the Sacré-Coeur in Paris. *So romantic! So exciting! Can you believe it?* 'Yes,' I say; 'I know,' I say; 'No,' I say. The veil was Verity's idea; she raided the wardrobe department, and now we're all having our pictures taken with Kaz and her veil and her Cartier engagement ring. *Say cheese!*

I remember – as if I'd really forgotten – the threatening text she sent in the early hours of Saturday morning. Had Kaz known? Had she seen it coming as so many fiancées-to-be do? Was I a final fling? A last hurrah? Or was she as surprised on Saturday night as I am now? If so, I hope she feels as sick with guilt as I do.

I kiss Kaz on the cheek and wish her well. Her face doesn't flicker.

Anyone who's been on more than one shoot knows. Shoots are a stop-start process, intercutting periods of high bustle with long spells of inactivity. So you take a book. Or a magazine, a pair of headphones, a crossword, a sheaf of Sudoku, knitting. Bianca gave me a colouring book full of elaborately illustrated animals.

Our client on Little Horrors is a friendly but tightly wound woman called Judith, and although this is not her first shoot, it is the first one she's commissioned. So if it turns out terrible, it's on her head. Accordingly, Judith is frenetic with caffeine, nervous energy and questions – as such, this morning's schedule is more stop than start. The most recent stop involves a tight close-up of our little vampire. Ben is giving direction to Ruth, the DP is adjusting the lighting, and a small army of crew is rigging up lamps and reflectors. I'll only be called upon if there's a dispute or if something malfunctions. Likewise, the bulk of Verity's work has been in the preparation, so while Laura retouches Ruth's make-up, Verity quietly turns the pages of her novel. Today she's got a whole rock-chick thing going on: black jeans, torn at both knees; white high-top Converse; sleeveless Ramones T-shirt; a cluster of bracelets and a cloud of teased-out, mussed-up blonde hair. It's my favourite of her various looks so far.

I've finished colouring most of the stripes on a sleeping tiger when Verity yawns and closes the book with a sharp snap.

'That good?' I ask.

Out of solidarity with Ruth, our vampire starlet, Verity has run a green streak through her hair and fitted me with a pair of pointy ears.

'Lack of sleep,' Verity says.

Stuck for an answer, I nod and go over one of my tiger's stripes. We are sharing a small folding table at the back of the room; the nearest person to us is the best boy, but he's plugged into his headphones, learning French. It's not exactly an intimate spot, but now that I know Verity has a boyfriend, it's relaxed and cosy. Verity making the odd comment as she turns pages in her novel; me humming to myself, apparently, as I ink in my big cat.

'Your ear's slipping,' Verity says.

'My what?'

'Here.' She shuffles her chair next to mine, licks her finger and uses it to moisten the glue on my werewolf ear. 'That's better.'

'Not interrupting anything, am I?' says Holly as she approaches our table. She says this in complete innocence, but the heat rises in my cheeks all the same.

'No, not all, we're just . . . fixing my ear.'

'Ah, cute,' says Holly. 'Are you all right for tea? Coffee?'

'I'm fine,' says Verity.

'Me too.'

'Orange juice? Water?'

'No thanks,' I say. 'I'm all good.'

Verity shakes her head. 'Thanks. I'm all good, too.'

'Well, just yell if you need anything. Right, I'll . . . leave you to it.' Then she smiles – as if at a basket of kittens – and walks away.

Verity is smirking.

'What?'

'I think Holly's got the hots for someone.'

'Me?' I say, feeling as though I'm walking a precipice. 'Don't be daft.'

'She's a nice-looking girl,' says Verity.

'She's seeing Rob.'

Verity beams. 'Ah, that's so sweet. They're just right for each other, don't you think?'

The truth is, I hadn't thought about it. Not from their point of view. On the tube journey home last Friday, after my clumsy hit on Holly and her revelation that she was 'going with Rob', I wallowed briefly in a stew of self-made embarrassment. But subsequent events and subsequent wallowings pushed the Holly-and-Rob thing to the rear of my mind. But now that I do think about it, I can appreciate Verity's point.

'Yes,' I say. 'They are.'

'Sweet,' she says again. 'Doesn't it just make you feel . . .' She pushes the fingers of both hands into her hair and gives it an absent-minded tousling.

'It's a good look,' I say.

'What's good luck?'

'No – *a* good look. A good style. The whole' – I make rock horns with the index and little fingers of my right hand – 'wild-chick thing.'

'Wild?'

'I mean rock chick, wild child.' I actually wish I'd kept my mouth shut. 'You know . . . the knackered jeans and' – miming big erratic hair – 'mad hair . . . thing.'

Verity regards me through semi-squinted eyes. 'You make it sound so glam.'

'So what's that all about anyway?'

'Sorry?'

'The dress-up thing. The rollergirl; the sailor get-up; the vintage thing; the *wild chick*.'

Verity laughs. 'Didn't know you were paying so much attention.'

I gesture vaguely about myself; it's completely meaningless but in the absence of something clever to say it will have to do.

'Anyway,' says Verity, 'I already told you. Verity is . . .' She nods at me to continue.

'The spice of life.'

'There you go. Besides, most of it's shoot loot. You know, leftover wardrobe and whatnot, so it's a shame to just have it hanging at home feeding the moths. The' – painting quote marks in the air – 'sailor thing was from an Amex shoot; the vintage thing was a cider commercial; and the rollergirl thing was a bit of fun for that bloody awful roller disco. So now you know.'

'And this?' I say, again with the rock horns.

'This?' Verity says, pointing two index fingers at herself. 'This is me,' she says. 'Me getting up early for a shoot and not having time to think about what I'm wearing or what I'm going to do with my hair. My knackered jeans, my "mad hair", just . . . out of bed and out the door.'

I grimace an apology, but Verity is smiling.

'I like it,' I tell her. 'It's a good look.'

The problem with bright moments, such as the one just expired, is the awkward silence that invariably follows. As if the high borrows oxygen from the following pocket of time. At a dinner party, someone will generally fill the void with a comment about the quality of the food. *Great potatoes. Thanks, we got them from the organic market at Putney. Now isn't organic just a great big con . . . and you're back on track. There* are no organic potatoes to discuss here, so I direct my attention to Verity's book, *The Secret History*.

'Any good?' I ask.

Verity picks up the novel and weighs it in her hand. 'Yeah,' she says. 'Very. Not what I'd normally go for but . . . yeah.'

'Verity is the spice of life, right?'

Verity smiles. 'A friend of mine – hair and make-up – she goes to a book club, so now and again, I go too. Although we never seem to cross over. I'm wittering, sorry.'

'What's it about? The book.'

Verity blows out air as she thinks how to answer the question. 'Growing up, fitting in, class, snobbery, intellectualism . . . sexuality. Maybe.'

I pull a face.

'I'm not doing it justice,' Verity says. 'You can borrow it when I'm done, tell me what you think.'

'Maybe I'll watch the movie.'

'There isn't one,' Verity says, shaking her head. 'You'll have to do it the hard way. Or not at all.'

She passes the novel to me and I read the back-cover blurb. 'It's a bit . . . heavy,' I say, weighing the fat volume in my hands.

'Oh, come on. When was the last time you read a really good book?'

An old memory floats to the surface and I laugh involuntarily.

'What?' asks Verity. 'Are you taking the—'

'No, no, sorry, just remembering something. Silly.'

'Well, now you have to tell.'

'Ha ha! Well' — wondering if I should take the conversation in this direction and instantaneously deciding *what the hell* — 'I was young.'

Verity glares at me, exasperated.

I check over my shoulder, and then say quietly. 'It was called *Sexus*.'

Verity laughs. 'Now there's an ambiguous title. Who was it by?'

'Henry Miller,' I say, cringing at the name and its old associations. 'Any good?'

I remember that I'm wearing a pair of pointy plastic ears. My cheeks redden, but I don't mind and it doesn't seem to matter – after all, Verity has a boyfriend now, so I have nothing to lose, gain or fear.

'Bits of it were . . . good enough,' I say. 'If you know what I mean.'

'I do if it's anything like *Lady Chatterley*.' Verity screws up her eyes as if she's made a terrible faux pas. 'Oh my God,' she says from behind her hand. 'Too much information, Verity.'

'The joy of books,' I say.

Verity shakes her head and opens *The Secret History*.

I pick up my felt-tip pen and start on the tiger's tail.

We wrap the shoot at six, and Ben pops a bottle of champagne in honour of Kaz's engagement. I'm out of the door and heading for home before the cork hits the ground.

Chapter Twenty-Three

'Sixty,' says Doug, pulling his darts from the board. 'Steady enough.'

I haven't seen him since Eileen came to visit, and what with this packet of Viagra in my back pocket, I'm finding it hard to concentrate on the game.

'How's the shoot?' he asks.

I'm looking for an opening, a nice segue into: *Talking of which, I've got three tablets of dead man's Viagra here.* But it's not as easy as you might imagine.

'Off to a good start,' I tell him, hitting the lower section of the four.

'Do you need your eyes testing?' Doug asks.

Talking of eyes, look at these beauties.

'Just tired,' I say.

I lean at the waist as I take aim, pushing my bottom out slightly and hoping the Viagra will work their way out of my back pocket and onto the floor.

'You look uncomfortable, lad.'

I am.

'Bad back,' I say.

'Perhaps you need a new bed,' says Doug. And then, as if to himself, 'Well, I wouldnae be surprised.'

I turn to Doug, mouth half open, dart still gripped in my fingers.

'Only joking,' he says, holding his hands up in surrender.

'Ha,' I say.

Talking of my bed . . .

'You all right, lad?'

I turn back to the board. 'Yeah,' I tell him. 'Sorry.'

'Oof,' says Doug. 'Double top.'

It's hopeless.

Chapter Twenty-Four

I'm a dog, Verity is a tiger, Albert is an octopus.

In animal snap, you deal out the full deck and all turn over one card at the same time. If anyone turns over the same value card as you, you have to make their noise before they make yours: a bark, a growl, or – according to Albert – a *schplorbble*.

We all turn a card.

No matches.

Outside our trailer, rain is hitting the ground so hard it bounces back to knee height. The weathermen are saying we're in for one of the wettest summers on record, and if today is anything to go by they might just be right for once.

Well bring it on.

The majority of Frankenstein's Albert was to be shot outside, but there's no way that's happening in this weather. Even if we wanted to brave the rain we couldn't, on account of Albert's make-up. Plus we have poor light and bad contrast. We've got more chance of raising the dead than shooting this commercial today. When it became apparent we were looking at a washout, we rearranged the shooting order and filmed our single indoor set-up – the resolution scene in the dungeon. Albert nailed it in one take.

Kaz is livid, as if the rain is my fault, was somehow my idea.

And while Kaz is going ballistic, the crew – me and Ben included – can barely contain its delight. Thanks to the wonder that is weather insurance, me, Ben, Verity and every other member of contracted crew pocket an additional day's wages for doing little more than drinking coffee on the catering bus and doing the crossword. All that the agency and client get is a wet bum and a day out of the office. By midday Kaz had become unbearable, so Ben took her and the client for a posh lunch while I stayed behind to rearrange next week's schedule and supervise the equipment. Albert's mother has gone out to buy souvenirs from the gift shop, but we need to keep Albert's make-up dry, so in addition to my other duties, I'm babysitting. The agency creative still hasn't taken the hint – yesterday he invited Verity to a preview screening of some indie movie – so Verity has joined me and Albert in the art-department trailer, rather than eating lunch on the crew bus where she is susceptible to further embarrassment.

'Why don't you just tell him?' I ask.

'Tell him what?'

Verity is wearing a Smashing Pumpkins T-shirt today. She has run a red streak through her wild-chick hair and attached a wart the size of a peanut to her nose.

I'm wearing red eyeliner, and a trickle of blood runs from the corner of my mouth. 'I dunno. That you're . . . not available.'

'Bit blunt, isn't it? Anyway, shoot'll be over in a week.'

The idea deflates me somewhat.

We all turn another card.

No matches.

And again.

And again.

There's a false start with a nine of hearts, an eight of hearts and a seven of diamonds – we all get a bit excited and growl, bark, schplorbble, but no cards change hands.

'Going anywhere nice for your summer holidays?' I ask Albert.

Albert's face is thick with blue make-up. He shakes his head a little sadly. 'No. Well, I'm going to see my dad, but I don't know anyone where he lives.'

'Oh, I see.'

'Mum says Dad's priorities are confused, and that some men never grow up. And he says it's not about growing up but growing apart, but I don't know what that means. She says he takes her for granted and he said she let herself go, but she never goes anywhere. Dad has a girlfriend, but Mum says she doesn't have the time or energy for anyone else. And anyway, all men are the same.'

'Blimey,' says Verity. 'That does sound like a pickle.'

'Schplorbble,' I say, taking Albert's three of clubs.

'I used to feel left out at school,' says Verity, 'because both of my best friends' parents were divorced.'

Albert smiles a big goonish grin. 'Really?'

Verity nods. 'I thought it was very . . . dramatic, I suppose. And my friends had this *thing* in common, talking about all the arguments their parents had. Plus, both of their dads completely spoiled them with dresses, shoes, games, ice creams.'

'Dad bought me a new football,' Albert says. 'But Mum says that's typical of him and I shouldn't expect the same from her. I should be grateful she cooks my meals and washes my underpants, she says.'

'I guess she's right,' I say.

'It's hard on everyone,' says Verity.

'But your parents are married,' Albert says.

'*Were.* They got divorced when I was twenty-six. So I guess we should all be careful what we wish for, hey?'

Albert nods, rattling the zipper glued above his eyes. 'It'll work out, Zipperhead,' Verity says, kissing Albert on the forehead. 'One way or another.' And when she pulls back, she has blue face paint smeared across her lips.

'Blue lips,' says Albert, pointing.

'Yes, and now we're going to have to redo your Frankenface, aren't we?'

Verity winks at me. Smiles.

I want to kiss those lips.

Verity's brow furrows slightly, and I realise that I'm staring.

I turn to Albert. 'So, Zipperhead, I've got a question for *you*.'

'What?'

'You go to school with Ruth the vampire?'

Albert shrugs.

'I saw you two chatting at the make-up tests.'

'So?'

'She's very pretty, don't you think?'

'How would I know?' says Albert.

'You mean you hadn't noticed?' asks Verity.

Albert wrinkles his brow and shakes his head emphatically.

'Are you sure, Albert?' I tease.

'I know what you two are doing,' he says.

'I'm not doing anything,' I say, all mock-offended. 'I just thought that maybe you . . . liked Ruth, that's all.'

'She's only eight,' says Albert. 'I'm nine.'

'A younger woman!' teases Verity.

'I'm warning you,' says Albert, taking hold of his zipper. 'If you don't stop being silly I'm going to pull my zipper off.'

'Doesn't matter,' I say. 'It's not like we can film anything.'

'And anyway,' says Verity, 'your brains will fall out. And then how are you going to make Ruth your girlfriend?'

'I mean it,' says Albert. 'I'll do it.'

My phone rings. I listen to what Ben has to say, hang up the call, walk over to Albert and peel the zipper from his head, leaving a pink horizontal scar in his blue make-up.

'It's a wrap,' I tell him.

The time is approaching three in the afternoon, and even if the weather does break, there's not enough day left. We'll try again next week. And if it rains again, Ben says, we'll cover Albert in lettuce and call him Swamp Thing.

Verity is removing Albert's make-up. 'What are you up to this weekend, Zipperhead?'

'Playing football tomorrow.'

'What's your position?' I ask.

'Defender.'

'Figures,' I say. 'I used to be a goalie. Cos I'm so long.'

'Are you married?' asks Albert.

I laugh. 'What's that got to do with football?'

'Well, you said you *used* to play,' says Albert. 'And my dad used to play football, but he says after he got married, Mum wouldn't let him play anymore.'

'Right, I see. No, I'm not married.'

'Have you got a girlfriend then?'

'Yeuch. Horrible things.'

Albert laughs and Verity throws a dirty cotton ball at me.

Albert turns to her. 'Are you married?'

'Not married, no boyfriend, don't play football. Next question, please, Zipperhead.'

No boyfriend?

Verity has 'no boyfriend'.

I rehearse a question in my head, attempting to give it a casual aspect but conscious that if I don't spit it out in the next few seconds, it'll sound anything but. 'So . . . the, er . . . ?'

'Yes?'

'Didn't you say something about a . . . second . . . date?'

'Did I?' asks Verity.

I shake my head, shrug – *no big deal, just asking, it's really nothing* – 'I thought I overheard . . . something. Probably nothing.'

'Overheard, did you? What did you overhear?'

This trailer is smaller than it seemed ten minutes ago. I look at Albert and he shakes his head: *Don't ask me.*

'Carpenter? Maybe?'

'Joiner,' says Verity.

'Right, and you didn't . . . it didn't . . .' I make a gesture intended to indicate two pieces of wood being connected, in a dovetail joint perhaps, but I realise it might be misinterpreted and abandon the charade. 'Click,' I say.

Albert picks up the deck of cards and shuffles them clumsily.

'No,' says Verity. 'It didn't click. Without a drink in his hand – in his system – John—'

'John the joiner?'

'I know, right? Anyway, without the help of alcohol, John the joiner is as dull as a plank of wood. Do you know how long it takes the London Eye to turn through a single revolution?'

'Ten minutes?'

'God knows. But it felt like forever. Moral of the story – don't drink too many mojitos on a first date. It mangles your judgement.'

'Noted,' I say, holding a finger to my temple. 'So what are you doing with next week's . . . frog?'

Verity laughs. 'Not cocktail-making, that's for sure. Anyway,' she says, ruffling Albert's hair, 'we're shooting this fella next Tuesday, aren't we? So I guess I'll leave off the frogs for a week.'

There is a temptation to croak like a frog, but I resist.

A temptation to do a silly little dance.

A temptation to ask Verity what she's doing one week on Tuesday.

Verity and Albert are talking. '. . . if the rain holds off,' says Verity. 'What about you, Tom?'

'Sorry?'

'Plans for the weekend?'

Mum's memorial service.

Verity begins packing away her sketches and notes. 'I'm sure we could find a spare sausage for you,' she says, 'if you're at a loose end on Saturday, that is.'

'A sausage?'

'My barbecue,' says Verity, and I've never seen her look so bashful. She turns her back, organising items into a metal case.

Albert stares at me expectantly.

'I'd love to,' I say, 'but it's . . . I . . .'

Any other weekend, any other plans, I'd cancel. In a heartbeat. But that's not how Sod's Law works, is it?

'Don't worry about it,' says Verity, pulling on her coat. 'Really, it's no big deal.'

'I'm going away for the weekend,' I tell her.

'Sure,' says Verity. 'No worries. I only mentioned it because, you know . . . it'll probably rain, anyway.'

'Yeah. Probably.'

And Verity steps out into the rain.

Albert smiles apologetically, the way a doctor might when delivering a bad diagnosis.

Chapter Twenty-Five

Doug's Triumph Herald is younger than its owner, but about twenty years older than me. The classic car groans plaintively as I rattle north, and I can feel the texture of the motorway through the seat of my Levi's. There is no CD player and the radio isn't receiving. When Doug offered me the use of his car for the weekend I accepted immediately, but with hindsight, perhaps I should have taken the train. With the accelerator pressed firmly to the floor mat, I have achieved a speed of almost seventy miles an hour, but it's hard to be accurate with the old analogue needle vibrating like it's about to come loose.

I glance in the rear-view mirror and wince at my own reflection.

I couldn't face Alyson at The Edge, not today, but I needed a haircut for Mum's anniversary so I went to a local barber's. You wouldn't think 'just a trim' could go particularly badly. But you'd be wrong. I'd been thinking about Mum. Replaying yesterday's exchange with Verity. And before I realised what was going on, there was an ASBO thug staring back at me from the barber's mirror. Everything below the level of my temples was clippered grade-one short; the rest was gelled forward into a drug dealer's fringe. The hairdresser held up a mirror and asked what I thought. I told him to wash out the gel and clipper the lot. My head looks like an orange tennis ball.

On a good day in unjammed traffic, the drive to Dad's takes between three and four hours. The traffic is fine, but the Herald sounds like it's coming apart, so I ease off the gas and move into the inside lane. I guess I'll get there when I get there. Tomorrow there'll be a service for Mum at St Francis's Church, and we'll have all day to feel sorry for ourselves. Tonight, I'll cook supper and we'll have a quiet night, looking at old photographs and remembering the good times. Mum's been dead for almost nine years now, and it feels like my memories of her become harder to access with every passing year. On Friday nights we'd all have fish and chips and play knockout whist around the kitchen table. I remember sitting on Mum's knee in my Superman pyjamas. I remember the two of us making cakes with red icing. I remember the four us in homemade Sergeant Pepper costumes. There are photographs of all of these things in mismatched albums on the bookshelves, and maybe I don't really remember them at all.

I pull into Dad's driveway at ten past six, and he's at the door before I'm out of the car. He kisses my cheek and rubs his hand over my shorn head.

'What's this?' he says, and already his breath has a faint tang of whisky. 'New look?'

'Something like that,' I say.

'Is this yours?' Dad says, fingering the chrome letters on the bonnet of the Triumph. 'I had one, once.'

'Borrowing it,' I say. 'Sadie's got the Mini.'

Dad pats me on the shoulder. 'I'll make you a cup of tea and you can fill me in.'

'Bianca home?'

'In her room,' he says, his expression adding: *Let's leave it at that for now.*

It's still bright and warm so we drink our tea in the garden. We talk about work and the weather, London and here, and a summer holiday in Devon when Mum – exasperated with the miserable and relentless weather – put on her swimming costume and lay out in the rain just to make us all laugh. Bianca – four at the time – was the first to join her, then Dad and finally me. It was my last summer at home. In a way, it was our last summer as a family.

We're sitting quietly, when out of nowhere I find myself crying. And it takes me entirely by surprise. It's not as if I'm thinking maudlin thoughts; I'm not thinking anything at all. Just listening to the birds, staring abstractedly at the rose bushes and sipping my tea. And just like that, there are tears rolling down my cheeks. Dad pulls his chair next to mine and puts his arm around my shoulders. 'I'm just tired,' I tell him, and I go inside to take a shower.

Heading down the stairs twenty minutes later, I can hear Bianca and Dad arguing in the kitchen.

'But I'm seven*teen*!'

I anticipate Dad's reply and subvocalise it as I walk into the kitchen.

'And when you're eighteen, you can decide for yourself.'

'Hey,' I say, putting my arm around Bianca and kissing her on the cheek.

'Will you tell Dad?' she says, twisting out from under my arm.

'Hello?' I try.

'Hi!' says Bianca. 'How was the drive?' Pulling a face in case I missed the sarcasm.

'Well, it was a long way, that's for sure.'

'Not my fault you live in London, is it?'

Dad shakes his head in the dismissive way parents do but really shouldn't.

'I don't know what's going on here,' I say, 'but there's no need to have a go at me.'

Bea glares at me. Dad crosses his arms across his chest.

'If no one's going to talk to me, I'm going to the pub,' I say.

'All right for you, isn't it?'

I remember Bea and Dad texting me in the evening after the make-up tests. Bea to tell me Dad was being a 'dick', and Dad telling me we needed to talk about Bianca. Whatever this is, it's been brewing for a fortnight, so I try again, taking extra care to sound as reasonable and patient as possible.

'So,' I say, 'what's going on?'

'Bianca is refusing to do the work experience her teachers organised for her.'

Bianca turns to Dad. 'I don't even want to be a lawyer.'

'That's not the point, Bianca.'

'Oh, really? So what is?'

'It's good for your university applications.'

'Well, maybe I won't go to university.'

'You bloody will,' Dad and I say in unison.

Bea snaps her head around to direct her ire at me. 'Don't you start. Anyway, I can't do my work experience, because he' – returning her focus to Dad – 'has grounded me.'

Dad leans back in his chair, his body language making it clear that this is a decision he neither regrets nor intends to reverse. 'You know very well it doesn't apply to you doing your work experience.'

'Unground me and I'll go. Don't and I won't.' And Bea's body language is a perfect mirror of my father's.

'Why' – I take care to keep my voice calm – 'are you grounded?'

'Because Dad thinks I'm on drugs.'

'I don't think, I know!'

'Drugs?' This from me.

Bianca shakes her head with petulant contempt. 'It was a bit of hash. Two spliffs' worth at best.'

'Drugs are drugs,' Dad says, banging his palm on the table.

Cold relief washes over me, but I'm not about to show it and undermine Dad. He's overreacting, for sure, but it would be unkind and probably irresponsible for me to say as much.

The sound of Dad's hand striking the table is still reverberating in the air.

'How often?' I say, hoping the tone of my voice will work for both my sister and my father – a combination of calm pragmatism and mild disapproval.

Bea shrugs. 'Now and then.'

'*Now an—*'

'Anything else?' I cut Dad off before he works himself back into attack mode.

Bea softens minutely. Her frown relaxing by perhaps one and a half furrows. 'No. Honest. I'm not an idiot.'

Dad takes a breath, and I send him a psychic message, urging him not to respond the way I'm sure he wants to.

'You're lucky I'm still letting you go to Kavos,' he says.

'Yeah, well, only cos it's paid for.'

'No, because a deal's a deal. Something you should think about.'

'What's that supposed to mean?'

'I bought you a suit,' he says.

'I don't want to be a lawyer.'

'How long before the applications go in?' I ask.

'January,' they both tell me.

'So we've got six months?' I say.

Both my sister and my father dial their tension down by another couple of wrinkles.

'If I'm going,' Bianca says.

'You're going,' I say, saving Dad the trouble.

'So can I go out?' Bianca asks.

Dad holds Bianca's gaze for a second, before turning to me. 'You seem to have all the answers,' he says.

We walk the half-mile to the Old Bull, a small village pub with all the traditional trappings – dreary locals, pork scratchings, underage drinkers.

'Recognise the barmaid?' asks Bianca once we're settled at a table with our drinks.

'Should I?'

'Susan Chambers, isn't it?' she says.

'Who?'

'Used to be Susan Cooper, she married Declan Chambers.'

'Wasn't he a friend of yours?' Dad asks.

I remember Deck Chambers sticking chewing gum in my hair, putting me in a headlock until I saw stars, asking if my mum was 'a screamer' as he re-enacted his version of Bianca's conception.

'Not exactly,' I say. 'How do you know her?' I ask Bianca.

'I don't. But we have this mentor thing – they give the sixth formers a nem to look after.'

'A nem?'

'Nematode, worm, first-former.'

'Wait a minute. Are you . . . are you saying Deck Chambers has reproduced?'

'Nice kid, actually,' says Bianca.

I huff incredulously. 'Must get it from the barmaid, then.'

Dad laughs fondly. 'We used to call them blats,' he says. 'First-formers. Something to do with cockroaches – Blattodea, maybe . . . It was a long time ago.'

'Wicked,' says Bianca. 'Might reintroduce that.' She takes a sip of her Guinness and blackcurrant. 'Cheers.'

We clink glasses.

'Sorry about the suit,' Bianca says to Dad.

'I kept the receipt,' he says. 'But I stand by what I said – it would be good for you to do some work experience.'

Bianca sighs, but it's a small gesture that might include a degree of agreement. 'Can we talk about it later, Dad?'

Dad nods and lays his hand on top of Bea's. 'So,' he says, turning to me. 'You're on a shoot?'

'Skittles,' I say. 'They're quite good fun actually; we did one with a vampire this week, and next week it's zombies, a werewolf and Frankenstein's monster.'

With Verity.

'Wicked,' says Bianca.

'Literally,' I say, but it's a bad joke and nobody laughs.

My phone pings with an incoming text.

Eileen: Have you spoken to Douglas yet?

I send a message back: Sorry, haven't had a chance.

Eileen: I can't hang around forever, Thomas.

'Fancy woman?' asks Dad.

'Old dear from across the road,' I say, turning my phone to silent.

'Whatever turns you on,' says Bianca.

'I'm doing her a favour.'

'That's what you call it, is it?'

'Oi, Daffy, keep your beak out.'

'Daffy?' asks Dad.

Bianca blushes.

'Old joke,' I say.

'I'm in no hurry,' Dad says, gesturing at his full pint.

So I tell him about my old nickname for Bianca, and the transition from The Mistake to The Gaff to Gaffy to Daffy. Dad laughs so hard he turns red. He tries to take a sip of his drink but starts laughing again, drawing a good deal of attention in the small pub. 'Daffy?' he says, after he's regained around eighty per cent of his composure. 'Oh, that's funny. Like the duck,' he says, then he quacks, then he loses it all over again.

'It's not *that* funny,' says Bianca.

Dad takes a deep breath and a drink. 'Beg to differ,' he says, and he pulls Bianca to him, kissing the top of her head. 'You weren't a mistake, sweetheart. You were entirely deliberate. Tom was all surly and covered in spots and we thought it would be nice to have a baby in the house again.'

Bea blushes all over again, and you get the sense that despite being touched, she is a little disappointed at losing this small edge from her backstory.

'This one, though,' says Dad, clapping a hand on my shoulder. 'Complete accident.'

I pause with my drink halfway to my mouth. 'What?'

Bea's eyes go wide, and she points a finger at me. 'Daffy!'

'An accident?'

Dad shrugs. 'We were planning to wait a few years, but . . . here you are. Daffy.'

And now the pair of them are laughing like fools. And then I join in, too.

I'd never considered what it must be like to be an unplanned baby – an unplanned person, for that matter. Our parents never treated Bianca or me any differently from each other, and there was never a shortage of love, attention or affection in our house. But now that I've been outed as a gatecrasher at the big party of humankind, if I feel any different at all, I feel inordinately lucky.

After the teasing eases off – and it takes a while – the conversation winds its way back to Mum, which in turn leads to school, leads to Bianca.

'Have you thought about teaching?' Dad says. 'Your mother loved it.'

Bianca shakes her head. 'Don't know what I'd teach,' she says. 'I don't mind school, as such, but . . . I dunno if I want to spend my life in one.'

Dad picks up his glass, realises it's empty and goes to stand up, but I beat him to it.

Susan the barmaid is talking to some guy perched at the end of the bar; he nods in my direction and she comes over to take my order. And it's not until she starts pouring the Guinness that I recognise him. Heavier, older and thinner-haired than in my memory, Deck Chambers tilts his pint in my direction and smiles.

In the toilets of the Old Bull, looking in the stained mirror above the sink, if I twist my shorn head and bend my ear forwards, I can see the smooth white scar where the hair doesn't grow. About as long as the top joint of my finger and as thin as a match.

I was thirteen.

Declan Chambers thought it would be just hysterical to have me stand in the middle of the playing field with my arms held out from my sides as if I were hanging from an invisible cross – three or four books balanced in each hand. His goons stood around me in a semicircle, each holding a stone or a rock to throw at me if I let my arms drop. Deck called this game 'Stoning or Crucifixion'. Just another benefit of a Catholic education.

I played along, certain that at any moment a teacher – even Mum would have been welcome – would come and rescue me. After maybe two or three minutes, my arms burning and trembling, I pleaded with Declan Chambers for mercy – and, almost twenty years on, I'm angry and embarrassed at how pathetic I was. 'My arms are killing,' I whinged. 'Let us off.' Laughing, Deck held up a stone and tossed it from one hand to the other. A couple of the other kids laughed with him – *at me* – and I realised no one was going to save me but myself.

I relaxed my shoulders, dropped my books and shook out my arms.

'Get back on your fucking cross, Ferguson.'

I wanted to tell Deck Chambers to fuck off but my bravery had its limits. I was prepared to take what was coming, but I didn't want to make it any worse than it was already going to be. I might even have said I was sorry.

I bent down to pick up my bag. But before my fingers closed around the strap, a rock smacked into the back of my head, sending me sprawling onto my hands and knees. The pain was bright and immediate, seeming to fill the entire right side of my head. I held my hand to the spot behind my ear, and when I took it away the palm was slick with blood. Deck and his crew crowded around me. 'You know we was only messin?' It was Chambers that helped me to my feet. He told someone to collect my things and put his arm around my shoulders as we all walked off the field. 'Fuckin'ell, Tom, it was like you'd been got by a fuckin sniper.' Deck laughed and slapped me on the back. I laughed back. My hair was long enough to hide the cut, but I had a headache for the rest of the afternoon.

Now, glaring at my reflection in the Old Bull, I am consumed with a notion. I will follow Declan Chambers into these toilets tonight. I'll wait for him to start pissing, then smash his head into the tiled wall – once, twice – then leave him bleeding and unconscious in a trough full of urine.

The door opens. I snap my head around towards the sound, and I must look like a psychopath to the old boy who walks in. He nods at me warily, and I have to unclench my jaw so that I can smile back.

When I collect my drinks from the bar, I tip Chambers's wife the change from ten pounds.

'Took your time,' says Bianca. 'Thought you'd drowned.'

'I've got an idea,' I say.

'About what?'

'About your work experience.'

206

Over the past eight years, Mum's anniversary must have fallen on every day of the week; this year it's a Sunday and it's nice that we can all be together.

I was twenty-two when she died, and had just started working in the job I still do today. I suppose I thought I was pretty grown up at the time, but looking back I was little more than a child. Only a handful of years older than Bianca is now. Dad cried so much at the funeral that it embarrassed me to the point where I wasn't able to cry myself. It was summer-holiday sunny and I remember Dad's head getting so sunburned it peeled for the whole week I was home. Mum was thin when she died, her ribs showing at the open neck of her nightie; stark clavicles, sunken cheeks, lost eyes. I was one of the pallbearers, and I remember being surprised by the weight of the coffin that couldn't have contained more than a wisp of my mother. What I remember of the service was a lot of readings and hymns. They talked about life and death and life everlasting. Heaven. God's only son dying for our sins. But they didn't really talk about Mum. Mother, daughter, loving wife, yes; but they never mentioned how funny she was, how she'd blow raspberries on my tummy, dance while she cooked breakfast, sing while she drove.

The priest told me, squeezing my shoulders, that Mum had gone to a better place.

In a sense, today is nothing special. Just a regular Sunday Mass, dedicated to Katherine Jane Ferguson, wife of James, mother of Bianca and Thomas. The congregation offers up a silent prayer. And that's it.

We stand graveside, holding hands all in a line with Dad in the middle. Today is not as sunny as the first time, but it's warm and still and quiet. Bianca places flowers on Mum's already well-tended grave: *Katherine Jane Ferguson. Our world is less bright without you.*

She was forty-eight years old.

I think my mum would have liked Verity, and that makes me sadder than anything else about today.

Dad has lifted Bianca's grounding, and after supper and a pleasant but competitive game of Monopoly in the garden, she went round to a friend's to watch a film and stay overnight. 'No funny business,' Dad warned her, but he winked and Bianca hugged him long and hard before she left.

The Fergusons have all had a bit to drink today, but by nine Dad's passed out in his armchair and he must have put away close to a pint of whisky. I help him up the stairs, and in the doorway to his room he cries and says he misses my mum every single day.

Chapter Twenty-Six

Bianca will be staying with me for four nights, gaining three days' work experience on the Little Horrors shoot, which now that I think of it is rather fitting. She's packed enough gear for a month and the Herald is feeling the strain as we haul south down the motorway.

'Didn't you used to have a Mini?' asks Bianca.

'Sadie's got it.'

Bianca grunts. 'You never said why you and her broke up.'

'We just weren't right for each other.'

'Did you cheat on her?'

I sigh.

'Men are such wankers.'

'Language.'

Bianca tuts.

'But, yes,' I say, 'men are, by and large, wankers.'

'If Perx cheated on me I'd cut his cock off.'

'That's nice, dear, so how do you think your exams went?'

Bianca makes a noise somewhere between a laugh and a grunt, which could mean anything between wonderful and dreadful.

'Thank you for this,' she says.

'Well, couldn't very well have you doing work experience as a lawyer, could we?'

'Nuh-uh. Was a mistake saying I was even interested. Talking of,' she says, 'how does it feel to find out you're an accident, *Daffy*?'

'Feels awesome. I'm the rebel now. How does it feel to be legit?'

Bianca shrugs. 'Same same.'

'You and Dad seem better,' I say.

'What's he going to do if I leave home, do you think?'

'I dunno. Same as he is now, I suppose.'

'He'll be lonely,' Bianca says, and I feel like a bad son for not considering this myself. 'And he drinks too much.'

'You sound like his mother,' I say.

Bianca laughs. 'We should fix him up.'

'With a woman?'

'Unless you know something I don't.'

'I don't know if he wants fixing up,' I say.

Bianca tuts. 'Everyone wants fixing up.' And she glances sideways, looking for a reaction.

'Maybe,' I tell her. 'Good idea for a website: Date my Dad.'

'Already exists,' Bea says.

'You haven't?'

'Not yet. But I probably will.'

I'm reminded of Phil describing El's attempts to convince him into dating, and it makes me feel sad and optimistic at the same time.

'I told you I'm seeing El tonight, didn't I?'

'Your mate that's . . . you know . . .'

'Yup. I'll only be a couple of hours. Promise not to smoke any wacky baccy and burn the flat down?'

'Have you got Wi-Fi?'

'It's London.'

'Might see if I can fix Dad up,' she says.

'Yeah, there's a lot of it about.'

El's ankle is bandaged and there's a crutch balanced beside his chair. He has a red mark on his forehead and the back of his hand is grazed. There's an awkwardness to the atmosphere and, so far, all anyone's told me is that El fell. He isn't nimble on a good day, and today he's propped up on crutches and heavy painkillers . . . so here we are, eating Lucky Dragon takeaway and drinking mango lassis around El and Phil's kitchen table. The absence of beer and the presence of Phil are welcome variations to our routine. Lately, it seems that every time I see El, a little more of his disease shows up and a little more of my best friend is left behind. And, love him as much as I do, I was dreading tonight.

'Shagged anyone recently?' he asks.

Phil wags his finger. 'Manners, Laurence.'

El pokes his tongue out at Phil. ''xcuse me, Thomas,' he articulates camply. 'Have you had much cunt lately?'

Phil sighs and continues eating.

'Thomas?' pursues El. 'Any cunt, Thomas?'

Phil looks at me expectantly. It feels like the scrutiny of an authority figure, and I feel suddenly embarrassed. Ashamed.

'Well?' says El, prodding me with his crutch.

'El,' chides Phil. 'Don't poke the guests.'

'Thomas?' insists El.

I hold up one finger.

El bangs his fist on the table, making the plates jump. 'I knew it.'

'El,' says Phil. 'You'll hurt yourself.'

'How mny you on now?'

'Ninety-eight,' I say to the tablecloth.

'Tart,' says El, and Phil shakes his head.

I groan into my mango lassi.

'Don't beat yourself up about it,' says Phil. 'A hundred isn't so many.'

'No?' I say. And although I'm sure it isn't Phil's intention, I'm ever so slightly – and ever so pathetically – deflated by his lack of awe at my sexual prowess.

'Not in my circle,' says Phil. 'No pun intended.'

'Up yr bum,' says El.

'Quite,' says Phil, acknowledging El's reaction with a smile and a little bow. 'I knew one gentleman,' he goes on, 'who threw a party to mark the occasion of his five hundred and first. Everyone, including his latest conquest, wore Levi's 501s.'

El laughs and stamps his feet. 'Who's 'at?'

'Kevin Thompson.'

El hums out a short indulgent laugh.

'How many's he on now?' I ask.

'Dead,' says Phil with a sad smile. He articulates the word with a significance that seems to imply both the method and the inevitability of Kevin Thompson's demise.

El's arm twitches sideways, as if he's swiping at a fly only he can see. Head wobbling on top of his thin neck, he mutters something under his breath – 'fuckig dead' it sounds like – and his face is a mask of anger and frustration.

Phil blows his nose into an ironed handkerchief.

'So, Laurence,' says Phil, 'shall I tell Tom about your ankle, or will you?'

El stuffs a forkful of curry into his mouth.

On Sunday, Phil went for a meal with Trevor and Michael, a couple he's been friends with for several years. Also present was Oscar, a friend of Trevor's – good-looking, recently single. Not exactly a blind date, but not exactly not. Before he left the house, Phil cooked a pan of Bolognese for El. All El had to do was boil the spaghetti.

El opened a bottle of wine. He decided he didn't want Bolognese, so he dialled a pizza. Thirty minutes later there was a ring at the doorbell. Fortunately, El was nearer the bottom than the top of the stairs when he tripped. When Phil got home El was passed out in his armchair. He'd finished the bottle of wine and his foot had ballooned and turned purple. Phil skipped concern, worry and panic, flew straight into blind hysteria and called an ambulance. They hobbled out of casualty at something after two in the morning with a 'disappointing X-ray', a pair of crutches and a prescription.

I think Phil blames himself.

'Don't get me wrong,' Phil says. 'I don't blame myself. I'm not *that* melodramatic—'

El laughs, throws his hands in the air and screams, 'Amblance!'

'*But*,' Phil continues, 'the fact remains . . . it wouldn't have happened if I'd been at home.'

'You can't think like that,' I tell him.

'Yeah,' says El. 'I might've choked on that bsgetti Bolnese.'

'Throttle you myself in a minute,' says Phil.

El turns to me. 'You gonna let him talk t'me like that?'

'So, Phil,' I ask, 'how was the meal?'

He waves a hand in the air. 'Fine fine.'

'He's goin to see Oscar again,' says El.

'I am bloody not. Why do you insist on . . . I'm not, and I never said I was.'

El laughs. 'You should.'

'Oh, should I? For all you know, he could be a fat whale with a moustache and body odour.'

'Is he?' I ask.

'Actually, no. He's rather handsome. *But*' – Phil holds up a finger as El opens his mouth to interrupt – '*but* . . . he's not my type. Too tall and sophisticated.'

El blows a raspberry.

'Quite,' says Phil. 'And besides, I'm too old for dating. I never enjoyed it first time around. And I'm far less tolerant and way more particular now than I ever was then.'

'Juss haven met the right one,' says El.

Phil looks at El and shakes his head. 'That's the problem, isn't it, love? I have.' He uses his little fingers to wipe the tears from the corners of his eyes. 'I met him five years ago.'

'Fuckig hell,' says El, shaking his head. 'I thought you said you wern melodratic.'

I had imagined that I'd get back to the flat and find Bianca curled up asleep on the sofa. All I find in the living room, however, is an empty pizza box, a greasy plate and a dirty wine glass. Bianca is in the spare room, door closed, talking to someone on her mobile. The words are muffled but I get the intonation, which is alternately argumentative and pleading. I'm guessing Perx.

'Home,' I say, knocking on her bedroom door.

Grunt.

'Okay then.'

I clean up Bianca's mess and switch on the news.

Twenty minutes later she's still in her room, still on the phone.

I give the door another knock. 'I'm going to bed in a minute.'

''kay.'

I brush my teeth.

Knock knock. 'Right, I'm off then . . . Goodnight.'

''night.'

'Early start tomorrow, okay?'

'Yes, o-kay.' A little narky.

'I'll give you a knock at six.'

'Fine.'

Kids, who'd have 'em?

Lying in bed, with Bianca snoring lightly in the next room, I think again about the revelation that I was an unplanned baby. All of us are ten-trillion-to-one shots; all of us have a responsibility to make the most of our lucky break. But those of us who snuck past the guards of intent, us rebels on the fringes of design, we have that added pressure to make it count. And I feel it keenly tonight. I've wasted too much time already this year, chasing numbers under the pretext of chasing El's bet. But that's over now, and when the shoot is over I'm going to make my time count. I don't know exactly what I'm going to do, but inviting Verity for a glass of wine, a coffee, a meal, a walk in the park, a night at the flicks . . . any of those things would be a good place to start.

Chapter Twenty-Seven

At six fifteen there's still no sign of life from Bianca's room, so I'm forced to enter and open the curtains, which is a little awkward because Bianca has changed shape since I changed her nappies – something that is cringingly evident as she eats her Coco Pops in a vest top and short shorts. It used to take Sadie twenty minutes to apply make-up that looked like it wasn't there. It takes Bianca five minutes to layer on enough black to print a broadsheet newspaper. It's not an elegant look but it is quick, and we're out of the door only a few minutes behind schedule.

Bianca is fantastically excited during the drive to the Tower of London. I try to manage her expectations by explaining that her main job is to ensure everyone has coffee, but her enthusiasm remains undampened. I'm kind of excited too – after all, Verity doesn't have a boyfriend. We're taking a second swing at Albert's Frankenstein today, and if the white-wisped Wedgwood sky is any indication, we won't be needing the weather insurance.

After our awkward exchange last Friday, I had expected Verity to be coy this morning, but when I knock on her trailer door she is exactly the opposite.

'Hey,' she says. 'Looks like good weather.'

'We might even have to do some work,' I say. 'This is my sister, by the way. Bianca. She's going to help us out for a few days.'

'Pleased to meet you, Bianca. Pretty name.'

'Thanks. Mum was an English teacher.'

I see a minuscule reaction on Verity's face – a tightening at the corners of her eyes, maybe – at the word *was*. 'Not after whatsit from *EastEnders*, then?'

Bianca laughs. 'Well, I get that a lot. Obviously. But it's from *The Taming of the Shrew*. Bianca Minola was – at the end – sort of a late arrival. Like me. And not just cos Mum and Dad were . . . you know, knocking on. Mum was in labour forty-seven hours.'

'Been trouble ever since,' I say.

Verity runs a hand through a lock of Bianca's blue-streaked hair. 'Maybe I'll go blue too.'

Bianca glances at me.

'First things first,' I tell her. 'Go see if you can find your brother a cup of coffee. Verity?'

Verity shakes her head. 'Just put one out.'

Bianca looks hesitant.

'Don't be shy,' I tell her. 'Anyone bothers you, tell them you're my sister.'

Bianca goes in search of coffee and Verity begins unpacking a box full of props. 'So, what do you fancy? Fangs, pointy ears, wart?'

She's wearing skinny blue jeans today that show off the shape of her legs – runner's legs maybe, or yoga; whatever it is, it works – and a Pixies T-shirt that finishes maybe half an inch above her leather belt.

'How about stitches around my neck?'

'I have just the thing,' says Verity. 'I like the new hair by the way.'

'Well, it's not what I asked for. How was the barbie?'

'Yeah, it was good. Stayed mostly dry, didn't burn anything, drank too much.'

'Sounds like a success.'

Verity produces a strip of precast latex stitches. 'Here's one I prepared earlier,' she says, leaning in to measure the strip around my neck.

Close up, I notice that the tips of her dark eyelashes – thick, dark brown – are in fact very pale blonde, and longer than they appear at first glance.

'How was your weekend?' she asks.

I'd anticipated this, but the question still wrong-foots me.

'It was the anniversary of my mum's . . . nine years ago . . . she died nine years ago.'

Verity steps back to look at me, her brow creased with concern.

I smile. 'It was a nice day. We had a nice weekend.'

Verity returns my smile, continues gluing the stitches to my neck, and her hair is soft against my face.

'I feel bad,' she says. 'For putting you on the spot on Friday.'

'How?'

'You know, the barbecue?'

She's moved behind me now, and I feel emboldened by the pseudo-anonymity. 'I'm glad you asked me,' I say. 'I wish I could have made it.'

'Maybe next time,' says Verity.

I turn around to face her. 'Definitely next time.'

By the time Albert arrives on set, I'm fully stitched up, Verity has a gash on her cheek, and Bianca is sporting evil eyebrows and a nose wart. Ben gets a bullet wound between the eyes, Kaz gets fangs – they suit her.

I introduce Bianca to the crew, and at least half of them affect a cockney accent and shout 'Rickeeeeeey!'

And despite the well-practised sigh-and-eye-roll combination, I think Bianca is enjoying the attention.

Rob spent yesterday shooting establishing and incidental shots, and in between set-ups I look at the footage. It's all excellent. I could use every shot, I tell him, the only problem being it might make my own stuff look bad.

'Thanks,' he says bashfully. 'I appreciate the opportunity.'

'Don't be soft,' I say. 'We only asked you cos you're cheap.'

Rob laughs, smiles, opens his mouth, closes it, frowns as if there's something on his mind but he's uncertain whether or not to let it out of his mouth. He takes a deep breath, 'I mean, what with you and . . . Holly . . . and stuff.'

I'd never considered whether or not Rob knew about me and Holly. It hadn't entered my head that he knew I knew about the two of them. And now that it's out there, I'm not nearly as embarrassed as I might have imagined I would be. Maybe it's because Rob is uncomfortable enough for the two of us – for all three of us.

'Piss off,' I tell him. 'And go and see if you can shoot some ravens.'

'Nice one.' Rob starts away, hesitates, then turns back and pats me awkwardly on the arm. 'Yeah, nice one.'

The shoot progresses swiftly and painlessly. Which is perversely annoying. I was looking forward to spending time with my new buddy Albert, but the day is flying past in take after take after perfect take. Ben shoots more variations than we need, changing angles and lighting and direction, but we continue to cross shots off the storyboard with miserable efficiency. I mutter a prayer for rain, but God isn't listening. It's a perfect summer day, and the Tower is overrun with happy sightseers and couples and families. And, if you can't beat 'em . . .

At lunchtime I ask the catering manager to make four packed lunches, and while Ben babysits the grown-ups, Verity and Albert and Bianca and I wander among the crowds, eating ice cream and generally behaving like tourists.

When we return to set ten minutes late, Ben and Ruth and Kaz are sitting all in a row, eyes closed, faces tilted to the sun. If anything, they seem disappointed that we're back so soon.

And still we can't seem to avoid lurching ahead of schedule. The shoot is clockwork wound fast, and by four o'clock we're all but finished. And I know it's unprofessional and possibly pathetic, but I have a quiet word with Ben and he contrives a camera malfunction that will take roughly the same amount of time to fix as it takes to play one good hand of animal snap. And so, while Rob pretends to fix the imaginary problem, Verity and me and my little buddy growl and bark and schplorbble and laugh ourselves daft one last time. When we wrap for the day and I wave goodbye to Albert, there is a cold pebble of sadness in my belly. Maybe I'll look him up when he turns eighteen. It's only eight years and forty-four weeks away.

I'm back at my flat, chopping onions for a chilli.

'See if you can find some garlic,' I say to Bianca, pointing my knife at a cupboard. 'So, did you have a good day?'

'It was brilliant. I thought everyone'd be wankers, but they're all really cool.'

'I'm not entirely sure how to take that. Mushrooms, please. Frigidaire.'

'Can I have a glass of wine?'

'With your tea.'

Bianca hands me a tub of mushrooms. 'I think that old man thought I was your bird.'

'Doug?'

'Yeah,' says Bianca. 'So have you?'

'Have I what?'

'Got a bird.'

'Nope. Here, put these back in the fridge.'

'Verity's nice,' says Bianca.

'She is, isn't she? Chillies, please. Freezer compartment, top drawer.'

'How many?'

'How hot can you handle it?'

Bianca hands me two chillies.

'She's, like, really pretty, but doesn't act like she thinks she's all that. You know what I mean?'

'I think so, yes.'

'Has she got a boyfriend?' Bianca looks at me, trying to read me.

'No, I don't . . . What is this? Twenty questions?'

Bianca claps her hands together. 'Ha! Busted!'

'What? Who's busted?'

She shakes her head. 'You are so busted.'

'You,' I say, advancing on Bianca with a dripping wooden spoon, 'go and give Dad a ring. Food in thirty minutes. And give him my love.'

Bianca backs towards her room. 'I'll tell him how busted you are.'

I leave the chilli to simmer, put on a pan of rice and go to my room to change into a clean set of clothes. On the return trip, I notice a square of folded-up paper on the living room coffee table. My name is handwritten on the top.

Inside: *I know you don't owe me anything, but courtesy costs nothing. I suppose I overestimated you.*

Yvette answers her phone on the first ring.

'Yes?'

'Yvette, hi, how are you?'

'Been better.'

'I know the feeling,' I tell her.

'Can you make it quick,' says Yvette, 'I'm watching *EastEnders*.'

'Okay. I take it we had a viewing today?'

'That's generally how we sell our properties, yes. I did text you this morning.'

Did she? Phones are turned off on set and messages are dealt with in batches in between set-ups. This morning I had a message from Dad, checking on Bianca. Something from my phone company, offering an upgrade. And . . . yes, a text from Yvette.

'And you didn't reply,' Yvette goes on, 'so I assumed it was all right to go ahead.'

'And did you also assume it was all right to leave an abusive note?'

Silence.

'Yvette, listen, I think there's been a misunderstanding.'

'Really? So your girlfriend hasn't moved back in, then? Does she know about m—'

'Hold on a second, Yvette. She's my *sister*. She's helping out with the shoot, and . . .'

And it's none of your fucking business!

'Oh my God. I feel so stupid.'

'Yes, well.'

'Tom, I'm so sorry. I just . . . it was a bit of a shock, that's all.'

'Clearly.'

'I know it's silly but' – Yvette takes a deep breath – 'well . . . I thought we connected.'

I say nothing. What *would* I say? *'Yes, we did'*? *'No, we didn't'*?

'Well, didn't we?' Yvette prompts. 'Connect?'

'Well . . . I, er . . . I suppose.'

'I knew we did. And I know you're busy and everything, but I got the idea you were avoiding me. And then I saw her clothes everywhere—'

'Yvette, her clothes are in the *spare room*.'

'I know, but I . . . I like you, Tom.'

I know danger signs when I see them. And this one is red and flashing and comes with a klaxon. It's simple: I need to find a new estate agent, sell up quickly, get the hell out of here and don't leave a forwarding address. Now, though, isn't the time to get into it. Bianca's in the next room and the rice is about to boil over.

'I've got to go. I'm cooking supper for Bianca – my sister.'

'I'm so sorry, Tom, I feel like . . . like . . .' Brilliant, now she's crying. 'Like such an . . . idiot.'

'I finish shooting on Thursday,' I say, shouldering the phone as I take the rice off the heat. 'We can talk about it after that. In the meantime, will you do me a favour?'

Bianca comes out of the bedroom and mimes a glass of wine.

'Of course,' says Yvette. 'What?'

I nod to Bianca, indicate a small one, and walk through to my bedroom to wrap up the conversation.

'I think it would be a good idea if we put the viewings on hold for the time being.'

'You don't need to . . . I mean, now that I know what's going on. It was just a misunderstanding.'

'I know,' I say. 'But the flat's a mess, my head's all over the place. We can talk about it after the shoot. After my sister has gone.'

'Are you pissed off with me?'

'No. It's fine.'

'You're sure?'

'Positive.'

'So how is the shoot?'

'It's fine, thank you.'

'And you finish on Thursday?'

'Yes. Listen, Yvette, I've got to go. We'll talk soon, okay?'

'Promise?'

'I promise.'

This is what it must be like being a parent. You cook the meal, watch it gulped down without the slightest appreciation of the effort that went into making it, and then clean the dishes while the ungrateful bugger goes to her room to call her bloody boyfriend. No wonder Dad's uptight.

While Bea calls Perx, I pop downstairs to see Doug. Ostensibly to borrow a cup of salt, but in reality, to see if I can casually hand him a box of prescription drugs for erectile dysfunction.

'I've made a pot of tea,' says Doug. 'You got time for a cuppa?'

'A quick one; I've left my sister upstairs.'

'Sister?'

'She's here doing some work experience.'

Doug pours two cups of reddish-brown tea. The box of blue pills in my back pocket feels as big as a hardback book.

'How was the weekend?' Doug asks.

'Fine,' I say, and Doug knows all about Mum's anniversary so he leaves it at that. 'Jesus, Doug! What sort of tea is . . . Sorry, but that tastes like . . . I don't know what it tastes like, but it isn't PG Tips.'

'Bit bitter, aye.'

'Bitter? It tastes like twigs.'

'Hawthorn,' he says. 'Good for the circulation, apparently.'

And you have to wonder what would drive a man to drink tea that tastes like something collected from the floor of a stable. I shift in my seat, taking some of my weight off the three diamonds of sildenafil citrate.

'And how is your . . . circulation?'

'I'm seventy-one, lad. How d'you think it is?'

'Fair enough. Maybe you should get a . . . I dunno' – as if it's just this second occurred to me – 'a check-up.'

'Why would I guddle about with all o'that, lad?'

I slide my teacup to the centre of the table. 'Save you drinking this muck, for one thing.'

And if I'm going to cut to the chase tonight, then now's the time to cut. The question is: how?

Eileen suggested pretending they were mine, but even if they were, why in the hell would I offer them to Doug? And what of honesty? *So,*

Doug, I was talking to Eileen the other day, and she said you'd had a wee bit of bother getting the old caber up.

No. Just no.

A door bangs upstairs, footsteps stomp from one room to another. A fridge door opening and closing. Feet stamping back to the living room. The muffled thud of a body dropping onto the sofa.

'The sound really travels,' I say.

'Aye,' says Doug. 'Every squeak.'

'Right, well, thanks for the salt and the swamp water.'

Doug raises his cup, takes a sip, tries and fails to disguise a wince of horror.

Bianca is sprawled across the sofa, ignoring something on the TV, fiddling with her phone, a face like a very long and rainy day.

'Any more wine?' she asks.

I squeeze onto the end of the sofa and mute the TV. 'Nuh-uh. Early start tomorrow.'

'Can't wait till I'm eighteen,' Bianca says. 'Do what I like.'

Bianca's eyes are puffy, and it looks as if she's been crying. 'Hey, what's up?'

She wipes her nose on the back of her wrist. 'Nothing.'

'Perx?'

Bianca nods.

'Come on, what's going on?'

Bianca inspects her chipped nail varnish. 'It's just that some of them, Perx and Vince and Grozzer and that lot th—'

'Sorry, did you say *Grozzer*?'

Bianca rolls her eyes, but otherwise ignores my interruption. 'They're all going down the White Horse—'

'In Chester?'

Bianca nods. 'The barmaid gives them free drinks. She's such a slag.'

'Right. But that doesn't make her a slag.'

'No, but I know for a fact three different blokes she's shagged. At least.'

And what would you think of your big brother if you knew how many people he'd slept with? What would you think if you knew about his bet with El?

On the TV, a superimposed weatherman looms over a British Isles dotted with sunny icons.

'So she is a slag, see?' says Bianca.

'Did she and Perx . . . ?'

Bianca nods.

'So you're worried he might cheat on you?'

Bianca loops her little finger into the wedding ring – our mother's wedding ring – that hangs from the chain around her neck. She tugs on the gold band, pulling the chain tight so that it digs a shallow furrow into the flesh of her neck.

'It wouldn't be so bad if I was eighteen,' she says.

'But you go to the pub anyway, right?'

'Yeah, but last time, Slag-features grassed me up to the manager for being underage.'

'You're right,' I say. 'She is a slag. So what did' – I drum-roll my fingers on the tabletop – 'Perx do?'

'Gave me his van keys.'

'He what?!'

'So I could wait for him.'

'He stayed in the pub?'

Bianca's chin dimples as she tries not to cry. The TV weatherman beckons to a group of concentric blobs sitting over France and they float towards him.

'Come here,' I say, sliding up the settee and putting my arm around Bianca's shoulders. 'Can I ask you a question? Just between you and me.'

Bianca nods.

'Do you think Perx is trying to pressure you into having sex?'

Bianca laughs and wipes her nose on my clean T-shirt.

'What's so funny?' I ask.

'Nothing.'

'Come on?'

'Just between you and me?' she says.

'You're already sleeping with him, aren't you?'

'You won't say anything to Dad?'

'Not if you make me a promise,' I say.

Bianca chews her bottom lip.

'You'll be careful,' I say.

'Duh. I'm not *stupid*.'

'No.' I laugh. 'Far far from it.'

Bianca glances at her mobile. But it doesn't beep or ring or offer any other comfort.

'It sounds to me,' I say, 'like Perx is buggering you around. Actually, he sounds like a fucking dick, but that's your call. Either way, you don't have to play his silly games.'

'Don't really have a lot of choice, do I?'

'Do you trust me?' I say.

'What?'

'I'll tell you what to do,' I say. 'But you have to trust me. You have to do exactly what I say, okay? Or it won't work.'

Bianca regards me uncertainly.

'Guaranteed results,' I tell her.

Bianca nods, but as I reach for her phone, her expression turns to panic and she tries to snatch it away from me.

'Be calm,' I say, holding her at arm's length. 'It's a magic trick.'

Bianca groans. 'Do you have to?'

'You used to like them.'

'I used to like rusks.'

'Touché. Now shut up and watch.'

'Yeah, but how—'

'Shhhh.' I take the back off Bianca's phone, hand it to her. 'Inspect that,' I say. And as she does, I remove the phone battery and slip it into my jeans pocket.

'What am I supposed to be looking for?'

'Power,' I say, quite pleased with my accidental quip, and I hand the rest of the phone to Bianca. 'Now replace the back.'

She starts to clip the phone together then stops, holds out her hand. 'Okay, where's the battery?'

'Magic,' I say, with what I'm sure is an annoying flourish.

Bianca slaps me hard on the thigh. 'Give.'

'Ouch.'

She raises her hand threateningly.

'Don't hit your brother, Bianca. Anyway, you can't have it; it's vani . . . *shed*.'

'All right, I'm not kidding now,' Bianca says, clenching her fist. 'What if he tries to—'

'That's the point. When Perx phones and you don't answer, he'll go nuts imagining what you're up to in the big city on a film set with loads of cool guys and sexy actors. It'll do his little head in.'

'But what if he thinks I'm cheating on him and then he cheats on me?'

'Then you cut his cock off.'

Bianca laughs. 'Seriously. What if he does?'

'Do you think he might?'

Bianca pouts and shrugs.

'Him being able to get you on the phone won't stop him cheating on you, Bea. If he's going to do it, he's going to do it.'

'What if he *needs* to speak to me?'

'He can wait. Like you had to in his van.'

Bianca thinks about this.

On the TV, a commercial for something baffles me, and it probably would even with the benefit of a soundtrack and a voice-over. It reminds me that tomorrow I'm working with George the zombie brat and I hit the off button.

'What will I say when I see him?' Bianca asks.

'Say you forgot to pack a charger.'

'What if Dad needs to phone?'

'He'll call me.'

'Think you're clever, don't you?'

I hold out my hand. 'Do we have a deal?'

Bianca slaps me a low five. 'Can I have a glass of wine now?'

Chapter Twenty-Eight

We're shooting zombies. It's raining outside, but we're dry on Stage 4 of Pinewood Studios. Today I am the evil doctor – pointy beard, monocle, hillbilly teeth. Verity and Bianca have elfin ears and orange streaks in their hair. Kaz is part werewolf, Ben is Frankenstein's monster, the creative is an alien, Judith is mummified, Rob bewarted, Holly has a hunchback, the cameraman is a zipperhead. Plus, of course, our two zombies, Alice and George. It's like all hell is shooting a commercial. Which is pretty consistent with the prevailing mood. In one sense the day has been relatively straightforward – there's plenty of film in the can, we're marching through the storyboard and keeping to schedule. In another sense, it's been a bloody grind.

George has undermined Alice, been insensitive to Verity, dismissive of me. Rude, stubborn and awkward. Sometimes you're just right about people. All your first impressions and leaped-to conclusions, they turn out to be bang on the money. The fucker even complained about his lunch. He's like a little life-Hoover. A droning machine that sucks every speck of fun and joy out of the room.

So here we are, dressed as vampires and witches and ghouls, and all of us with the matching demeanour. Like the world's most miserable fancy-dress party. And it is with no small sense of relief that we set up for the final shot of the day, in which the zombies revert back to kids, enjoying the sweets and smiling at the camera. Simple.

Alice sits patiently as Laura the make-up artist removes George's zombie make-up and applies a dusting of natural colour. This is the system we have found causes minimum disruption. Attend to George while Alice reads a few pages of *Harry Potter*, then get rid of the bugger and sort out Alice. Except now, at the end of a long day, she is sitting with the book closed in her lap and an expression of pure glumness on her undead face. George leaves without saying thank you (as usual) and Alice climbs up onto the stool in front of Laura. We joke with her and she laughs politely, but the day has had the better of her.

Laura has finished Alice's make-up and is tying pink ribbons into her hair when tears begin to well in the little girl's eyes.

'Hey,' I say. 'What's up, sweetheart?'

Alice shakes her head. It dislodges the burgeoning tears and two thick streams curve over her fat cheeks.

'What's the matter?'

Alice's breath comes in staccato in-in-outs and she clutches at the front of her jumper, grabbing little fistfuls of material.

'It's okay,' I say. 'You can tell us.'

'G— G— George. He said Harry dies.'

'Harry Potter?' says Verity.

Alice nods her head. 'He said that Voldemort, he kills Harry and he turns into a zombie wizard.'

'Which one is this?' I say, taking the book from Alice. '*Chamber of Secrets*. It's a scary one, for sure.'

'Have you read it?' she asks.

'See that girl,' I say, pointing out Bianca, who seems to be flirting with the electrician. 'That's my little sister.'

'Really?'

'Really. And I read this book to her when she was about the same age as you are now.'

'Honest?'

'Yup. It's the one with Moaning Myrtle, right?'

Alice nods.

'Well, listen, I don't want to give anything away, but aren't there a few more Harry Potter books after this one?'

'I think there's four more,' says Alice.

I show her the fingers and thumb of my splayed hand. 'Five. Now, do you really think Harry is going to die in book two and drag himself around like a' – I tickle Alice's ribs – 'creaky old zombie for *five* more books?'

Alice chuckles and shakes her head.

'No. Me neither. So I wouldn't necessarily believe everything George says.'

Alice nods, wipes her nose and drags a trail of snot through her make-up.

'If only we had some Puking Pastilles,' says Verity. 'That'd show him.'

And Alice laughs.

'Right then,' I say. 'If we ask Laura to redo your make-up, do you promise not to get any more snot on it?'

Alice sniffs. 'I'll do my best.'

Maybe it's because we've shot three out of four commercials and she is now bored, or maybe it's because we've got two kids eating her 'candy', but Judith the client is scrutinising every aspect of this final sequence. On the previous scripts, we've covered this shot early in the schedule in order to appease her. We have deviated today because I was worried about the George–Alice dynamic, and I wanted Ben to shoot as much zombie as possible before the monsters got tired and cranky. Instead, I've got a tired and cranky client. And then Kaz gets involved, and then the creative, and everyone's got a suggestion about how we should shoot this simple shot. Eat and smile. Smile and eat. Eat and chuckle. Giggle and chew. Take after take after take after take. It's kids eating sweets, it is what it is, but . . . Take 8, Take 9, Take 10. 'Maybe if we had just one kid as hero,' suggests someone. And while the word *hero* is still ringing in the air, George has shouldered himself forward.

'Mate,' says Ben, taking me aside, 'I've got a bastard migraine coming on like a galloping elephant; I'm seeing double, and if I have to look at the little shit's face for another second I might throw something at it.'

'Want me to finish off? I mean, it's not like we're going to use it, right?'

'I owe you one,' says Ben.

I wave it off. 'All I have to do is shout "Action" and "Cut". Any idiot could do it.'

George is not a bad actor, but after each take – partly to convince the client I care and, yes, partly to punish George – I act vaguely dissatisfied and suggest a new direction. *Give me yummy, give me happy, ecstatic, enraptured, overjoyed. Chew fast, chew slow, chomp.* Sweet after sweet after sweet after sweet. One at a time, two at a time and by the handful.

They say people turn green when they're going to be sick.

George turns blue. It's as if the zombie he's played all day has possessed him. He turns blue and his eyes water. I'm watching this down a camera lens and I zoom in tighter. Sweat bubbles up beneath the make-up on his forehead and top lip. He retches in his throat, blinks, regains some composure.

'Give me one more, George,' I say.

Give me something from deep inside.

George stares at the red and green and yellow sweets in his hand, licks his dry lips, his eyes bulge. He gulps, opens his mouth wide enough to swallow his fist. George's jaw trembles under the strain; half closing, half opening, stuttering a silent *O-O-O-O*. He puts a hand to his mouth but the pressure forces a geyser of Technicolor vomit from the corners of his mouth and between his fingers. I zoom back to capture the spectacular extent of George's upchuck as his body spasms and he releases a fist-wide column of semi-digested, E-numbered slurry.

And who needs Puking Pastilles when you've got Skittles.

When she's finished mopping up George's insides, Bianca skips up to me in a better mood than I would be under the circumstances.

'Guess what,' she says.

'You've got spew on your boots,' I tell her.

'Ew, dirty little shithead,' she says, wiping the toe of her boot on the back of her jeans. 'Verity's giving me a makeover. If that's okay.'

''course it's okay. Now?'

'Well, to be honest, Tom, I'm a bit embarrassed.'

'What are you up to? Is this some ploy to get your phone back?'

'If I wanted that, I'd nick it out of your coat pocket. I just don't want Verity to make me over with all this lot around. They'll take the piss.'

'What about the trailer?'

'It's a bit pokey. I was wondering if we could do it at your flat? With a glass of wine.' Bianca shifts her weight from foot to foot in a childishly excited two-step.

'Oh, you were, were you?'

'It's still early.'

'Verity might want to go home and put her feet up.'

'She doesn't,' Bianca says, still dancing on the spot. 'I already asked.'

'Doesn't look like I've got much choice, then, does it?'

'Not really,' says Bianca. 'You can cook tea while she does my makeover.'

'Who said anything about tea? Verity might—'

'I already checked; she likes everything except aubergines.'

'Fine,' I say. 'And you've still got spew on your boot.'

Chapter Twenty-Nine

Bianca squeezes into the back seat of the Triumph and I drop the girls at my flat (Verity says it'll take her half an hour just to remove Bianca's existing layers of make-up) before driving to the supermarket to gather ingredients for the finest chicken carbonara Verity has ever tasted. Shallots, pancetta, fresh herbs, organic chicken thighs, chestnut mushrooms, a Pinot Grigio for cooking and an expensive Gavi di Gavi for drinking.

The groceries cost over fifty quid, and I cut my thumb chopping the shallots. And what do I get in return for my efforts? I get to sit here like a turnip while Bianca and Verity compile a list of Hollywood's hunkiest hunks. For all they're concerned, they might as well be eating a Pot Noodle.

'Clive Owen,' says Verity.

'What about Daniel Craig?' asks Bianca. Gone is the overdrawn eyeliner, the swathes of mascara, the gaudy lipstick, the blue streak. She looks calmer, fresher, more approachable. More like my sister.

'Bit too . . .' Verity barrels her chest, juts her elbows. Today she's wearing the Supersuckers – a skull over crossed cutlasses – and I find myself wishing I knew more about the bands Verity appears to listen to.

'Brad Pitt then?'

Verity eats a mouthful of carbonara and makes a noise of appreciation. Whether it's aimed at the food or Brad, I don't know.

'Okay,' says Bianca. 'Brad in *Fight Club*, or Brad in *Ocean's Eleven*?'

Verity sips her wine and takes a moment to savour it. '*Thelma and Louise*,' she says.

'Never seen it,' says Bianca.

Again Verity makes that noise of appreciation. 'You should. This really is amazing, Tom,' she says, showing me a forkful of pasta.

'The trick,' I say, 'is to get the balance right between the wine and the cream.'

'Have you ever been out with anybody famous?' Bianca says to Verity.

'I dated an actor from *Casualty* for a few months. Not exactly famous, though.'

'*Casualty*!' says Bianca. 'Cool. Which one?'

'He was only in a few episodes.'

Bianca turns to me. 'What about you?'

'Market trader from *EastEnders*. Two dates.'

'So cool,' says Bianca, without any irony.

'The problem with actors,' says Verity, 'is they're terminally needy. Jason – the *Casualty* guy – was constantly asking me if he was handsome, how was his hair, how was his skin, was he talented, should he work on his pecs, get his chest waxed.'

'They do that?' asks Bianca.

Verity nods, 'Oh yes.'

'Hattie the market girl,' I say, 'couldn't walk past a window without checking her reflection.'

'I know,' says Verity. 'It's like, you don't need me, you need a mirror with a recorded message: *You're gorgeous. You're gorgeous. You're gorgeous.*'

'A vanity mirror,' I say. 'You should patent that.'

'I'd buy one,' says Bianca.

'You don't need one,' says Verity, and Bianca blushes.

After blueberries with crème fraîche and poppy seeds, Bianca offers to clear the table and load the dishwasher, so Verity and I take our drinks through to the living room.

'Nice flat.'

'Thanks, I'm selling it,' I say, and a shudder runs through me as I recall the note Yvette left on the coffee table – in the exact same spot where Verity's wine glass is now standing. I jab my thumb in the direction of the kitchen, where it sounds as if my sister is systematically smashing my crockery. 'Thanks, by the way, for sorting Bea out.'

'Not at all,' says Verity. 'She's lovely.'

'Her dad might disagree with you on that one.'

'You're a good brother; she's lucky. Must have been strange. I mean, her being so young.'

'Thank you. It was nice,' I say. 'I'm sort of a hybrid brother, uncle, stepmum, I suppose. Keeps it interesting.'

Verity laughs. 'This Perx character sounds like a complete loser, though.'

'Total tosser,' I say. 'Definitely a frog, that one.'

The reference to dating seems to make Verity uncomfortable, and she takes a sip of her wine before saying, 'Good idea, taking her phone off her, though. Could have done with someone taking mine off me a few times.'

'You're not the only one,' I say.

'Do you think it was easier before phones, the Internet, all that . . . stuff?'

'Well, you'd have to talk to each other, which is . . .'

'. . . not always a good thing.'

'It's why the cinema's such a big draw.'

She picks up her wine again, 'And anywhere with alcohol.'

'Dating sucks,' I say, clinking my glass against Verity's.

'I'll drink to that.' She indicates my glass of sparkling water. 'You're making me look unprofessional.'

Bianca walks into the room and yawns theatrically. 'Who's unprofessional?'

'More importantly,' I say. 'Who are you? And what have you done with my goth sister?'

'Ho ho,' says Bianca. 'So funny. And it's not goth, it's emo.'

'Like the . . .' I hold my hand up to mime an Emu puppet.

Verity grabs my wrist, lowers my arm. 'Don't do it,' she says *sotto voce*. 'Dad joke.'

'*Bad* joke,' says Bianca. She yawns again and stretches her arms. 'Think I'll go to bed; I'm knackered. Thanks for this,' she says, circling her face with a finger.

'Pleasure,' says Verity. 'I'll leave you a few bits and bobs.'

Bianca kisses Verity, and then she kisses me.

As if she's connecting us.

'Night, bruv. Don't stay up too late.'

Bianca disappears into her bedroom, leaving a subtle hum of tension behind her.

'She must be tired,' says Verity, smiling.

I laugh. 'So it seems.'

Verity yawns and arches her back left and right in a single fluid movement. 'Sorry. Bianca's got me at it now. I suppose I should call a cab.'

'I'll drive you,' I say, holding up my glass of sparkling water.

'No, it's late. You've got an early.'

'It's not even eleven. I won't sleep for at least an hour.'

'Are you sure?'

'Positive. It's drive you home or watch crap telly for an hour.'

'Well, I wouldn't wish that on you.'

I'm nervous and happy and there's something in the air – anticipation, maybe – as we drive though the night-time streets of south London.

We talk about tomorrow's shoot with Elijah. We talk about Verity's brother, my sister, my dad, my mum. Verity tells me about a two-day shoot she is working on, starting next Wednesday. What I'm going to do next, I don't know. As we travel west, cut through empty back streets and quiet green spaces, the conversation fades, giving way to a prosaic sequence of *lefts*, *rights*, and *straight-aheads* as Verity directs me towards her flat. We'll be there soon, and I'm kind of dreading it in a kind of looking-forward-to-it kind of way. While we're driving, the pressure's off – there's nothing we can do but sit, talk and look at the lights. But when we stop, something has to happen. Either I kiss Verity or I don't kiss Verity. Both deliberate, definite courses of action.

This is the first time I've had Verity to myself, and I don't want it to be the last. We talk easily, without having to think about what to say next. And when it's quiet it's comfortable. The last thing I want to do now is misread the signals and mess it all up.

'Second on the right,' Verity says. 'See that one street light that's more orange than the others? That's me.'

My stomach clenches as I take the right onto Verity's street. True to her description, one of the street lamps glows a different colour, flickering slightly as if this will be its last summer. I could stop in the middle of the road, let Verity jump out, wave goodbye. Or I could pull into the parking space on the wrong side of the road and find out what happens next. Verity too, I sense, is aware of these options.

I pull into the space on the opposite side of the road.

Verity unbuckles her seat belt. 'Thanks for the meal.'

'Thank you. For sorting Bianca out.'

Verity shifts around in her seat, so that she's facing me. 'I suppose it's a little late for coffee,' she says, and sort of laughs. Or maybe she just clears her throat.

In the faint orange glow, Verity's face is in partial shadow.

'Yeah,' I say. 'We don't want to be up all night.'

I'm replaying how that might be interpreted when Verity leans forward and . . .

She is going to kiss me.

. . . Verity kisses me. And her lips are warm. Verity kisses me and her lips are gently wet as they slide across my own. I push into the kiss and her lips are soft and deep. I don't remember my first kiss. I know who, when, where . . . but the details of the kiss itself are lost.

Kissing Verity now . . . in the flickering lamplight, the only sound the clicks and ticks of the cooling engine . . . this I will remember.

Verity's hand is on the back of my neck, she isolates my top lip, takes it between hers, runs her tongue across its surface. I put my hand against the side of her face, my fingers sliding into her hair, my thumb tracing the shape of her cheekbone.

I only want to think about this kiss, but my mind has made a connection it's determined to pursue. The night of my first kiss was the same night I lost my virginity to Trudi Roberts. And after Trudi there was Lisa; after Lisa, Samantha; then Jennifer, Debbie, Joanne, Kelly, and so on and on and on.

Verity's lips surround my bottom lip, and maybe she senses my distraction. She breaks off the kiss, slowly, says, 'I'm looking forward to finding out all about you, Tom Ferguson.'

And after Sadie there was Holly, and Yvette, and Kaz, and 98 . . . and . . .

Verity smiles, broad and true, but I send the wrong smile back – a smile distorted out of shape with doubt and hesitation. Verity reads it instantly, her embarrassment fills the space between us and there is nowhere for her to hide in this tiny car.

'I had a nice night,' I say.

'Yeah,' says Verity.

'I'd better . . . better get back to Bianca.'

'Sure,' says Verity.

I lean in to kiss her goodnight and she twists her face away, offering me her cheek.

When I get back to the flat Bianca is in her room. I should go to bed too but my mind is chattering, replaying, deconstructing. I pour myself a glass of Gavi and take it to the sofa.

'What happened?' shouts Bianca through her bedroom wall.

'What do you mean, what happened?'

Bianca *d'oh*'s loudly. 'Did you get off with Verity?'

'Nothing happened.'

'Berk.'

'Goodnight, sister.'

'Goodnight, berk.'

Bianca's right.

My bedpost is notched to matchwood but my bed is empty.

Chapter Thirty

I bang on Bianca's door and she opens it one second later, already dressed, packed and caked in emo make-up.

'Morning, berk.'

'Good morning, sister. What happened to the makeover?'

Bianca shrugs. 'Not really my thing.'

I turn away from her door, stop, turn back. 'That was very devious,' I tell her.

Bianca smiles.

Today it's a full moon in Ad-Land and the set is crawling with monsters. No one is without a pair of fangs, a wart, an eyepatch, pointy ears, a dagger through the head. The script has a teenage couple snuggling on the sofa in front of a scary movie. They begin to kiss. Upstairs, Elijah's ears prick up. As the kiss develops the teenagers recline further and further into the sofa. Elijah the werewolf creeps downstairs. And the moment the snoggers hit horizontal, Elijah pops up from behind the settee, scaring the bejesus out of the pair of them. They give him sweets, et cetera and so on.

There was no kissing at the casting, which, with hindsight, was a mistake. The emphasis was on finding good monsters and a supporting cast who could act convincingly terrified – which our teenagers, Ray and Kelly, did. The kiss, though, it just isn't happening.

Take 1 is a dry clumsy effort that's more of a lip collision than a kiss. Take 2 is not much better. Take 3 is a whole lot worse. We go again and again and again and it's terrible and awful and woeful. When Ben calls 'Cut' for the fourteenth time, sections of the crew groan loudly. The actors' embarrassment is escalating to the level of a fire hazard, and if we don't get this kiss soon, we never will.

'Fuck!' Ben says. 'What's wrong with them?'

My mind flashes to last night, me kissing Verity, her reading my mind through the pressure of my lips. And I have nothing but sympathy for our actors.

'Want me to have a word?'

Ben nods. 'Well, they're not listening to me. Knock yourself out.'

I walk on to set and tell Ray and Kelly to relax and have fun. I try to make them laugh, but they're beyond being amused. We film two more takes and they're so awful I'm blushing out of sympathy. It's after four in the afternoon now, and the crew are restless. They can smell the weekend – we all can – and even without the catcalls their impatience is tangible.

Crouching beside the prop sofa in the two-walled, studio-lit sitting room, in front of three dozen braying crew, I'm telling Kelly and Ray to forget they're shooting a commercial. And then Kaz strides onto the set.

'The client's getting twitchy,' she says, glancing at Ray and Kelly.

'Any suggestions?' I ask.

'Just give it some enthusiasm,' Kaz says to Ray. 'Just get stuck in,' she says to Kelly. And Ray and Kelly look more terrified than they ever did in the casting.

Someone, it might be Ben, shouts, 'Demonstration!'

Everyone, even Ray and Kelly, laughs.

Someone else shouts, 'Show 'em how it's done.'

Kaz shrugs nonchalantly and raises her palms in a gesture that says, *I will if you will.*

Someone wolf whistles. Someone else howls.

Kaz looks at me: *Well?*

Ray and Kelly look at me: *Well?*

Ben and Judith and the creative and Rob look at me: *WELL?*

A demonstration is not a bad idea, and it seems the entire room knows it. Not so much that the kids need to be taught how to kiss, more that the tension has reached a point where a sharp pin is needed to burst it.

Kaz cocks her head to one side. 'Since when were you so coy?' she whispers.

'Okay,' I say to my actors, beckoning them off the sofa. 'Stand there.'

Kaz and I take their places on the sofa. Kaz wets the front of her teeth with her tongue and, despite myself, I experience a tingling frisson.

'Ready?' I say to Kaz.

'You know me,' she says.

'Would somebody like to give me an "Action",' I shout to the gathered crew on the other side of the lights.

Forty voices shout, 'Action!'

Kaz and I turn to face each other. She winks. I smirk. Kaz brushes her hair from her face, blinks lazily, parts her lips enough to show a flash of enamel. As I lean in to kiss Kaz, she grabs my face in both hands and pushes me back onto the sofa. Her tongue enters my mouth, finds my tongue, says hello and retreats.

'Call it old times' sake,' Kaz whispers, holding my lip between her teeth. And she springs off me like a dismounting gymnast.

The chorus of whoops and whistles sounds like something from a football terrace. Kaz takes a bow to ferocious applause, while I make a big deal of wiping my lips and drying my hand on my jeans.

Kelly and Ray nail it in the next take.

We break for the final set-up of the entire campaign – Ray and Kelly's horrified reaction to Elijah the werewolf. It's a simple shot, but

I'm nervous as hell. So far today Verity and I have done a fine job of being polite and professional and pretending we didn't kiss last night.

But we did. I thought about it all night, and I want to do it again. Verity deserves better than me, for sure, but if I'm with Verity, I think I can be better than me. I know I can.

I intercept Verity on the way out of the art department office.

'That was a little awkward,' I say, nodding towards the sofa.

'What was?' says Verity coldly.

'You know, Kaz . . . and me . . . kissing.'

She's wearing an AC/DC T-shirt and the band sneer at me from beneath the heavy red letters.

Verity shrugs. 'Seemed pretty convincing.'

'Yeah.' I force a laugh. 'I suppose.'

'Awkward,' Verity says. 'Do you remember when we first met? That kiss-handshake thing.'

'Yeah,' I nod.

'Awkward!' Verity says, throwing her hands in the air, re-enacting our introduction from a hundred years ago. 'Typical Verity,' she says, the humour appearing to ebb out of her.

'Last night,' I say. 'It's just . . . I've been so busy and my head's . . .' I swirl my hands around my skull to indicate *all over the place, messed up, distracted.*

'Are you seeing someone?'

I shake my head.

Verity stares at me, as if trying to assess the honesty of my answer.

'Cross my heart,' I tell her, doing exactly that. 'I'm not seeing anyone.'

Verity shakes her head. '*I'm looking forward to finding out all about you, Thomas Ferguson,*' she says, her voice breathy and self-mocking. 'Talk about cornballs. No wonder you freaked.'

'Hey, no, it wasn't you.'

'It's not me, it's you, right?'

'Yes. I mean, no, well not like that. Sorry, mixed messages.'

Verity half opens her mouth, half forms a word.

'And I'd hardly say I freaked.'

She holds her thumb a few millimetres from her forefinger. 'Lil bit,' she says.

I shrug that this may be a fair point. 'But here's the thing,' I say, moving half a step closer to her. 'I want to learn all about you too. If that's okay?'

'Yeah,' says Verity, nodding. 'That's okay.'

'Are you going to the wrap party tonight?'

'I could force myself.'

I take hold of Verity's hand. 'Good. And just in case that was another mixed message . . .' I lean in and kiss her, and for a moment everything else fades into the background.

*

We shoot the final shot. Ben gathers everyone into a circle, tells them they've been great, round of applause, *it's a wrap*.

Bianca has a train to catch and we're reversing out of our parking space when Verity knocks on my side window – there's no automatic switch and it takes what seems like an age to manually wind the bugger down.

'I was going to give you this earlier,' Verity says, holding up a paperback. 'But the opportunity never . . . you know. And then I thought I'd give it to you in the pub, later, but I didn't want to embarrass you. So, anyway, here.' Verity passes the book through the open window.

It's shop-new, never read.

They say you can't judge a book by its cover, but, judging by the sprawled bare-breasted woman on the front of this one, it seems the publishers have set out to prove the contrary.

'Henry Miller,' says Verity. 'He wrote that book . . . the one we were talking about last week.'

'What book?' says Bianca.

Sexus.

'And, well, I know how much you like him,' says Verity with a sly smile.

'You're blushing,' says Bianca. 'Why are you blushing?'

'Thank you,' I say to Verity. 'It's perfect.'

Bianca snatches the book from my hand. '*Tropic of Capricorn*? Ha. Uncle Tom's a Capricorn.'

'Is he really?' says Verity with contrived surprise.

'Yeah, Mum used to call him Goat Boy.'

Verity laughs and I put the car into gear.

'I think I'd better get this one to the station,' I say.

Verity blows a kiss across me to Bianca. 'Take care, Goth Girl. See you later, Goat Boy.'

At Euston station I return Bianca's phone battery, and by the time we've unloaded her bags and carried them to the platform, her mobile has beeped the arrival of at least a dozen texts, missed calls and voice messages.

Bianca laughs. 'Sad really, isn't it?'

'Give you something to read on the train,' I say.

'Suppose,' Bianca says, shrugging. 'What was that book all about?'

'The one off Verity?'

'Dur. Which other book would it be?'

'Just a present,' I say. 'For being such a cool guy.'

Bianca rolls her eyes. 'It looked a bit pervy to me.'

'D'you think?'

'I think,' says Bianca, 'that if you don't pull Verity tonight, you're a total and utter div.'

Chapter Thirty-One

The Little Horrors party is at the Goose – maybe twenty people gathered on and around a rough circle of assorted pub furniture in a corner of the pub. A cheer goes up as I approach the group. I hold up my palms in appreciation, take a bow, and Ben shoves a pint of Guinness into my hand.

'*Twixes of Eastwick*,' says Marlon as I nudge into the circle.

'Sweets in movie titles,' says Ben in response to my nonplussed frown.

'You've got to say one or down your drink,' adds Marlon.

'Fair enough,' I say. 'Er . . . *Mars Attacks?*'

'Had it,' says Holly from atop Rob's lap. There's a shortage of seats, but does she really need to bounce up and down on his knee like that?

'*Mutiny on the Bounty?*' I try.

'Had it,' says Ben.

'Ditto *Galaxy Quest, Flake Placid, A Clockwork Terry's Chocolate Orange, Kit Kat on a Hot Tin Roof* and *The Malteser Falcon*,' says Marlon.

'Plus *The Bourneville Identity, Supremacy* and *Ultimatum*,' says Rob from beneath Holly.

'*Marathon Man.*'

'They're Snickers now,' says Marlon.

'But they were Marathons.'

'Overruled,' says everyone.

'*Three Men and a Jelly Baby,*' says Verity.

'Good one,' says Ben.

'*Point Breakaway.*'

'Had it,' says everyone.

'This is a stitch-up.'

'Drink, drink, drink,' they chant.

'*Revels Without a Cause.*'

'Drink.'

I raise my Guinness to my lips as twenty-odd people chant, 'Down in one!' I down it in three, but they cheer nevertheless.

'Bar!' shouts Marlon, holding up an empty glass.

'Come on, big fella,' says Ben, 'I'll give you a hand.'

I raise my eyebrows enquiringly at Verity. She waggles a bottle of Sol and gives a semi-sympathetic smile.

'Meester Tom,' says Christina. 'A long time.'

'He'll have the same again,' says Ben. 'And a London Pride and a Star, cheers.'

'*Muito obrigada.*'

'And a bottle of Sol,' I say.

Ben gives me an appraising look.

'For Verity,' I explain.

Ben persists with the look.

'What?'

Ben shakes his head. 'Nothing.'

'Go on, what?'

'She's a nice girl,' says Ben.

'*And?*'

'*And* nothing. She's an extremely nice girl. That's all.'

My phone rings and I fish it out of my pocket.

'One of your women?' asks Ben.

'No,' I say, turning my phone off. 'Estate agent.'

'Not leaving us, are you?'

'Just need a change,' I say.

Ben puts an arm around my shoulder and pulls me into a tight hug. 'What's that for?' I ask.

'For sorting this out.' Ben takes in the party with a sweep of his arm, sloshing beer from his pint in the process. 'I know I was in two minds about the shoot, but it was . . . not as shit as I expected. So thanks.' And he kisses me on the ear.

'How pissed are you?' I say.

'Don't get any ideas,' Ben says. 'I'm not that kind of girl.'

Christina lines up our drinks and Ben hands me my Guinness.

'I mean it,' Ben says. 'Thanks.' Then he hands me Verity's Sol. He nods at the bottle and looks at me significantly. 'And try not to be a tosser.'

'Well, it won't be easy, Benjamin, but I'll do my best.'

Verity is talking to the cameraman when I hand her her drink, and I end up stuck in a conversation with the soundman, who wants me to read a screenplay he's written. The soundman goes to the toilet, but before I can get to Verity I'm cornered by Rob. And after Rob it's the gaffer, and after the gaffer the spark. Holly appears, kisses me on the cheek and tells me Verity is a 'special person'. 'I know,' I tell her, and glance towards Verity, who is now talking to the soundman, presumably about his screenplay. She smiles and I smile back. Judith the client drags me to the bar and we do a round of tequilas. When we rejoin the gang, Verity is sitting on the sofa between Ben and Marlon. Holly is perched on Rob's knee and the pair of them shift along to make room.

'Oopsy,' says Holly, as Rob shuffles sideways.

'Brace yourself,' says Rob, and the pair of them laugh at their not-entirely-private joke.

'Room for one more on top?' asks Kaz, sitting on my lap and wiggling herself comfortable.

'*The Usual Suspects*,' says Marlon.

'*The Fast and the Furious*,' says the soundman.

'*Mission Impossible*,' says Ben, and everyone laughs.

'What are we playing now?' says Kaz, from on top of my lap.

'Movies that describe your sex life,' says Marlon.

Kaz claps her hands. 'Excellent. Er . . . *For Your Eyes Only*.' And she wiggles just enough for me to feel it.

'*King Kong*,' says Holly, bouncing up and down excitedly.

'*Scream*,' says Rob, and the pair of them kiss.

'*Toy Story*,' says Judith.

'Tom?' says Kaz. 'You're awfully quiet.'

And where to begin? *The Jerk, It's Complicated, The Good, the Bad and the Ugly.*

Verity is obscured from my view by Kaz's back, which helps a little but not enough.

'Thomas?' says Ben. 'Not shy, are we?'

'Would be a first,' says Kaz, half under her breath.

And this must be how it feels to walk a plank.

'*A Series of Unfortunate Events*,' I try, receiving a mixture of groans, laughter and a sympathetic coo from Holly.

'*Enter the Dragon*,' says a voice I can't identify.

'Meester Tom,' says a Brazilian voice, and for a second I think it must be a movie I have never heard of.

'Phone call for Meester Tom,' says Christina.

I slither out from under Kaz to a chorus of boos and jeers and whistles, and follow Christina to the bar.

'A woman,' says Christina, pouting.

Yvette!

'Shit,' I say. 'Can you say I'm not here?'

'Too late, Meester Tom.' Cristina hands me a cordless handset, winks, and sashays to the opposite end of the bar.

I hold the phone like a giant poisonous insect, and bring it slowly, reluctantly, to my ear.

'Hello?'

'Meester Tom,' says the voice on the other end of the line.

Christina is still behind the bar, serving drinks.

'Sorry? Hello?'

'About those mixed messages,' says the voice.

I glance around the bar, looking for a clue.

'Outside,' says the voice.

Standing on the opposite side of the road, phone to her ear, is Verity. She waves. I hang up.

Yes, snogging on public transport is embarrassing. No, I don't care. We're not devouring each other like European backpackers, but we definitely deserve it when some wag suggests we get a room. And that's when the nerves kick in. Standing outside the Goose, I suggested we find a quiet bar somewhere. Verity laughed and reminded me that this was central London on a Thursday night in the middle of summer. So I suggested my place. If not the last thing on my mind, sex wasn't the first thing either. And I think – *hope* – Verity understood that. Now, though, with the words *get a room* ringing in my ears, there is a palpable, charged anticipation between us.

We walk to my flat hand in hand, and despite the warm night I find myself shivering gently. It feels good – intimate somehow. When we arrive it's dark behind the glass panels of Doug's front door. I hold a finger to my lips.

'Secret woman?' whispers Verity.

'Secret man,' I say, carefully shutting the porch door. 'I'll introduce you tomorrow, if you like.'

Verity inclines her head. 'A little presumptuous, aren't we?'

Still whispering: 'I didn't mean . . .'

Verity widens her eyes and purses her lips in an expression of indulgent cynicism. I place my hands on her shoulders, push her, gently, against the wall, kiss her. Verity presses her face into me and there's something different in this kiss, something that incites me to hook my fingers into the waistband of her jeans and pull her hips hard against mine. My fingertips brush what might be an embroidered bow on the front of her underwear and her belly is cold and tight against the backs of my fingers. My free hand drifts up the side of Verity's body and before I get where I intend to go, she puts a hand on my chest and pushes me a step backwards.

'I don't want to say I don't normally do this kind of thing, but . . .'

'Sorry,' I say, 'I don't mean to . . . I'm in no hurry.'

'Sometimes, it takes a while to see a person,' Verity says. 'The *real* person. That's all. I like to know who I'm with before I . . . before I'm with them. If you follow.'

'Yeah,' I say. 'Sure. I didn't mean to be pushy.'

Verity takes hold of both my hands in hers. 'People are weird on dates. They say what they think you want to hear. Chew with their mouths closed. Pretend to be interested.' Verity shrugs. 'Thing is . . . we haven't been on any dates.'

'We could?'

Verity shakes her head, but she's smiling. 'I've seen you with your sister, though. With Ben, with the kids at the casting. And . . . well, I feel like I do know you. Getting to, anyway.'

'And you're still here?' I say.

Verity kisses me. She presses her hips forward into mine. She whispers in my ear: 'Let's go upstairs.'

I open the door at the foot of the stairs. 'They creak,' I whisper, tiptoeing upwards. 'Especially the fourth one up.'

'Déjà vu,' says Verity as we walk into the flat.

I kick off my trainers and drop my keys into the glass bowl. 'Drink?'

'Would tea be terribly unromantic?'

'Depends how you drink it,' I say, leading Verity through the living room and into the kitchen.

I click on the kettle.

And something is . . . wrong.

'Julie Andrews,' says Verity.

'Did you just say "Julie Andrews"?'

'Milk no sugar,' says Verity, pointing at the mug in my hand. 'White nun.'

'Funny,' I say distractedly.

Because something . . . is not quite right.

I open the fridge and remove the milk. Verity pushes herself up to sit on the countertop. Beside the sink is a corkscrew and an open bottle of red wine, half drunk.

Last night we drank white . . .

'Something the matter?' asks Verity.

'Just tired,' I say, opening a cupboard to get teabags.

'This is a bit embarrassing,' says a voice behind me.

The voice isn't Verity's and I turn around so fast that I crack my head on the cupboard door.

'Shit!'

'Mind your head,' says Yvette from the kitchen doorway. She is holding an empty wine glass, one of my T-shirts hanging halfway down her bare thighs. 'Are you going to introduce us?' she says.

My mind reels as it tries to process what's happening. My heart rate spikes as if at a violent threat, my balance feels precarious, I feel like I'm going to throw up. And at the same time a rational part of me is saying, *You did this, you caused this, you deserve this.*

I look from Yvette to Verity, who is holding one hand to her mouth and the other across her belly, a gesture of incomprehension and alarm. She looks at me as if I am a complete stranger.

'What is this?' she says. 'What's going on here?'

I turn on Yvette. 'What are you doing here? What the *hell* are you doing here?!'

'Me?' asks Yvette. 'What about her!'

'She's . . . she's my . . .'

'She's Verity,' says Verity, sliding off the countertop. She walks straight at Yvette, who shrinks back against the door frame to let her past.

'Verity,' I call after her. 'Verity, wait. Just give me a second.' I go to follow Verity but she halts me with an outstretched palm, and her eyes reflect the absolute depth of my own self-loathing.

'You two have a lovely night,' Verity says, and walks out of the kitchen.

I wait, braced, for the door to bang, but the sound doesn't come.

Yvette touches my arm. 'Tom, I th—'

I jerk my arm away from her. 'Put some clothes on,' I say through gritted teeth. 'And get the fuck out of my flat.'

Yvette winces. 'I thought we could talk. I thought we were going to talk.'

'I mean it,' I say, pushing past her. 'If you're here when I get back I'm calling the police.'

I snatch up my keys and thunder down the stairs.

There's no sign of Verity. My first thought is that she must have jumped into a cab, or run, but then I check behind me and see her heading the wrong way down the road. I shout after her but she doesn't stop or turn. Just shrinks further and smaller away from me.

Running in my stocking feet, I never take my eyes from Verity, regardless of what I might step in or on. I call her name twice more before I catch up.

'Verity,' I say, drawing level with her, 'please.'

Verity doesn't look at me, doesn't acknowledge my existence.

'Verity. Can we please talk?'

She turns left – the way you'd go if you were looking for drugs or for trouble.

'Verity, let me at least explain.'

The air has become chilly and the pavement is cold and hard beneath my socks.

'You said you weren't seeing anyone,' Verity says, and her voice is hard and hurt. 'You stood there and crossed your heart. You're just a selfish, manipulative liar.'

'She's my estate agent,' I say.

Verity laughs, a short exhalation without any trace of humour. An expression of disdain.

'I slept with her. Once. But it was weeks ag—'

Verity stops, turns to face me. 'Lucky her.'

'It was j—'

'You don't have to explain yourself to me,' says Verity. 'I just wanted someone to . . . to take me to bed, okay? And you seemed the easiest option.'

'Verity, pl—'

'But it looks like I got you wrong, after all. Doesn't it?'

She starts walking and I follow.

'Verity, it's not safe out here,' I say.

'Thank you for your concern. Now will you leave me alone, please.'

'I'll walk you to the tube.'

'I'd rather you didn't. I'd rather you weren't anywhere near me.'

'Verity—'

'Tom,' she spits the word and it stops me like a steel trap. 'Leave me alone *right now*, or I'll scream.'

I watch her walk away until she turns the corner. I don't call her name again but follow at a distance until she reaches the station, and Verity doesn't look back once.

Traipsing back to the flat, I'm just approaching Chaucer Road when the silence is shattered by the violent bang of a slamming door. I trot the last few paces, turning the corner just in time to see a small figure scurrying into the distance. Dread lurches through me, and I pat frantically at my jeans before locating the lump of keys in my pocket. It does little to stem the surge of adrenalin pumping through me, though, and I jog the rest of the way to the flat.

Yvette has left the porch unlocked and there is a light on inside Doug's flat now. I hear him curse and a door bangs. I stand rooted to the spot, waiting for something to happen, but nothing does. A toilet flushes inside Doug's flat, a door bangs again and the light is turned off.

In the darkened porch I find the key to my door, and I know, even before I attempt to push it into the lock, that it's wrong. That part of my brain that recognised something was rotten just ten very long minutes ago, now that same lobe covers its eyes and shakes its head. The key doesn't fit. I try to force it into the keyhole nevertheless, but it won't go. Of course it won't go; I've picked up Sadie's old set of keys. The keys she gave me when I gave her the Mini. Keys that fit the old lock – the lock I had changed a month ago.

Doug has a spare. I stand in front of his door, fist raised, ready to knock, frozen like a dummy. He would give me hell, but he would give me my key. Whatever else I do tonight, though, I'm not getting Doug out of bed again.

Yvette, of course, has a key. But my mobile is in the flat along with my keys and my wallet. The door at the bottom of the stairs is a heavy-duty fire door. It's unlikely I could knock it off its hinges. But even if I could, I'd make so much noise I might just as well knock on Doug's door. I could walk to El's house, six miles in my socks, throw stones at his window, sleep on his sofa. It's eleven forty-three, I'd be there by, what, one thirty a.m.? Two?

Verity will be on the tube now, accelerating away from me.

And I've caused enough of a disturbance for one evening.

Short of risking my life and climbing the drainpipe in my socks, I'm out of options. If I extend my arms left and right I can touch the walls on either side with my fingertips. Front to back the porch is smaller, maybe four feet deep. A cell. I lie down on the floor, curl up in a tight ball and fold the doormat double into a pillow. It's cold but it's not freezing; I'll most likely live.

I count to one hundred, forwards and back. I count in French and then in Roman numerals. And then I start all over again until I slip into something approaching sleep.

I wake as the porch door slams closed.

I feel like I've been clubbed across the temples; the right side of my body – the side I'm lying on – is six feet of bruise; my spine is twisted junk. Even if I wanted to jump up and run after Doug, I couldn't do it. It takes me several minutes and failed attempts to get upright and crack myself into something like a straight line. I bend at the knees and my joints creak and pop. I reach for my toes but they're too far away. I stretch my thighs. I kick the fire door at the bottom of the stairs and I think I break my toes.

I don't wear a watch and it could be anything o'clock as I limp to the high street. It must be early – not all the shops are open, not all the tramps have crawled from beneath their hedges – somewhere between eight and nine a.m.

I'm sitting on his doorstep when the locksmith turns up to open shop.

'Locked out?' he says, glancing at my filthy socks.

'How did you guess?'

It takes him less than ten seconds to pick my lock, and five minutes to write an invoice for eighty quid.

'You have to see the funny side,' he says.

I shut the door on him, and I've almost made it to the toilet when I step on a jag of broken glass.

Yvette has been busy. The wine bottle, the wine glass and two mugs float in a billion shards in a pool of milk and red wine. I limp bloody footprints through the living room to the bathroom, run a bath and lie in it until long after the water has lost its heat. I keep my phone beside me at all times, but it doesn't ring, no one calls. My big toe has turned purple and I should probably get an X-ray, but what difference would it make?

My old diary is in the bedside drawer, where it's been since Sadie found it six months ago and added her own pithy entry: *Eighty-six, fuck your sad self.* It was good advice and I should have taken it. I tear the diary into pieces and throw them into the bin with the mess of broken glass and blood-soaked kitchen roll.

I don't call Verity. Because what would I say? Surely the truth is worse than any conclusion she might have already come to.

I phone Dad, and he goes straight into: 'Who's this Verity I've been hearing about?' *Just someone,* I tell him. No, she's not my girlfriend. When I say I'm thinking of coming home for the weekend, Dad says Bianca is staying at a friend's and he has plans for tonight – something at the church. He offers to cancel, but I tell him not to.

Maybe it's best that no one's around tonight – I'm not in a particularly gregarious frame of mind – but I do feel the need to be far away from here, so I pack a bag and head out the door.

Chapter Thirty-Two

I still have Doug's car keys, but I was too embarrassed to face him, not shameless enough to ask if I can borrow his car again. Besides, I can drink coffee on the train, stare out of the window, think. As the scenery rolls past I listen to the Supersuckers on my iPhone, the Pixies, the Ramones, Smashing Pumpkins. It's not really my thing, but then again, it would seem neither is Verity. Or at any rate, I'm not hers.

Henry Miller has been riding beside me, not saying much, but I sense his disapproval wafting up through the pages of *Tropic of Capricorn*. Perhaps he still resents me for allowing my father to discover and subsequently burn him two decades ago. Or perhaps his contempt stems from my utter ineptitude as a debaucher. Well, I hear ya, Henry. I guess my heart wasn't in it, after all. Another lump of flesh, for sure, but not my heart.

I pick up the book and start reading.

No sex happens in the first twenty pages. The language is pretty ripe, particularly considering the book was written eighty years ago, but other than that there's not much to get excited about. On page twenty-eight, in a casual aside, the author mentions his prolific and indiscriminate sexual appetite, but there's no detail, no titillation, no satisfaction. I'm determined, however, to see this through to the bitter three-hundred-and-seventeen-page end. It's my only link to Verity – maybe it contains answers, clues, redemption, an epiphany, I don't know. A family-sized packet of Opal Fruits and litre of coffee later, Henry Miller has fucked six women (one of them his wife) and practically fisted another. But it's not as romantic or as enlightening as it sounds.

※

Dad is excited to see me and offers again to cancel his arrangements, but I tell him I'm exhausted and planning on having an early night. He opens a bottle of wine anyway, and we drink a glass in the garden before he leaves for a fundraiser at the church hall. Bianca, he says, has talked non-stop about the shoot, and is now considering applying for courses in media studies, and film production and cinematography. I apologise for this, but Dad is in fact delighted. He says that Bianca was also 'particularly taken with a certain . . . Verity?' But I don't take the bait and Dad lets it be. Bianca is going clubbing tonight, with her father's consent, and will be staying overnight with a friend, so neither of us will have to witness or deal with the aftermath.

Dad leaves a little after seven, and I take the wine through to the living room and open a box of unsorted photographs.

There is a snap of me at a family farm in Brittany. I'm twelve years old, sitting on an upturned box, milking a goat with matted brown fur. I'm clearly terrified, milking at fully extended arm's length, leaning so far back that it looks as if I'm about to fall off my crate. But I didn't. I remember it vividly. Mum laughed in that infectious way she had – biting her bottom lip; her hands clasped, palms together, between her thighs. What was I afraid of, she asked. After all, wasn't I a Capricorn? She called me Goat Boy and made little horns with her fingers. A real memory, not just a reimagining of the photograph.

I put the photo back in the box, pour myself another glass of wine and flick on the TV. A game show, a panel show, a hospital drama, a talent contest, a canned-laughter sitcom, repeats from the '80s, repeats from last week, the hundred-best somethings, celebrities making arses of themselves, a romantic fucking comedy. I turn off the TV with one hand and empty my glass with the other. Dad buys crap wine and I'm nowhere near done for the night, so I pull on my trainers and limp off in the direction of the Old Bull.

From my table in the corner, I count fourteen people including Susan Chambers and Steve, the proprietor. They're all in groups of two and three and four. And then there's me. Tonight I could have been with Verity. Maybe we spent the day sunbathing in Brockwell Park. Or rowing a boat in Putney. Ice creams and cold beers, that kind of thing. Or maybe just stayed in bed. Tonight we could have gone out for cocktails. Dressed up for a posh meal. Ordered a pizza and rented a movie. But no, none of that. I fucked it all well and truly up, and now I'm drinking on my own like little Jack no mates. I check my phone for messages, and it's no big surprise to find there aren't any. Yvette called earlier, twice, and I let it go through to voicemail each time. I sent a text saying we'd talk next week and in the meantime to post my keys through the letter box.

I open a blank message, key in Verity, Hi, and immediately delete it.
I'm sorry
Delete.
I'd like to explain
Delete.
I'm a fucking idiot
True, but delete.

I order a second pint from the bar and ask Susan for a piece of paper and a pen. 'Not going to give her your number, are you?' jokes Steve. 'Declan won't be happy.' Steve laughs at his own joke, while Susan tears a sheet of paper from an order pad and passes it across the bar along with a chewed biro.

At my table I write the numbers *1* to *98* in four columns, two on each side of the page. Number 1 – *Trudi Roberts*. Could Trudi have been the one for me? I run a horizontal line through her name. Number 2 – *Lisa McAllister*. Was Lisa my soulmate? Another crossed-out name. Number 3 – *Samantha Fawcett*, score her out. After Dad told me I was an accident, it occurred to me how lucky we are to have the time we have, and it irritated me that I'd wasted half a year on a puerile pursuit. But as I fill in names on my list, it occurs to me that I've wasted a good deal more than six months. I'm up to Number 49 – *Gale ???* when Susan appears at my table and asks if I'd like another.

'Excuse me?' I say, covering the list with my elbow.

'Another Guinness?' says Susan, picking up my empty glass.

'Right,' I say. 'Why not?'

'I'll bring it over,' says Susan, smiling.

'Are you sure?'

'It'll give me something to do,' she says, taking in the quiet bar with a nod of her head.

Susan is everyday pretty – off-blonde hair gathered into a tight ponytail, small nose, even teeth. Nothing to stand her out in a crowd, but there's no crowd here. She's certainly a damn sight more than Deck Chambers deserves.

I pick up the pen, print *Keeley Alexander* next to the number 50, then cross her out with a wiggly line. I'm about to turn the page when I see it . . .

Number 1 – *Trudi Roberts*

. . . and my mind makes the connection.

I remember how things changed after Trudi. How I acquired a degree of popularity at school, leaving behind the timid teacher's son who dreaded lunchtimes in case someone threw rocks at his head. I arrived at university with three notches on my bedpost and my ego located firmly between my legs. And it's not my fault. Blame Deck fucking Chambers, but don't blame me.

I screw up the list and take the borrowed pen back to the bar, where Steve is holding court with a couple of regulars.

'Thought I'd save you a trip,' I say to Susan as she tops off my Guinness.

I ask if Deck is planning to pop in tonight, and Susan says he's driving a lorryload of kitchen fittings to London. Probably passed him on the way up, I joke. Steve asks what I've been up to in 'the big shitty', and I tell everyone about the Little Horrors shoot. They listen with a flattering reverence. 'You're practically famous,' says Steve, and insists on buying me a drink. Eleven thirty comes and goes and Steve locks us in, me and him and his two buddies who laugh at his quips and concur with his shifting opinions. Susan's kids are staying overnight at their granny's, so she agrees to join us for a drink. I'm buying, I say.

Susan's top rides up her waist as she reaches for the vodka optic. The black trim of her bra shows around the neckline of her vest; she has freckles on her white cleavage.

Someone asks if I have a girlfriend, and I say no.

Steve starts to pour a new round of drinks but Susan has to go; drink goes straight to her head, she says, and she has to pick up the kiddies first thing in the morning. She calls a cab but both the local firms' cars are out on jobs. 'I'll walk you home,' I tell her, 'it's hardly even out of my way.' Everyone agrees that I'm a proper gentleman.

'It's not as warm as I thought,' says Susan shortly after we set off walking.

'I'd give you my jacket,' I say, 'but I don't have one.'

Susan laughs.

'Here' – I hold out my arm, crooked at the elbow – 'we'll keep each other warm.'

Susan hooks up next to me. 'Are you limping?'

'Stubbed my toe,' I say.

We walk and limp on for a minute before Susan breaks the silence. 'So what brings you home?'

'Just fancied getting away from London.'

'I've never been,' she says.

'To London?'

Susan's ponytail lashes right, left, right as she shakes her head.

'Deck never taken you?'

'Too expensive,' says Susan.

'You don't know what you're missing,' I say, and where her arm is threaded through mine I squeeze her incrementally tighter.

The moon is bright enough to see a fox saunter across the road fifty yards ahead of us. I steer Susan through a twisting, hedge-lined cut-through, and it's not for the one minute we'll shave off the walk time.

'Scary,' says Susan, leaning in closer against me.

'And you all alone in that house,' I say.

'Stop it,' she says, elbowing me playfully.

I stop walking and Susan, anchored to my side, jolts to a halt beside me. 'What's up?' she says in a frightened whisper.

I turn her to face me. 'I wondered if you needed any company tonight.'

It's darker here than on the street but our faces are close enough that I can smell the vodka on Susan's breath, and I can see the trepidation in her eyes. Susan doesn't ask me what I mean by 'company'. She doesn't say she's married. She doesn't say anything. I hold her by both biceps, and we stand like that in silence for a count of seconds.

I kiss her, tentatively; politely almost.

Susan looks up at me. 'I shouldn't,' she says.

I kiss her again and her lips are stiff and dry . . .

Not like Verity's lips.

. . . our teeth clash and we both apologise.

'I don't know if we should,' Susan says, but her hands are still on my waist, mine still holding her arms.

'It's just a kiss,' I say.

That's what I told Sadie after I kissed Holly. *Just a kiss*. And look where it led. Here, kissing a married mother-of-two in a back alley.

'I remember you from school,' says Susan. 'You were tall.'

'Still am.'

She laughs nervously. 'You seemed nice.'

Declan Chambers deserves this, but not Susan.

And what about Verity? What about me?

'Yeah, well, looks can be deceiving,' I say. 'Come on, I'm supposed to be walking you home.'

'You won't tell your sister, will you?'

'Just a kiss goodnight,' I say. 'Nothing to tell.'

'Yeah,' says Susan. 'Just goodnight.'

We walk the rest of the way with our hands in our pockets, and I watch Susan to her door from the end of the road.

It's almost an hour into Sunday when I get back to Dad's place. He's asleep in his chair, a bottle of whisky and an empty glass beside him. The glassware clinks when I pick it up, and Dad wakes with a start.

'Thomas,' he says, rubbing his eyes. 'Time is it?'

'Nearly one.'

'Pinch punch first of the month,' Dad says – one of my mother's tics, and we both smile at the reference. He nods at the bottle in my hand. 'You want a drink, son?'

'I'll make tea,' I say. 'Do you want tea?'

'Aye, go on.'

Dad follows me into the kitchen. 'You're out late,' he says. 'Thought you were staying in.'

'Went to the Bull.'

I take two mugs from the cupboard beside the sink and drop tea-bags into them. 'Déjà vu,' Verity said last night as we walked into the flat. I touch my head and there's a lump on my temple where I banged it on my kitchen cupboard twenty-four hours ago.

Dad hands me a carton of milk from the fridge. 'Steve have a lock-in, did he?' His voice is groggy with sleep and drink.

Over the few days I've spent in this house this year, Dad must have consumed an entire bottle of whisky. Maybe more. Plus wine, plus beer.

'Dad?'

'Son?'

'I'm worried that you might drink too much.'

Dad rubs a big paw back and forth across his face, and his stubble rasps against his palm. 'I could drink less, son, aye. But you don't need to worry. That's my job,' he says, laughing.

'I do, though – worry.'

Dad smiles. 'I don't drink for a long time, son, and then . . . some-times, I do. Had a few yourself, hey?'

'It's not about me, is it?'

'You can get pissed and I can't, is that right?' Dad's voice is calm.

The kettle boils and I pour water into the mugs.

'Other than tonight,' Dad says, 'I haven't had a drink since . . . not since last time you were down.'

'Mum's anniversary?' I say.

'And before that . . . I don't know when.' He nods to the whisky bottle on the countertop, blows air out the corner of his mouth and shrugs. 'But, aye, sometimes . . .'

'So what's the occasion tonight?'

'Saw the photographs out,' Dad says. 'Reminiscing, I suppose.'

I spoon out the teabags, add milk to both mugs, sugar to Dad's.

'You and that goat, son. You were terrified, hey?'

'Pretty scared, yeah.'

We carry our tea through to the living room. Dad sits on the sofa instead of his armchair. I sit down next to him.

'You're limping, son.'

'Stubbed my toe.'

'Show me.'

'It's fine,' I say. 'It's nothing.'

'Let your da see his boy's foot, Tom.'

I kick off my trainer and put my foot in Dad's lap. He rolls down my sock and winces when he sees the swollen toe. 'Looks broken,' he says. 'You should have an X-ray.'

'They'd only tell me to rest it.'

'You've cut it too,' he says, gently touching the wound on the ball of my foot. 'Does it hurt?'

'It's fine.'

Dad waggles his mug. 'Probably anaesthetised?'

I laugh. 'Probably.'

'You've been in the wars, son,' he says, stroking my foot.

'You could say that.'

Dad goes to stand. 'I'll get the TCP.'

'It'll keep,' I say. 'Drink your tea.'

We're quiet for a while, sipping our tea, and I feel somehow calmed by this contact. Like stepping off a fairground waltzer onto solid ground. I'm tired, and sore, and stupid, and I'm getting an early hangover, but I feel . . . I don't know, *lighter*. The box of photographs is sitting beside Dad's armchair; maybe tomorrow I'll take a few back to London.

'Penny for them,' says Dad.

He rubs my toes absentmindedly, and even now, nine years after Mum's death, he still wears his wedding ring. I put my other foot into his lap.

'Do you think Mum was, you know, "The One"?'

'Yes and no,' says Dad. 'I don't know if there was someone else in God's whole wide world I could have been equally as happy with.

Loved. Probably there is.' He shrugs, apologetically almost. 'But no one more than your mother.'

'How do you know?'

'It just isn't in me, Tom. To love anyone more than I loved her.'

'How can you be positive that there wasn't someone who . . . I don't know . . . someone else?'

'I was engaged to be married before I met your mother, you know.'

'Yeah, when you were in college.'

'Theresa Howells, aye. And she wasn't my first girlfriend either, you know.' He says this in a way that implies 'girlfriend' is a euphemism. 'I'd slept with other girls, son,' he says, just in case I didn't get it.

I nod my head in a way intended to demonstrate that I find this neither surprising nor shocking. I doubt it's very convincing, but it feels like the appropriate thing to do.

Dad continues: 'And then I met Theresa Howells. And she was confident and clever and funny, she made all the girls before her seem like . . . well, like girls. Do you understand me?'

'I think so.'

'Well, when I met your mother, it was like that times a hundred.'

'But how do you know you wouldn't love someone else a hundred times more than you loved Mum?'

'Because it simply isn't in me, son. The way I couldn't jump out of that window and fly. It's . . . it's like laughing, I think. You can only laugh so hard, you know. Or cry. You have your limits. And your mum was mine, son.'

There are tears in Dad's eyes when he says this, but he's smiling too. And I believe him completely.

'Sadie left me because I cheated on her,' I say.

Dad doesn't say anything, just rubs my feet.

'Well, I told her, and then she returned the favour, and then she left me.'

'Had her pound of flesh, did she?'

'You could say that,' I say, trying not to dwell on Dad's unfortunate turn of phrase. 'No more than I deserved.'

'Do you miss her, son?'

I shake my head, and Dad smiles. 'Someone else?'

'There might have been. But I think I've . . . I think I've fucked that up, too.'

Dad stares at me for a moment. He looks tired.

'You're not going to smack me for swearing are you?' I say.

Dad slaps my leg playfully.

'Maybe you should pray for me.'

'Always do, son.'

'You know I don't believe in' – I point upwards – 'all of that?'

Dad nods, smiles. 'Doesn't matter, son. Just be good. Be honest.'

'I was honest with Sadie, and look where that got me.'

'Got you out of the wrong relationship, didn't it?'

'Yeah, I suppose it did.'

'So, Daffy . . .' He smiles. 'What's the plan?'

I hold up my mug. 'Another?'

'Yeah,' says Dad. 'That'd be nice.'

JULY

Chapter Thirty-Three

'Muggins?' says Doug, collecting together the dominoes, turning them face down and mixing the set. He's referring to a variation of gameplay, rather than to himself or, for that matter, me.

'Whatever tickles your fancy,' I tell him, placing two fresh pints on the table.

'Less loose ends,' he says. 'All threes or fives?'

'Let's do threes?'

We draw our tiles and Doug kicks off with the double three. 'Six,' he says, scribbling the score in his small notebook.

Eileen texted again while I was on the train down to Dad's, and again while I made the return trip. The woman has a one-track mind and she's issued a deadline. And the deadline is today.

'How's Eileen?' I ask, opting for direct.

'She seems fine.'

'You know what I mean.'

'Nine points,' says Doug, noting down my score.

'I mean how are *you* and Eileen?' I try, opting for even more direct.

Doug inspects his tiles, makes a gruff sound that could mean anything or nothing at all.

'Sorry about the other night,' I say. 'All the . . . you know, *drama*.'

'Aye, you said. It's fine. You're young.'

'And stupid?'

Douglas sips his bitter, wipes foam from his top lip. 'We were all weetchils once,' he says.

And I tell him everything. I don't leave out a detail. He is the only person I have talked to about the whole sorry mess. El knows about the numbers, Ben knows about Kaz and Holly, Bianca knows about Verity, Dad knows about Sadie. But this is the first time I've laid the whole thing out, bare, if you like. Doug listens and nods and sips his drink. He calls me a fool, a dope, an eejit, a doitit divil and a daft beggar – but he does so sympathetically. And anyway, he's absolutely right. When I get to the bit about Yvette and Verity and sleeping in the porch and breaking my toe and standing on glass, Doug calls me a halfwit but he says it in a paternal, compassionate way. I tell about him going to my dad's, about Susan from the Old Bull.

'Ye've been busy,' Doug says.

'That's one way of putting it. Another way would be I've been . . .' I try to think of a suitable description, but I thinks Doug's exhausted all the available options. 'I've made a lot of mistakes,' I tell him.

'Did ye learn anything?'

'Other than the fact I'm an eejit?'

Doug pats me on the shoulder. 'Don't be too hard on yeself. That's what I'm here for.'

'Thank you,' I tell him. 'Can I ask you a question?'

'Aye.'

'What went wrong in Lyme Regis?'

'Who said anything went wrong?'

'No one. It's just that, up until then everything seemed tickety-boo.'

'Tickety-boo? Do folk still say that?'

'Just trying to get down to your level.'

Doug smiles, shows me the back of his hand. 'I'll knock ye doon a level.'

'Lyme Regis,' I say. 'You're avoiding the question.'

I hate putting Doug on the spot like this, but I can't think of another way to move on.

'Doug, we're friends, right?'

'Aye, I like to think so.'

'What would you have said, if I'd told you all that bullshit about the bet? About one hundred women?'

Doug plays a domino but doesn't score. 'I'd've told ye t'screw your head on right,' he says, shaking his head. 'That's for sure.'

'And you'd have saved me a shitload of trouble, Doug. You'd have liked Verity.'

'Aye, she sounds like a guid yin.'

'She is. And if I'd told you what I was doing four months ago, maybe you could have got to meet her.'

'Would ye have listened?'

I shrug. 'Who knows. Maybe. Twelve points. So?'

'So what, lad?'

'So what happened in Lyme Regis?'

'Precisely' – Doug plays his own tile, another no score – 'nothing.' He looks at me, letting his gaze give his words context.

'Because? Is Eileen not . . . interested?'

'Oh, she's interested, lad. Very interested.'

And this is it, Thomas: now or never time.

I reach into my back pocket, produce the box of Viagra and place them among the dominoes. 'Do you know what these are?'

Doug looks at the tablets like they might be lethal. He looks at me but his expression is as blank as the back of the domino in his hand.

'Viagra,' I say.

'What are you doing with those?'

'A friend gave them to me,' I say.

'What? Do ye have . . . issues?'

'Not exactly. Not like that. But they're . . . recreationally,' I say, 'they're kind of *in*.'

'In?'

'Popular. With clubbers and whatnot.'

Doug lays down his domino and picks up the pack of pills, turning it over in his hands as if examining an item of intricate marquetry. 'I'm no much of a clubber,' he says.

I'm just about to congratulate myself when Doug's expression changes, first into bewilderment, then hardening into frustration and anger.

'Y've a damn nerve,' he says, slapping the box down on the table with enough force to slop beer from both our glasses. 'A barefaced bloody nerve. The pair o' yous.'

Pair of us?

'Doug?'

He stands up from the table, points a finger at me, goes to say something then changes his mind, clenches his hand into a tight fist and walks away. I call after him one more time, but Doug is gone. My life seems to be stuck in a repeating pattern of people walking away from me, more often than not disappointed, angry, upset, or all of the above.

I pick up the box of tablets to put it in my pocket. I have never examined it before, but now my eyes land on the small adhesive label stuck to the side. As well as the instruction to *Take as directed by your doctor*, is the patient's name. *Frederick Turnbull.* Eileen's husband Fred died before she met Douglas, and like most widows she has retained her deceased partner's surname – so you really don't need to be a professional sleuth to connect the name on this box to the woman Doug's been dating.

Chapter Thirty-Four

'So,' says Ben, 'what happened?'

We're sitting in a darkened room, drinking too much coffee, watching dozens of takes of dozens of shots, looking for the best bite, scream, smile, kiss. There's up to an hour of footage per commercial, and we're trying to find the best thirty-second combination. Attempting to stitch it all together so it makes any kind of sense.

What happened?

Took Verity home, humiliated her, slept rough, broke my toe, pulled my former bully's wife, cried over old photos with Dad.

'Not much,' I say.

The only light in the editing suite comes from a playback monitor about the size of a small portable TV, and even this is largely obscured by the silhouetted head of Vernon, our editor.

It's too dark to see Ben sneer, but I'm certain I hear his lips curl.

'She went back to yours, though?'

I say nothing.

'Right?' Ben tries again.

'Right,' I say. 'She came back to mine.'

'And?'

'How about this one?' says Vernon's silhouette, a pencil bobbing up and down in his mouth. On screen, Albert looms along a torch-lit dungeon corridor.

'Perfect,' says Ben to Vernon. 'Fuck her?' he says to me.

'Fuck you.'

'Is that a yes?'

'Not that it's any of your business,' I say, 'but, no, I didn't *fuck her.*'

Ben grunts. A sound that says, *Well, there's a turn-up.*

I think about what Dad said about honesty.

'I've got a confession,' I say to the black outline of Ben, and I have a flash of me at twelve telling Father McKinley about the mucky book I hid under the carpet in my bedroom.

'You shagged Kaz,' says Ben.

Vernon spins dials, clacks his keyboard. Maybe it's the darkness, my invisibility, but I'm unperturbed by his presence. The professional discretion of priests and doctors and editors.

'You asking or telling?'

Ben laughs. 'I'm knowing. You're many things, my friend, but difficult to read isn't one of them.'

'Right.'

'Here's a good one,' says Vernon, as Albert gurns from the playback monitor.

'Nice one,' says Ben. 'Try it in between the close-up and that wide shot on the walkway.'

'Right-o,' says Vernon. 'Funny little bugger, isn't he?'

'You can say that again,' says Ben.

I sigh long and noisily through my nose because it seems like an appropriate thing to do.

'I like her,' I say into the darkness.

'Which one?' says Ben.

'Oh, piss off. You know who I mean.'

Vernon clears his throat. 'Take a look at this,' he says, and runs a thirty-second edit of Frankenstein's Albert.

The film isn't graded yet, there are no sound effects, no music, no voice-over, but that's not what's bothering me. The film feels awkward. Disjointed.

'Not working, is it?' I say.

Ben ho-hums. 'I think it's the close-up. It throws the rhythm all out.'

'Well, we can't have our rhythm all out,' I say. 'It's not decent.'

'Want me to shave a few frames off?' asks Vernon.

'Go for it.'

Vern twiddles knobs and presses buttons. 'Right-o, how's about . . . this . . .'

'Much better,' says Ben.

And it is. It's remarkable, in fact, just how much difference the loss of even the smallest moment can make.

'So,' says Ben, 'what are you going to do about it? About Verity?'

'I'm really not sure.'

Because the only thing I can conceive of that might possibly work is figuring out a way to shave a substantial number of frames from the bloody awful mess that is my bloody awful life. But I don't think that machine's been invented yet.

Chapter Thirty-Five

One thousand pounds in one-pound coins weighs nine point five kilos. It doesn't sound like much, but my backpack feels like it's dragging my arm out of the socket. Maybe it's all the psychological weight on top of the physical.

'Whass in the bag?' El asks.

'Surprise,' I tell him.

'Not movin in, are you?'

Phil has been chilling a miniature bottle of Moët for me – two hundred millilitres of bubbles between the three of us; it's not much, but El can't handle much. And besides, it isn't much of a celebration.

On Sunday I spent the train ride back to London psyching myself up to call Verity. But my practice run-through sounded like so much insincere, low-budget romcom horseshit . . . and every time I ran through it the budget became smaller and smaller until, eventually, there was nothing left and the sound of my voice made me want to pull my teeth out. Last night, I spent two hours writing a six-page letter. More than a thousand handwritten words that sounded more incriminating than mitigating and ended up in shreds in the bin. I'm running out of time and options.

Phil carries the bubbly and three glasses into the living room on a silver tray.

'Explanaishun,' says El, both feet tapping, head jiggling like a nodding car ornament.

Phil shrugs as he opens the bottle, a plastic screw cap that gives with a hiss not a pop. 'I am merely a dumb but beautiful assistant,' he says.

'Half right,' says El.

'I am rather intrigued, though,' says Phil, distributing the glasses. 'I thought perhaps you'd brought proof of a mission accomplished.'

'A head,' says El.

'You're not far wrong,' I say, standing and unzipping the bag, and I begin to pour the coins onto the sheepskin rug. 'A thousand heads, every one a queen.'

Neither Phil nor El speak as the coins shish and clink into a spreading pile at my feet. Phil looks confused but amused, El merely delighted – although he shows no sign of having grasped the significance of the bronze spill forming on the carpet. I shake the last few coins out of the bag and raise my glass.

'Cheers.'

'Is iss real champagne?' asks El.

'Sure is.'

'D'you rob an ice-cream van?' He points a finger pistol at my head. 'Gimme the niney-nines or'll blow y'brains out.'

'Ninety-eights,' I say.

'Ahh,' says Phil, 'the penny drops.'

I kick my foot through the mound of pound coins. 'Tell me about it.'

El continues brandishing his invisible pistol. 'An the Strawberry Mivvis, an the Zooms, an all y'choc ices.'

'Bet's over,' I tell him, dropping a handful of money into his lap. 'You win.'

'Bet?'

'One hundred women by C-Day. One thousand pounds.'

'The bet!' says El, scooping and dropping the coins. 'The bet, the bet, the bet.'

I raise my glass. 'Cheers.'

Phil laughs and sips from his glass, but El regards me with suspicion.

'What daysit? Whassa date?'

'July the second,' says Phil.

'C-Day's in July. July . . .' El snaps his fingers in the air, trying to summon the date.

'Nineteenth,' I tell him.

'How farway's at?'

'Seventeen days.'

'Senteen days!' El points at me accusingly. 'Quitter! You cn easy do a hunred.'

'I hope I never do.'

El scowls at me as if I've said a dirty word. 'Whass he on about, Phil?'

'Yes,' says Phil. 'What are you on about, Tom?'

'I think I've met someone. Well, I have met someone, I just . . . It's a long story. I've met someone.'

'A girl?' says El, as if we were thirteen-year-old boys.

'A girl.'

'Niney-nine!' shouts El.

I shake my head. 'Nothing's happened. Well, lots has happened, actually, but not that.'

El throws a pound coin at me. 'Cn you talk some fuckig sense? I'm cnfused enough without you talkin in . . . cnfusions.'

'Can we just say, for the time being, that I've met a girl, I'm conceding the bet, and you, El, are now one thousand pounds richer.'

'What in the f—'

'I think we can manage that,' says Phil. '*For the time being.*'

'Name?' says El.

'Verity.'

'Pretty,' says Phil.

'Is the spice of life,' says El.

'You don't need to do this, Tom,' says Phil, gathering up pound coins into stacks of ten. 'It really isn't necessary.'

'Oh yes it fuckig well is,' says El.

'A bet's a bet,' I say.

'Too fuckig right.'

'So, what are you going to do with it?'

El doesn't hesitate. 'Take him t'Disneyland,' he says, pointing at Phil. 'Dress up as sailors. Say hello to Mickey.'

Phil tells El not to be silly, but his voice betrays his excitement.

'Soon as possble.' says El. 'While I still can.'

'Bloody hell,' says Phil, palming tears off his cheeks.

'Donald Duck, Goofy, Snow White. Hey, we cn fix y'up with a dw. . . dw. . . dwarf.'

Phil kisses El on the top of his head. 'God, I love you, you little bugger.'

'Almost makes the whole thing worth it,' I say, and I empty my glass in one swallow. 'Thank God that's over.'

'C'mon,' says El. 'Y'must've enjoyed it at least a bit?'

I waver my downturned palm. 'I suppose it's had its moments. On the whole, though, I'd have to say it wasn't one of our better schemes.'

'Serves you right for lisnin to me then, doesn it?' says El, his head jiggling. 'I mean, do I look like someone in his right f. . . fuckig mind?'

❦

My bedside clock marks the transition into tomorrow, resetting itself to a neat line of zeros.

I've been in and out of bed since nine o'clock, but I haven't come close to anything resembling sleep. Still, I suppose it's only fair.

The morning after the Viagra incident, I knocked on Doug's door, but if he was in he wasn't answering. Neither has he returned my calls or answered my texts. I apprised Eileen of the way events unfolded, and she gave me a hot earful, as if the whole scheme had been my idea. I'd assumed the whole regrettable episode was over, but I had obviously underestimated Eileen's resolve. When that woman wants something, that woman gets something.

When I got back from El's I was so tired I could barely hold my toothbrush, and was in bed a few minutes after nine o'clock. I began to drift off as soon as my head hit the pillow – my mind running a scenario involving Queen Elizabeth II, Donald Duck and an ice-cream van. Donald had just asked Her Majesty if she'd like raspberry sauce on her ninety-nine when I was jolted awake by the sound of someone hammering on the door downstairs.

For a moment I thought I was under arrest for treason, but then I was brought to my senses by further banging, the doorbell ringing and someone shouting Doug's name through the letter box.

Footsteps downstairs; an internal door opening.

Raised voices – one gruff and indignant, one sharp and insistent.

A door closing; footsteps; silence.

. . .

The slow resurgence of impassioned discourse.

I pulled a pillow over my head – but the muffled grunts and mumblings were punctuated with more solid sounds now, as if Doug and Eileen were assembling a complicated item of flat-pack furniture at fifteen minutes past nine on a Tuesday evening. After several minutes the noises began to take on a more rhythmic quality.

I took *Tropic of Capricorn* through to the living room, turned on the radio and made a pot of tea.

Since Verity walked out of my flat five days ago, Henry Miller has been my constant companion – a self-destructive low-life whom I can neither bear nor ignore. Sitting on the sofa, I had to force myself to open the book at the folded page marking my slow progress through the author's sordid exploits. At the last count, Miller had slept with sixteen women, screwed a friend's sister in a doorway, molested a stranger on the elevated railway and picked up a dose from a hooker. The temptation to skim passages, skip pages or just drop the whole damn thing into the bin was hard to resist, but the book had taken on the weight of a penance and I was determined to complete it.

And so, while Doug and Eileen made whoopee, I opened *Tropic of Capricorn* and attempted to make amends. Twice I fell asleep. The first time I woke to the sound of the novel hitting the floorboards. The second time to the sound of Eileen hitting the roof. I cranked the radio up a notch, made more tea and pressed further forward. Around eighty pages later, the knock and thump from below subsided. I closed the book, washed my cup and returned to bed.

And ten minutes after I resettled my head on the pillow, Doug and Eileen began again. And again I rolled out of bed and turned on the kettle and switched on the radio. By now I was too tired to sleep, and with the end in sight, and more tea in the pot, I advanced again, determined now to end my ordeal.

The final assault was exactly that, and the old-timers had reached their climax long before I arrived at my own – rather less rousing – conclusion.

The closing words: *We must get going. Tomorrow, tomorrow . . .*

True enough, but hardly worth the effort. In the final pinch of pages, having inflicted himself on a total of seventeen unfortunate ladies, Henry Miller moves to Paris, meets the love of his life and lives, presumably, happily ever after.

If he can do it, why can't I?

It's been quiet in Flat 5a, Chaucer Road for over an hour now, and it would appear that the seniors' bedroom gymnastics is over for the evening. My mind, however, is swimming in tea and turning somersaults. I turn on my bedside light and reread the passage where my old mate Henry meets the woman of his dreams . . .

. . . and I throw the book across the room.

It leaves a shallow indent in the plaster, just below the spot where my poster – *Obstacles are what we see when we take our eyes off the goal* – used to hang. Taped to the wall in its place is Verity's sketch of me as a werewolf, howling at nothing and holding a purple umbrella.

And I laugh out loud because, finally, I know what I'm going to do.

Chapter Thirty-Six

I ring Doug's doorbell, and a female voice shouts for me to hang on a moment, she'll be right there.

This morning we presented the first Little Horrors edits. The client and the agency are, by and large, happy; they want to see more sweets, more eating, there are concerns over the ending. Other people's concerns, not mine.

A dappled figure grows larger in the frosted-glass panel, and it seems to me that she's taking an awfully long time to cross a short corridor. Finally, Eileen opens the door.

'Flowers,' I say, handing a gigantic bouquet to Eileen. 'And' – holding up a potted plant – 'for Doug.'

'Thank you, love,' Eileen says, taking the flowers. She kisses me on the cheek and holds a finger to her lips. 'Douglas is sleeping,' she says, and as she turns away I notice that she's blushing.

I follow Eileen as she shuffles into the living room, and hold her by the elbow as – with a good deal of wincing – she lowers herself onto the sofa.

'Hip again?' I ask.

Eileen nods sheepishly and makes herself comfortable in a nest of cushions. 'If you want a cuppa, you'll have to make it yourself.'

'Do you want one?'

'Go on, and bring some biscuits. And put those in some water while you're at it.'

'And your last slave died of . . . ?'

'Exhaustion,' says Eileen, and based on the kerfuffle coming from her bedroom last night, it might just be the truth. 'And none of that herbal nonsense,' she shouts after me. 'A proper cup of Typhoo's what I need.'

While the kettle is boiling I use the toilet. It stings when I pee and there is a pink tinge to my urine – but that's to be expected after the day I've had. I scrub my hands thoroughly before I make the tea.

'Has Doug forgiven me yet?' I ask once we're settled with our tea and biscuits.

'Doug's fine, love.'

'Sleeping, you say.'

'Yes, love,' Eileen says into her cup.

'Tired, then.'

Eileen dunks a custard cream.

I go on: 'Only, he's normally so energetic.'

'All right, smarty-pants,' says Eileen, finally looking up from her drink. 'Ha ha, very funny.'

'You gave it to him, then – the Viagra, I mean.'

An expression that manages to combine horror and relief passes over Eileen's face. 'Oh, Tom, I thought he'd never stop.'

'I know what you mean,' I say. 'So, how did you talk him round?'

'Didn't have to, love. He called me. Took himself to the doctor's yesterday, got his own prescription there and then.'

'No!'

Eileen nods. 'Turns out you're not entirely useless, after all.'

'You're too kind.'

'Cooked me supper, bottle of wine, took a Viagra with his rhubarb crumble. Very nice it was, too.'

'The crumble?'

'All of it, love.' Eileen shifts on her cushion and winces through her dentures. 'I'm not as limber as I used to be,' she says, and I cringe inwardly at the imagery my mind conjures up.

'How long's he been asleep?' I ask.

'He's been flat out since two,' Eileen says, and she can't resist a cheeky smile. 'What time is it now?'

'Almost four,' I tell her.

'You look worried, love. Is something up?'

Even after Eileen and Douglas had finished their rompathon, I couldn't sleep. I thought about Verity, fluctuating between excitement and despair and hope and frustration. I thought about Trudi Roberts, and Sadie, and Holly, and Yvette, and Kaz, and the woman with no name. I thought about El and Phil and their promiscuous dead friend. And it didn't help me sleep.

The p24 antigen test identifies a protein from the surface of HIV particles. This protein is detectable from approximately ten to thirty days post-exposure. I had unprotected sex nineteen days ago – briefly unprotected, but unprotected nevertheless. Another test, the HIV antibody test, detects infections contracted three months and more ago. I found a private clinic on Harley Street which offers both tests for £110 – they call it the 'peace-of-mind package'. Cheap at ten times the price. There is a plaster in the crook of my elbow where the nurse took my blood; she said the results take two to three hours. I'm still waiting.

When I told Dad about cheating on Sadie, I felt lighter. I experienced the same catharsis confessing to Ben and then to Doug. I'm getting a taste for candour, and after I tell Eileen about my afternoon, she kisses and hugs me, and I lose the plot and break down crying.

The nurse had a clipboard. *Is this your first time?* she asked. *How many sexual partners have you had in the last twelve months? How many in the last month? Do you use a contraceptive sheath? Have you ever had intercourse without a contraceptive sheath? Are you an intravenous drug user? Have you had surgery? A blood transfusion? Have you had unprotected anal sex as the insertive partner? As the receptive partner? Have you had sexual exposure in Africa? Southern Asia? Eastern Europe? Any tattoos or piercings? Have you employed the services of a sex worker?*

The nurse classified me as very low risk. Asked why I wanted the test. 'Peace of mind,' I said, with something resembling a laugh. The nurse jotted a note on her questionnaire. Blood and urine were taken. The membranous tube inside my penis was swabbed with a cotton bud. My genitals were inspected for warts. I was tested for chlamydia, gonorrhoea, hepatitis B and C, herpes simplex virus, human papillomavirus, urinary infections, non-specific urethritis, syphilis, HIV-1 and HIV-2. I paid extra for a throat swab.

Eileen checks her watch. 'You'll stay here until they call,' she says. 'I think there might be a *Columbo* on.'

Douglas emerges from his bedroom a little after five, limping a little and rubbing sleep from his eyes.

'Hello, trouble,' he says when he spots me on the sofa.

'Morning,' I say.

Doug and Eileen exchange a look, and – with not inconsiderable discomfort – she moves along the sofa to make room for her man.

I apologise all over again, but Douglas is more interested in putting his feet up.

'Ye meant well,' he says. Then, indicating the potted plant, 'What's this?'

'Passion flower,' I tell him.

Eileen looks aghast. 'Is that a joke?'

'Meant to help you sleep,' I tell her.

'Right,' she says. 'Good. Maybe have a little pot of that later, Douglas?'

'Aye,' says Doug, with something resembling relief. 'Aye.'

I say I'd best be leaving, but Eileen says I'll do no such thing and the three of us settle down to watch a quiz show called *Pointless*. Six o'clock comes and goes, and the clinic still hasn't called with my various results. Maybe they found something and they need to double-check.

Douglas goes to the kitchen to prepare supper. He's cooking pizza with allotment-grown tomatoes and fresh basil, and Eileen tells him to make one for me.

The clinic calls at seven minutes past six. And when the nurse tells me I'm not dying and that bits of me aren't going to turn green and drop off, I'm not nearly as relieved as maybe I should be. When the nurse said I was low risk, she wasn't telling me anything I didn't already suspect. Rather, it felt appropriate to put myself through the whole humiliating rigmarole out of due diligence and contrition. Even so, it's good to know I'm going to live for a little while longer.

Chapter Thirty-Seven

We go around the circle, introducing ourselves. From the left . . .

Agnes: silver hair, owlish spectacles, gouty fingers. Jim: married to Agnes, red-faced, mostly bald, walking stick. Helen: shoulder-length dyed-brown bob, glasses on a beaded chain, make-up clumped in the fine hairs on her cheeks. Vera, our host for the evening: miniature, Chinese, boyishly short hair one part black to three parts grey. Maureen: 'call me Mo', bifocaled, stripy-socked and woollen-skirted. Cora: an Ad-Land granny, pinks and browns and thick white curls. Agnes, Jim, Helen, Vera, Maureen, Cora – average age somewhere in the high sixties.

And then there's me.

'Tom,' I say. 'Hello.'

'Hello, Tom,' says everyone.

'Did he say Tom?' asks Cora. 'My husband was a Tom.'

Mo pats Cora's hand and winks at me. 'That's right, dear.'

'I never liked the name,' says Cora. 'Puts one in mind of cats.'

Eileen said I should have given Verity flowers, knocked on her door and said I was sorry. I'm beginning to think she was right. Because there is a piece missing from this puzzle and its name is Verity.

On Friday, via the Internet and a reconnaissance trip taking in several coffee shops and two libraries, I compiled a list of seven book clubs in and around Verity's neighbourhood. I called them all, but only one was reading *The Secret History*.

Helen explained that the group would be meeting on the coming Monday, which left me – an avid non-reader – with just three days to wade through six hundred and twenty-nine pages of literary fiction.

I spent the weekend cooking, reading, eating, reading, running, reading, drinking, reading, sleeping, reading. I finished *The Secret History* two hours ago, skim-reading the last fifty pages. And it's looking like I did it all for nothing.

'Have you had a chance to read it?' asks Mo, tapping her copy of the novel.

'Just about managed,' I say.

'Tom called on Friday,' says Helen. 'And he was quite undeterred when I informed him we would be congregating this evening.'

'Blimey,' says Jim. 'Fast reader.'

'I had a quiet weekend,' I say.

'Did he say he's local?' asks Cora. 'Are you local?'

'A few miles east,' I say. 'But I hope you won't hold it against me.'

'Why would I do that?' says Cora.

There's a little laughter and the interview atmosphere softens. Vera excuses herself to the kitchen to make tea, open wine, fetch glasses. Jim asks what I do for a living, and everyone's very impressed when I tell them. Everyone except Cora, who gets the idea that I make televisions. No one bothers to correct her.

'Look what I found,' says Vera, carrying a tray of drinks into the room.

Verity, bringing up the rear with a tray full of mugs and glasses, doesn't blink when she sees me. Everyone makes a fuss of her as she works her way around the circle, kissing cheeks and squeezing hands.

She's got a preppy thing going on for book club. Ankle-length chinos; flat brown brogues; plain, baby-blue polo shirt. Her hair is tied back in a neat ponytail and the only thing she's missing is a pair of glasses.

'Verity,' says Helen, 'this young gentleman is Tom.'

'Not local,' says Cora.

'Read it in three days,' says Jim.

'And this,' Helen says, 'is the lovely Verity.'

She looks beautiful.

'Pleased to meet you,' I say, desperately doubting the wisdom of this entire gambit.

Verity smiles politely, as if this is the first time we've met, as if we've never kissed, as if I didn't have a half-naked estate agent hidden under my bed.

'Drink, Tom?'

'I'll take a small wine please, Vera.'

And as I do so, my hand is shaking.

'Tom was saying he makes commercials,' says Mo. 'Verity's a . . . what is it, Verity? I can never remember.'

'Production designer,' she deadpans.

'Small world,' I say.

'Certainly is,' says Verity.

This is as far as my clever scheme extends; beyond this point I have no plan. I was so focused on getting here and getting the book read that I hadn't considered what I was going to do next.

The following two hours are a crossfire of literary jargon and allusions that mean as much to me as the technical specifications of a kitchen boiler. I spend the entire time stealing glances at Verity, trying and failing to think of clever comments or some witty, subtextual way of making everything all right between us. So far, however, my major contribution has been to say I thought Bunny was an interesting name for a boy.

My current strategy consists of waiting until the meeting has finished, following Verity outside, getting down on my knees and begging.

'So,' asks Verity, 'what do you make of it all, Tom?'

'I liked the ending,' I say.

After a pause, during which it becomes clear that this is the full extent of my literary criticism, Verity asks, 'Would you say it was a happy or sad ending?'

'Sad?' I try.

'Hmm. And you liked that?'

'Well, I suppose everyone got what they deserved . . . in the end.'

'Interesting,' says Verity, and she takes a swallow of her wine. 'Are you a fan of Tartt?'

'It's my first one.'

'Which authors do you normally read?' asks Helen.

All eyes on me.

'I just finished *Tropic of Capricorn*, actually.'

I might be imagining it – wishful thinking, probably – but something appears to yield in Verity's expression. A minuscule uplift at the corners of her mouth, a tightening around the eyes?

'Miller,' says Vera. 'I've never read him.'

'Rather bawdy,' says Helen.

'Might have to try that one,' says Jim, raising his eyebrows. 'Any good?'

Jim's well-meaning banter induces a feeling of weary sadness, and I hear myself sigh out loud. 'Not really, Jim. I found it all rather depressing, to be honest.'

Mo regards me over the top of her bifocals, as if neither of the options presented by her eyewear can bring me into clear focus. 'How so, Tom?'

Rather like *Tropic of Capricorn*, Verity's expression is hard to read.

'It's just so bleak and pointless,' I say. 'He spends the whole book drunk, miserable and entirely controlled by his . . . penis.'

The word – like the entity it represents – is out before I can stop it, as if it has a mind of its own, as if possessed by the ghost of Henry goddamned Miller.

'Penis?' asks Cora.

'I'm sorry,' I say, from behind my hands. 'I didn't mean to . . .'

'Quite all right,' says Helen. 'We're all adults. Besides, we can hardly critique literature if we're going to embargo its building blocks.'

'Hear hear,' says Mo.

'*Penis?*' says Cora.

Mo strokes Cora's hand. 'That's right, dear.'

'The thing is . . .' I say. 'The *truth* is' – and I look directly at Verity – 'I think I found *Tropic of Capricorn* so depressing because it reminded me of myself.'

The room is silent but for the sound of seven people leaning forward. And if this is my plan, I'm not convinced it's a good one.

'And this reminds you of you how?' asks Mo kindly.

'I've slept with a lot of women,' I say, and everyone leans back, as if retreating into the safety of their chairs.

I nod gently, as if to confirm this revelation, as if I'm granting myself permission to continue. 'All the time I was reading Henry Miller,' I say, 'I was thinking how sordid and pathetic and . . . and *hollow* his life was, but . . . well, that's me all over, isn't it?'

Jim nods as if, yes, he knows exactly what I mean. Vera's mouth is puckered into an expression that could be born of several attitudes, but I'd put my money on disapproval. Helen twiddles her glasses chain. Mo smiles. I don't know what Verity is doing because I don't dare look at her.

'And then I met someone,' I go on. 'And then . . . and then I ruined it.'

'You did the dirty on her?' asks Agnes.

'How many did he sleep with?' asks Cora.

'No,' I say, 'I didn't do the dirty. I didn't cheat on her or lie to her or anything like that. Things just sort of . . . caught up with me.'

'Mistakes make us human,' says Helen, looking at me then glancing, briefly, at Verity.

'Probably a misunderstanding,' says Jim; and Mo, Agnes and Vera mutter polite approval.

'Yes and no,' I say, and risk a glance at Verity. She is staring right through me, it seems, and I look away.

'Maybe you should talk to this girl,' says Helen. 'Explain yourself.'

'I was quite a one myself,' says Cora, taking hold of my hand. 'Is three an awful lot, do you think?'

Any other Monday, I'd shit myself laughing. But not today.

Verity rises from her chair and drops *The Secret History* into her handbag. Without looking up, she mutters 'excuse me' and leaves.

The front door clicks quietly closed, and everyone turns to face Tom. Cora still has hold of my hand, and if I were to obey my instincts and bolt after Verity, I'd likely yank Cora clean out of her chair and quite possibly into her grave. I unpick Cora's fingers from my hand, thank everyone for their hospitality and walk as casually as I can from the room.

When I get outside, Verity has vanished.

I jog the full length of the road but there's no sign of her. I'm about to kick a lamp post when I get the sense that I'm being observed. I turn on the spot and see six faces in Vera's front window. The book club waves. I wave back and plod around the corner to where I parked Doug's car.

I'm squashed behind the wheel, deciding whether or not I should drive to Verity's flat, when there's a tap on the window.

Verity opens the door and climbs into the passenger seat.

'I think they like you,' she says.

My heart is beating like I've just finished a ten-mile run instead of a slow trot up and down the street. 'And what about you?' I manage.

Verity pretends to think about this. She smiles. 'I think you're okay.'

'Eileen said I should have brought you flowers.'

Verity considers this and then wrinkles her nose. 'I like your way better.'

What I want to do now is reach across and hold Verity's hand, but it feels as though it might be presumptuous. I know I should simply be grateful that we're speaking, but I can't think of what to say next because all I can think about is reaching across and . . .

I reach across and take hold of Verity's hand. She doesn't recoil or scream or slap me. But the night is still young.

'That girl,' I say. 'She was my estate agent and I slept with her. Once. Before I met you.'

'And now we've all met each other.' Verity smiles, but I sense she is still reserving her final judgement. My hand feels conspicuous in hers now – heavy and clumsy.

'She had a set of keys and she let herself in.'

'What happened next?'

'I slept in the porch. She left while I was running after you, locked me out.'

'No! You're kidding.'

I shake my head. 'And I broke my toe trying to kick the door in.'

Verity laughs, an out-loud burst that appears to take her by surprise. It should be contagious but I don't join in.

She squeezes my hand. 'Any more surprises?'

'Well, you should probably know that I slept with Kaz, once. And Holly, a few times.'

Verity smiles and nods.

'You knew?'

'I guessed.'

And I screwed some anonymous drunk woman I picked up on the tube. But I don't think that's relevant. Honesty, I've realised, doesn't mean exposing every nasty detail. Only every important one. Sadie, for example – she never needed to know about Holly. That was me selfishly soothing my conscience and disregarding how it would make Sadie feel. What I should have done was admit to myself a damn sight sooner that Sadie wasn't the one for me. And then I should have admitted it to Sadie. Do I intend to tell Verity about my bet with El? *Do I hell*. And what about Susan Chambers? A drunken kiss that could have gone further but didn't. I can justify that triviality in at least three different ways and I'm fine with it. *Honestly*.

Still holding hands, we stare out of the car windscreen, and the sky has begun its slow fade to black. At some point it must have started raining and it's just dark enough to see the droplets in a dancing haze around the street lights.

'I like the librarian thing,' I say.

'All I need is a pair of glasses, don't you think?'

I laugh loudly and abruptly. 'Yeah, I was thinking the same thing.'

'Really?'

'Really. There's something else I should probably tell you.'

Verity turns to look at me.

'I don't like the Ramones,' I say. 'Or the Pixies, or the Supersuckers. I tried, but . . . not my thing, I'm afraid.'

Now Verity laughs. 'Me neither,' she says. 'I just like the T-shirts.'

'Really?'

'Yeah, really.'

It's another of those bright moments that precedes a lull.

Verity breaks the silence. 'That night,' she says. 'When you drove me back to my flat.'

'Yes?'

'You seemed . . . I dunno, hesitant. Unsure.'

'I was. Sure. I just . . .' I indicate the general vicinity of my brain. 'Too much thinking, I think.'

The dashboard on the Triumph Herald is a single piece of varnished wood, set with levers, knobs and various dials for displaying speed, temperature, volts, revolutions per minute. The second hand on the clock ticks its circular path.

'I know we don't *really* know each other,' Verity says, 'but I've kissed a lot of frogs, and' – smiling – 'I don't think you're a frog.'

'Some people might disagree.'

'It's a compliment, Tom. Accept it.'

'Thank you,' I say, turning to face her. 'And I don't think you're a frog, either.'

'I don't want to come off all . . .' Verity widens her eyes, grits her teeth, mimes stabbing me in the chest. 'You know, *intense*. I'm not. I'm honestly not. But . . .' She glances at our laced-together fingers. 'But I don't need a . . . a fling, you know?'

I nod that I understand.

'I want more than that,' Verity says. 'And if you've got your doubts, if you're on the rebound, if there's someone e—'

'There's no one else.'

Verity squeezes my hand. It seems to say, *Good*. Or perhaps: *There'd better not be.*

'There's no one else,' I say. 'I just convinced myself that I didn't deserve you. That you deserved someone better than me.'

Verity smiles. 'So what made you change your mind?'

'I didn't. It's just something I'm going to have to work on.'

Verity scooches up so that she's tight against me, and we lean into each other, staring out of the window at the dancing rain.

Chapter Thirty-Eight

It's two hundred and six days since I accepted El's bet. Seventeen days since I conceded it.

I lie with my head on Verity's chest, listening to her breathing as it slows . . . steadies. Beneath it I can hear her heart. Tonight we're cooking boeuf bourguignon for Eileen and Douglas – a double date. It's C-Day, but it's my secret and there'll be no champagne. El and Phil flew to Disneyland last Friday, but it's too soon for a postcard. My wish for Phil is that, after El has gone, he won't be like my dad. That he'll be like Doug, who is planning a summer holiday somewhere hot with Eileen.

Some people can love and love again, and I want Phil to be one of them.

My head rises and falls with Verity's chest, and one day her heart will stop beating. It's surely a long way off but it's as inevitable as tomorrow and it scares me sick – but that's a good thing; it makes me smile. The next time I see Dad, I'll tell him that I understand. The certainty that he couldn't love anyone more than he loved my mother – 'I know what you mean,' I'll tell him.

It's been twenty-one days since I first kissed Verity, ten days since we first made love.

But, hey, who's counting.

AUTHOR'S NOTE

A note on the chronology of *Girl 99* and *The Two of Us*:

If you've read my novel *The Two of Us*, you will have met the character El before. Regarding the order of the books, *Girl 99* came first and, accordingly, El's disease is less advanced in this story.

ACKNOWLEDGMENTS

As ever and forever, enormous gratitude and big love to Sarah, my wise, patient and supportive wife – you made this book better. And more of the same to my mother (and very own senior editor) for diligent, intelligent and creative notes, despite all the sex and naughty words.

Chris Mudge, Stephen Pipe and James Miller provided insight to matters of film production; Sarah Tabrizi gave generously of her valuable time and deep knowledge on Huntington's disease; Keith Juden was on hand with succinct and shrewd notes on later drafts.

To my agent and friend, Mark 'Stan' Stanton, for his pragmatism, positivity and unerring good humour – thank you, squire.

And finally, to my editors at Amazon, Sammia Hammer, Gemma Wain and Sophie Wilson – thank you for seeing the potential in this book, for recognising its strengths and highlighting its shortcomings. Thank you for razor-sharp notes, interesting juice recipes and for being thoroughly charming and totally lovely. It's been a joy.

Thank you all.

ABOUT THE AUTHOR

Photo © 2014 Daniel Allan

Andy Jones lives in London with his wife and two little girls. During the day he works in an advertising agency; at weekends and horribly early in the mornings, he writes fiction.

Follow Andy on Twitter & Facebook:

@andyjonesauthor

facebook.com/andyjonesauthor